ONWARD TO EDEN

DAYS OF WAR
BOOK 3

JONATHAN CULLEN

LIQUID MIND PUBLISHING

All rights reserved. No part of this book may be reproduced, distributed, or transmitted in any form or by any means, including photocopying, recording, or other electronic or mechanical methods, without the prior written permission of the author, except in the case of brief quotations embodied in critical reviews and certain other noncommercial uses permitted by copyright law.

Copyright © 2024 by Jonathan Cullen

www.jonathancullen.com

Liquid Mind Publishing

This is a work of fiction. Any resemblance to actual persons, living or dead, or actual events is purely coincidental.

ALSO BY JONATHAN CULLEN

The Days of War Series

The Last Happy Summer

Nighttime Passes, Morning Comes

Onward to Eden

Shadows of Our Time Collection

The Storm Beyond the Tides

Sunsets Never Wait

Bermuda Blue

The Jody Brae Mystery Series

Whiskey Point

City of Small Kingdoms

The Polish Triangle

Love Ain't For Keeping

Sign up for Jonathan's newsletter for updates on deals and new releases!

https://liquidmind.media/j-cullen-newsletter-sign-up-1/

1

OCTOBER 1942

It was strange that, despite all the shortages, sacrifices, heartaches, and hardships, Abby Nolan woke up some mornings forgetting there was a war.

The world had changed but, in many ways, her life had not. She still lived at home in the house her Irish great-grandfather had built, the same place her mother and grandmother had grown up. She still slept in the same small bedroom at the end of the hallway. When she went out, she would wave to Mrs. McNulty across the street or Mr. Braga a few doors down. She was still surrounded by the people she had known all her life.

If anything seemed different about East Boston, it was how quiet it had become. Most of the young men were gone. Timothy Enright, who owned Enright's Dairy, had joined the Navy, so now everyone had to walk to the shop to get their milk. Jimmy and Anthony Ianocconi had left for the Army in July. Libby Franchette was in Northampton training with the Naval Women's Reserve, and one of the Costello boys was missing in Guadalcanal.

After Pearl Harbor, the casualties had trickled in over the winter. Now it was like a flood. Every Sunday at Mass, Father Ward would read out the names of the dead or missing, eliciting cries and moans from the pews.

"Abigail!"

Abby opened her eyes. While her mother's voice was jarring, she didn't cringe like she used to. The only good that had come from the stress of the past ten months was that they had all become more forgiving of each other. Her father had died two summers before, and her brother George had joined the Army. The shock of death and war made any family bickering seem petty. Somehow they all knew, now more than ever, they had to stick together.

"Abigail!"

Abby yawned and pushed herself up from her bed. With no work and no classes, she could have slept till noon.

"Be right down," she called.

This was the first year Boston University had closed for Columbus Day. The official announcement made it sound like an act of patriotism, but it was probably to save money. With so many boys gone, the student body was a fraction of what it was before the war. If the college hadn't been hosting various Army training programs, it could have gone bankrupt.

Abby shivered as she got dressed. The nights were getting colder. Soon she would have to start wearing her wool gown to sleep. She put on a dress and walked out to the bathroom to fill the sink. As she washed her face, her eyes fell on George's toothbrush and she froze. Its frayed bristles and splintered wood handle were like a metaphor for his own troubled life.

Abby had never gotten along with her older brother. As a boy, he was mean and restless, always causing problems. By the time he was eighteen, he had been arrested twice. She had assumed he would end up in prison like some of his friends. But after their father's death, he had changed, even softened. For someone who only cared about himself, he'd surprised everyone by joining the Army. Now she worried about him more than anyone.

Abby reached for the Phillips toothpaste, its tube bent and split at the edges. With tin limited by the War Department, every container, from vegetable cans to shaving cream, was cheap and flimsy.

"Abigail!"

"Oh, for Christ's sake," Abby muttered.

She dried off her face and ran downstairs.

In the kitchen, her mother stood at the oven. She wore an apron over her nice dress, her dark hair in a pompadour. At fifty, Mrs. Nolan had the figure of a woman much younger.

Her mother glanced back, her face damp and frantic as usual.

"Were you gonna sleep all day?" she asked.

"What time is it?"

"Nearly eleven."

Mrs. Nolan took a tray of buns out of the oven and dropped them on the counter.

"I need more butter," she said. "The German market should be open today."

"Are you certain?"

"I saw Mr. Schultz yesterday."

"Okay."

"And be quick! The announcement is at noon!"

......

ABBY WALKED out to Bennington Street. Although most of the stores were closed, every window had an American flag. A neighborhood that had once been Irish and Jewish was now largely Italian. As a people viewed with suspicion, they were more patriotic than anyone. One deli even had an effigy of Adolph Hitler hanging from a noose until the police ordered them to take it down because it was scaring children.

As she crossed the street, she glanced over at Gittell's Tailor, a small shop between a pool hall and a paint store. It was where she had first met Arthur who had worked there for his father. He had been in the Air Force a year, and she hadn't seen him since Easter. Mr. Gittell was only open three days a week now.

Abby walked over to the German market. Mr. Schultz had owned the place for years, and everyone knew him. But it still didn't protect him from prejudice. As she opened the door, she could still see the word "Kraut!" someone had tried to scrub off the wall.

A bell jingled, and Mr. Schultz looked up from the counter.

"Abigail," he said in a heavy accent. "Happy Columbus Day."

"Same to you, Mr. Schultz."

As a girl, Abby always thought he was old. Now that she was an adult, he looked more like a distinguished gentleman. He had white hair and a handlebar mustache, the ends twisted with wax. Although short, his shoulders were broad and muscular. Most men Abby knew over fifty were hunched from hard work, but he was still fit. Rumors were that he had been a champion swimmer back in Germany.

The shop was small, with low ceilings and plank floors. In a neighborhood where most people didn't own a car, it sold everything from bread to bath salts. After the Rexall in Orient Heights closed during the Depression, Mr. Schultz got a license for a drug counter. The pharmacist was a young Romanian woman who Abby never saw because she only worked two days a week.

As she went down the aisle, she noticed some of the shelves were bare. At the back, she opened the cooler and wasn't surprised there was no butter. Food shortages had been on and off since the start of the war, and one never knew what to expect. A month before, pork chops were impossible to find. Sugar had been scarce since summer.

She grabbed a package of Nucoa instead. Her mother hated the stuff, saying it was lard with food coloring. But it was better than nothing, and Abby didn't have to waste a ration stamp buying it.

She walked back to the register, and Mr. Schultz said, "Margarine?"

"I didn't see any butter."

He held up his finger and went out back, returning a minute later with a block of butter.

"For your lovely mother," he said.

"Oh, thank you, Mr. Schultz."

At a time when everyone was struggling, his kindness meant a lot.

"Eighteen cents, please," he said, and she went into her purse. "Did you hear the good news?"

"What news is that?"

"We destroyed three Japanese boats in the Solomon Islands. That makes eleven this week."

Like any man, he viewed the war like a sport, something to be measured in a series of gains, losses, and comebacks. She tried to keep up with it all, but it only made her think about Arthur. The last letter she'd received from him was in September, around the same time they'd heard from George. He was somewhere in the Far East, although he hadn't said where. While she didn't know the Solomons from Siberia, she panicked anytime she heard about an incident in the Pacific.

"Hopefully it's one step closer to peace," she said, handing him two dimes.

He handed her the change with a smile.

"Tell Mrs. Nolan I say hello."

······

ABBY WALKED UP THE CIARLONES' steps and stopped on the porch. She was still uncomfortable with her brother living next door. That summer, Thomas had married Mrs. Ciarlone's niece Connie, an Italian girl whose first husband had died in the war. Two months later, Mrs. Ciarlone was killed by a car during a blackout and not long after, her son Sal left for the Army.

The door opened, and it was Connie.

"Have you been waiting out here?" she asked.

Abby shook her head and gave her the butter.

"For the rolls."

Connie had on an apron over a red dress, her hair in pin curls. Although flustered from cooking, she was no less beautiful. She had an exotic charm, and it wasn't just her accent. Mrs. Nolan said her eyes were too close together, but Abby knew her mother was just looking for a flaw.

"Can I help with anything?" Abby asked.

"No, thank you. The ham should be out shortly."

Abby walked in to see a dozen people, mostly neighbors and women from church. Thomas was kneeling by the radio, trying to get a signal. He had on his police uniform.

In the dining room, their mother was at the table with some older ladies. For a woman who used to complain about "all the foreigners," she now had more Italian friends than anyone.

Mrs. McNulty sat on the couch beside her husband, a tall man who always wore a bow tie and had a permanent grin.

"Hello, Abigail," she said, sipping wine. "Any news from George?"

Abby and her family hadn't heard from George in six weeks.

"He's still in the Aleutian Islands as far as we know."

"Let's pray he's safe."

Abby appreciated the sympathy, but it was easy for them to say. The McNultys' son Paul worked for the Department of State in Maryland, and their daughter Teresa was in the Women's Army Auxiliary Corps, stationed somewhere in New Mexico. Even if they were doing their part for the war, they were far from the battlefields.

"I hear the new barracks at Wood Island Park have been completed," Mr. McNulty said.

As a member of the Massachusetts Women's Defense Corps, Abby knew things other people didn't. But she couldn't say anything. She was saved from having to lie or avoid the question when Chickie came running down the stairs.

"*Uh-buh!*"

She had on a flowered dress, one sock pulled up to her knee and the other at her ankle.

"Hi, Chickie," Abby said, and they hugged.

At fourteen, Mrs. Ciarlone's daughter still acted like a young girl. She got easily excited and spoke in broken sentences. It was never determined exactly what was wrong with her. The doctors said she was *delayed*, and everyone else just called her *different*. After Mrs. Ciarlone's death, Thomas and Connie had adopted her.

"Play?" Chickie said, taking both of Abby's hands.

"Maybe in a little bit."

Suddenly, the radio got loud.

"Shhh!" Thomas said.

Connie ran in from the kitchen, and people gathered in the room. Moments later, the voice of Attorney General Francis Biddle came on:

"Here in America some six-hundred-thousand Italians…are working side by side with other millions who have in them the blood of the French, the Norwegians, the Belgians, the Dutch, the Poles, the Greeks….In each division of the United States Army, nearly five hundred soldiers, on the average, are the sons of Italian immigrants to America…Many more are of older Italian origin. I do not need to tell you that these men are abundantly represented in the list of heroes who have been decorated for bravery since December seven, nineteen forty-one."

"It is for this reason…I now announce to you that beginning October nineteen, a week from today, Italian aliens will no longer be classed as 'alien enemies.'"

THERE WAS a burst of heartfelt sighs. A few of the older Italian ladies wept. It was a speech everyone had expected the AG to make, but hearing it was a relief. After ten months of restrictions, curfews, and overall humiliation, Italians in America were finally free.

Thomas put his arm around Connie, and they kissed.

"C'mon," she said, wiping a tear from her eye. "Let's eat."

2

Thomas raced down Border Street past dockyards and warehouses. When it came to crime tips, speed and timing were everything. He kept the sirens off, but with another cruiser behind him, the raid would have hardly been a surprise.

"If anyone tries to run, crack 'em," he said.

Officer Carroll grinned, glancing down at his shiny baton. He was only two years younger than Thomas at eighteen, but with his head shaved and pimples on his chin, he looked like a kid. He had only been on the force for a month, which wasn't unusual. Their precinct was full of new officers.

They passed the entrance of East Boston Works where, even in the urgency, Thomas got sentimental. His father had worked there for thirty years until his crane collapsed in a windstorm and killed him. Since the start of the war, the facility had doubled in size. The fence had barbed wire, and MPs now guarded the gates. With so much military activity, all the shipyards had become like bases.

They stopped in front of a plain brick building and got out. Sergeant Silva and two patrolmen parked behind them, and they all walked up to the door. Thomas knocked three times, waited a few seconds, then knocked again. Finally, he heard someone undoing the lock. A bald man with a mustache opened it and peered out.

"Yeah?"

Thomas showed his badge.

"We've got a warrant to search the premises," he said.

"For what?"

"For mice."

When the man started to close the door, Thomas shoved it in.

"Hey, take it easy!" the guy said. "It's got a chain lock. I had to shut it to open it—"

Thomas ignored him, and they burst inside. Two other men stood up, and one even raised his arms.

The small office was shabby, with three desks and some old filing cabinets. The air was dank and oily, the overhead lamps emitting a dull light. Thomas could hear machinery somewhere in the back.

"What is this place?" he asked.

"Why don't you check your warrant?" the bald guy said.

Thomas frowned and looked over at the other men.

"We're a small manufacturer," one of them said.

"Of what?"

"We have a contract with the Department of Defense to produce cadaver pouches."

Thomas squinted in confusion.

"Body bags," the man explained.

The grim silence was broken only by voices behind the wall.

"Who's back there?" Thomas asked.

"We've got about a dozen guys on the line. Italians mostly. They've all been cleared."

"Look around," Thomas said, and the patrolmen began to search the room.

He still wasn't comfortable giving orders. With so many men leaving for the service, officers moved up fast. He had only been on the force a year and was already a sergeant. He was proud of the promotion but still felt guilty for not enlisting like his brother.

"Sarge?"

Thomas looked over and officer Carroll was standing by an open drawer, holding something up. When he walked closer, the sight of gas ration coupons made him smile. There were hundreds of them, all stamped with the letter "B", the most valuable kind. The spaces for the license numbers were blank, so he knew they were either forged or stolen.

"Are these counterfeits?" he asked.

With their heads slumped, the men just glanced at each other.

"Where'd you get them?" Thomas pressed.

They remained silent.

"You know this is a violation of the regulations of the Office of Price Administration?"

"I wanna talk to my lawyer," the bald guy said.

After a long day, Thomas didn't have the patience to interrogate them. Dealing contraband in wartime was a serious crime, but judges had been lenient, mainly because they sympathized. Everyone hated the restrictions. He knew the men probably wouldn't be prosecuted anyway. Or at least, that's what he told himself.

"Consider this a warning," he said, and he shoved the rations into his coat pocket. "Next time, we'll shut you down. Understand?"

The men hesitated.

"Understand?" Thomas barked.

"Yeah, yeah," the bald guy said.

Thomas nodded to Carroll, Silva, and the others, and they left.

......

EACH TIME THOMAS turned the wheel, the front of the car rattled. It was impossible to find new tires. The used ones he had put on over the summer were already flat. As a sergeant, he could've taken a cruiser home, but he liked the old Ford. George had given it to him before he left for the Army, a gesture that had surprised everyone.

After years of tension and spite, Thomas finally respected his brother. He might have even loved him.

He stopped in front of a corner shop on the ground level of a triple-decker. The sign in the window said, "Betty Ann Food Shop," but everyone called it Betty Ann Bakery. Although the owners were Cornish, they sold a mix of traditional and Italian pastries, from custard tarts to cannoli. Abby had been working there since high school and had gotten Connie a job after she was fired from the light bulb factory for not being an American citizen.

Moments later, Connie walked out. She had her pocketbook slung over her shoulder and a box in her hands. Thomas jumped out to get the passenger door for her, something his father had taught him. Thomas had never listened as a boy, but his father's life lessons continued to affect him. He had been gone over a year but in some ways, Thomas felt closer to him than ever.

"Hello," Connie said, kissing him on the cheek and sliding into the seat.

As he shut the door, he glanced over to the shop to see the counter girls looking out. He grinned to himself, walked around the front, and got back into the driver's seat.

"How was work?" she asked.

Thomas could control his emotions, but he could never hide his frustration.

"All the usual."

"What's all the usual?"

"What're those?" he asked, looking at the box on her lap.

She opened it, revealing cookies filled with chunks of red fruit.

"Victory cookies."

"Victory cookies?"

"Made with cranberries."

"How're we gonna win the war with those?"

She smiled.

"Cranberries makes sweet to them," she said, her English sloppy after a long day. "Only one cup of sugar for each batch."

Pulling out, a horn blared, and he hit the brakes. Connie gasped, and they watched an Army truck speed by. As it turned the corner, he saw black soldiers in the back.

"Where do they go?"

"The new barracks on Wood Island Park," he said, distracted.

They continued down Bennington Street, the traffic so heavy that it took fifteen minutes to go a mile. By the time they turned onto their street, it was already dark outside.

Thomas parked, and they got out and walked up the front steps. When they reached the porch, the door swung open, and Chickie ran out.

"*Conn-ah*," she said, jumping into Connie's arms.

They had discussed asking her to call them Mom and Dad, but they still weren't officially her parents. Until her brother Sal returned from the war—and they all hoped he did—her parental status was in limbo.

Mrs. Nolan walked out smiling, but Thomas could tell she was exhausted. Except for when Connie had off work, she picked up Chickie every day at school and watched her until they got home.

"Care to escort me back?" she asked, holding out her arm.

While she was only being playful, his mother really did need the help. She wasn't as steady as she used to be. After their father had died, she'd had a breakdown. No one was sure whether her drinking was the cause or just a consequence. Since getting out of the hospital, she had stayed dry and her mental state had improved. But she still wasn't like she used to be—none of them were. All his life, Thomas had dreamed of leaving East Boston. Now, he was glad he never had. He had come to realize that, especially in a time of war, there was nothing more important than family.

When they got to the porch, Mrs. Nolan walked up to the post box, a rusted iron relic from the last century. Thomas was surprised because she usually got the mail the moment it arrived.

"You didn't get the mail already?"

Her hand came out empty, the hatch closing with a ding.

"I did, but I figured maybe..."

The mailman never came twice, but Thomas understood her

angst. They hadn't gotten a letter from George since September and were all starting to worry. But correspondence in wartime was unreliable, and his brother, who had dropped out of high school in tenth grade, had never been much of a writer. They knew people who hadn't heard from their sons at all yet. Even Abby's boyfriend Arthur had only written to her a few times.

"Maybe tomorrow," Mrs. Nolan said.

"Maybe, Ma."

Opening the door, he put his arm around her back, and they walked in.

3

Holding out her arms, Abby dripped warm icing over the Danishes in long, steady sweeps. To save on sugar, they had to add molasses yet were still told not to use too much. The pastries were all apple which, aside from cranberries, were plentiful. Peaches were still hard to get, and Abby hadn't seen an apricot since spring. The government said any shortages were because there weren't enough men to work the fields. Out west, women were picking and canning most of the fruit.

Connie walked in from the front with an empty tray, and Abby helped her fill it. They didn't talk much at work, especially when it was busy.

Abby missed socializing at the bakery. Most of the girls she knew from high school were gone. Eleanor had married and moved to Medford, a step up from East Boston; Rosemary had gotten a job in the office at the Charlestown Navy Yard. Loretta had finished nursing school and was working at Mass General. The only one left was Eve, a constant gossip who had been made a manager because she had been there so long.

"Did you hear about the new Army base?"

Abby glanced back and saw Eve in the doorway, twirling her hair.

"On Wood Island Park?" Abby asked. "Who hasn't?"

"Eastie will be hopping with soldiers soon."

"We'll feel safer with them around then."

"I wasn't thinking about safety."

Abby made a sour smile, wiping her forehead. When Carlo walked over with more Danishes, she stepped aside. He dropped the sheet pan on the table.

"Hot, hot, hot!" he said with his heavy accent.

Everyone at the bakery loved Carlo. Short and stocky, he was as strong as a bull and could carry two bags of flour at a time up from the basement. He got there every morning before sunrise, six days a week, to mix and cut the dough. His big hands were dry and gnarled and reminded Abby of her father, who had worked hard his whole life.

Carlo had always been quiet, but lately, he was less serious. No longer "enemy aliens," Italians everywhere seemed more relaxed, even confident.

Abby looked up at the clock and saw it was close to eight. She quickly finished the last tray of pastries and then took off her apron. Someone was coming in to replace her, but she didn't know who. Ads for help were everywhere. Each week, some new girl would start, only to quit for a better job.

Abby walked down the hallway and got her coat off the hook. Hesitating, she looked over to see Carlo at the sink with his back to her. She stepped into the storeroom, a narrow space beside the basement stairs where the dry goods were kept. She went into one of the cabinets and found an open sack of sugar. Her heart pounding, she scooped some into a paper bag until it was full, and then she quickly shoved it into her pocketbook.

"Abby?"

Abby flinched and saw Angela Labadini standing at the back door. She stood and pushed her hair aside, trying not to seem flustered.

"Angela?"

"Did I scare you?"

"Hardly. What are you doing here?"

"I start work today."

"Here?"

Angela nodded.

She was taller than Abby, her figure lean but crooked from scoliosis. With her long dark hair, she was pretty, but in a troubled way. She always stood with her arms crossed, a look of wary defiance in her eyes. She lived in Jeffries Point, a poor neighborhood by the water, and they were in the same unit of the Massachusetts Women's Defense Corps.

"I'm supposed to see Eve or Margaret," Angela said.

"Margaret doesn't work Tuesdays. Eve is out at the counter. Leave your things here."

Abby led her through the kitchen, around the tables and equipment. Out front, the morning rush was over. A few older ladies sat sipping coffee by the window, but otherwise, the shop was quiet.

"Eve," Abby called out. "She starts work today."

"There're some clean aprons in the closet next to the washroom."

When Angela walked away, Eve lingered.

"I don't know how you stand it back there," she said. "All that heat and dust. Why don't you work the register with me?"

Abby never liked her questions, which were always critical and tinged with envy.

"Maybe I like the heat and dust."

"Can you work Friday?" Eve asked. "We're short."

"I might have a volleyball game."

"Would you check and let me know?"

"Sure," Abby said before she turned to go.

"Oh, wait."

Abby watched in horror as Eve wiped some sugar off her coat.

......

THE COMMUTE from East Boston to Boston University wasn't long, but it was complicated. Abby had to change trains three times, rushing to get to the next platform. In her first year, she was late for class a lot. Now she knew the system, when to make the connections, what to do if there were delays.

Still, she liked the excitement of coming into the city each morning. As a girl, she had felt confined, and not just because her neighborhood was so crowded. The streets were narrow, but the attitudes of the people were even narrower. Going to college was a relief, and she finally felt like an adult, even if she still lived at home.

When she walked into class, Mr. Glynn looked up.

"Miss Nolan," he said.

Thin with brown hair, the professor had come to America before the war. If he was over thirty, which Abby doubted, he looked young for his age, and he wasn't married. In his double-breasted suit and pocket watch, he was dignified, almost debonair, which was unusual. Most of the Irish men Abby knew were laborers and dockhands.

She sat down, smiling at the girl beside her. As an elective, the class was open to all grades, and Abby didn't know anyone. A few more students trickled in, but Irish History didn't seem popular. Maybe because enrollment was down in general.

"Now," the professor said, standing. "The next two weeks we'll be covering the Famine in Ireland. Who is familiar with it?"

Three-quarters of the class put up their hands, which wasn't a surprise in a city dominated by the Irish and their descendants.

"Miss Drummond?" the professor said.

"It was caused by a potato fungus."

"Good. *Phytophthora infestans* to be precise."

He then pointed to a young man in the back.

"Mr. Dwyer?"

"Millions of people died. The rest came to America."

Mr. Glynn made a tight smile.

"We don't know the exact number of deaths. What we do know, however, is that..."

He crossed his arms like he was waiting for everyone's attention.

"If it hadn't been for the stubbornness and cruelty of the British political class, much of the suffering could have been prevented. It's an ugly fact they still have not acknowledged or made restitution for."

The room got quiet, students glancing around. Considering the British were America's closest allies, the criticism was like blasphemy. In his weekly radio addresses, President Roosevelt called them "friends," reminding Americans they were the only barrier between freedom and Nazi tyranny. Abby's father used to make fun of the English, but it was all lighthearted.

After the controversial opening, the professor put the politics aside and talked about the event itself. Abby had always been interested in the Famine because her great-grandfather on her mother's side had immigrated during it. But Mr. Glynn spoke too fast, and she struggled to keep up. By the time class was over, she had five pages of notes.

"Please finish chapter three," Glynn said as everyone got up. "And with discretion. The textbook doesn't tell the whole story."

Abby closed her book, grabbed her bag, and left. She ran through the lobby and down the stairwell. With her next class at eleven, she had just enough time to get something to eat.

"Toodle-loo," she heard as she walked into the cafeteria.

Looking over, she saw Frances and Harold sitting in the corner. She got in line, bought some coffee and toast, and walked over to them.

Frances had on a beige skirt and jacket, which seemed too light for fall. But with her petite figure and spunky personality, she could pull off anything. Harold wore a navy pinstripe suit, his matching hat on the table. He was always just elegant enough to look refined without giving it away that he was queer.

Abby used to be intimidated by their style and sophistication. They were both from upper-class families. But she knew that wealth couldn't buy stability or protection from the problems of the world. Frances' parents were in the middle of a heated divorce, and Harold had lost both his mother and his brother to suicide.

"Don't you look a bit harried?" Harold observed, taking a long drag on his cigarette.

"I just got a lecture about British imperialism."

"Tsk, tsk," Frances said. "Dr. Glynn?"

"Doctor? We call him Professor."

"Whatever he is, the man should watch what he says."

"I didn't know you had him."

"Not for long. I took his class last semester until he started in about the Catholic Church."

"Darling," Harold said. "When was the last time you went to mass?"

She arched her back, making a cute frown.

"With my mother just two weeks ago."

"That's news to me."

"Speaking of news," she said, looking at Abby. "Sal might be coming back!"

"Might be?"

"He called last night from Virginia. There's a rumor his ship will be stopping in Boston before going over the Atlantic."

If Abby was excited for anyone it was Chickie. She never liked to envy someone else's good fortune, but it seemed unfair. Arthur hadn't written to her in over two months. All she knew was that he was in the Pacific, a region as wide and as mysterious as the war itself. Since the Army's landing at Guadalcanal, the Japanese had been bombing the American airfield. In the newspapers, Abby saw pictures of destroyed planes and runways in flames. The worry could have driven her crazy. The only thing that seemed to help was staying busy.

"I've gotta go," she said.

She shoved the last bit of stale toast into her mouth and sipped the bitter coffee. Whether it was from the food supply problems or her nerves, nothing tasted like it did before the war.

"Slow down lest you choke," Frances said.

Abby frowned.

"Do we have a volleyball game Friday?"

"No. Fire defense training."

"Fire defense training?"

"Ms. Stetson told us at practice Monday."

"Right," Abby said.

"If you're always going to be rushing about," Harold said, "then at least pay attention."

They always made fun of her frantic schedule, which was easy because neither of them had to work. Abby glanced at her watch and saw it was almost eleven. Standing too fast, she hit her knee on the table. Her pocketbook fell on the floor, and she cringed when she saw sugar pour out.

Frances and Harold looked at her, and she felt her face go red. She knelt down and swept as much as she could back into the bag, snapping it shut. Too humiliated to speak, she was relieved when Harold broke the silence with a joke.

"My dear, are you hoarding?"

"Thanksgiving is coming up..." she said, which was neither an explanation nor an excuse.

"That's certainly a lot of pies."

Abby tried to hide her embarrassment with a grin.

"See you all later," she said.

As she walked away, Frances blew her a kiss, waving like the entire world was watching.

"Toodle-loo!"

4

Thomas pulled into the lot behind the station, the bald tires sliding over trash and dead leaves. He turned off the engine and grabbed the lunch Connie had made him, a sandwich of leftover ham and bread from Sunday dinner. There was an apple too, bruised and dented. His mother had lived through the Depression, and Connie had lived through the war. Neither liked to waste food, but now they all ate things that even six months before, they would have thrown out.

As he got out, he saw two bums drinking next to the dumpster. In the past, he would have told them to leave, maybe hauled them in for vagrancy. But in wartime, the small day-to-day infractions were overlooked, not just out of sympathy. With blackouts, food shortages, and the threat of sabotage, the department had more to worry about.

The brick station outside Maverick Square had been there for decades. Thomas remembered his father bailing out George on more than one occasion. When he first got on the force, he worked the beat downtown, and he missed the excitement of the city. But being assigned to East Boston had its benefits too. His commute was short, and he could get home fast if his mother or Chickie needed help.

With the rear door locked, he had to go around to the front. He walked through the doors into the lobby, which was nothing more than a windowless room with a counter and two benches. Like most government buildings, it was hot in the summer and cold in the winter. He wasn't surprised to see the secretary behind the desk wearing a heavy sweater.

"Someone's here to see you," she said.

"Who?"

"A lieutenant from headquarters."

Thomas walked down the hallway, the floor creaky and slanted. The building was so old it should have been demolished instead of renovated, but everyone knew that wouldn't happen. The department budget was tight, and no one cared about a precinct in a rundown neighborhood.

When he entered his office, Lieutenant Nick DiMarco was standing at the window.

"You know you got some bums out there?" he asked.

"What makes you think they ain't staff?"

"'Cuz they look too good."

They laughed and shook hands. They had known each other since high school and had been on the boxing team. DiMarco was two grades ahead but four years older. As a child, he had polio and spent kindergarten in the hospital. But it was hard to tell by looking at him. With black hair and high cheekbones, he had always been a heartthrob. He had claimed to be the youngest lieutenant ever until someone from headquarters proved him wrong. While he could seem cocky, Thomas liked him and, more importantly, trusted him.

"What're you doing here so early?"

DiMarco held out a stack of checks.

"You forget it was Friday?" he asked.

"What's the difference?"

Their eyes locked. DiMarco gave him a sympathetic nod. Thomas hadn't had a day off in three weeks.

With a shortage of officers, everyone was working overtime, and not always getting paid for it. The budget that year was forty-four million, the largest ever, and it still wasn't enough. The department now had to train air wardens and auxiliary police officers and buy civilian defense equipment like shovels, ladders, generators, and pumps.

"How'd you make out with that gas coupon racket?" DiMarco asked.

Thomas searched through the car keys on the wall. None of the cruisers were in good shape, but he knew which ones had fewer problems.

"I wouldn't call it a racket," he said, distracted. "They make body bags for chrissakes."

"Good. We might need some."

Thomas gave him a sharp look.

"The chief sent out a memo this morning," DiMarco went on. "The OPA says there could be a serious oil shortage this winter."

"I use coal."

"It's not you he's worried about."

"That's obvious."

"It's the crooks and peddlers."

"We got enough of them without a shortage."

DiMarco frowned.

"He just wants everyone on the lookout. So keep your ears open."

Thomas finally found the key he wanted and swiped it off the hook.

"Is that even possible?" he asked, turning to leave.

"Is what possible?"

"Keeping your ears open."

They both laughed. If anyone had heard a sergeant talking to a lieutenant like that, they would have thought it was insubordination. But they had known each other long enough that rank didn't matter.

"Hey, Sarah and I are going to see *Across the Pacific* tomorrow. Why don't you and Connie come along?"

Thomas paused like he was considering it. But with his busy work schedule and a fourteen-year-old daughter at home, even a night at the movies seemed extravagant.

As he went to say no, DiMarco added, "I can get you the time off."

"Sure, let me ask her."

......

THOMAS DROVE through Maverick Square in the morning rush. The shops were starting to open, and fruit vendors were setting up their stalls. Packed streetcars and busses pulled into the train station. Kids scurried down the sidewalks with school bags over their shoulders.

For Thomas, the area had a warm familiarity. Having lived in East Boston all his life, he couldn't go anywhere without seeing ghosts of himself. The spot where, at nine years old, he had flipped his bicycle and broken his front teeth; the barbershop where he had gotten his first haircut; Sonny's barroom where, even after he had quit drinking, his father would go after work with men from the shipyard.

But he also saw how much the neighborhood was changing. Each time he came out to the harbor, he was amazed. From Chelsea Creek to the South Boston Annex, warships and other military vessels filled every wharf, pier, and dock. Over at the Charlestown Navy Yard, a giant new destroyer sat glistening in the sun, waiting to be launched.

He continued along the waterfront where areas that had been vacant when he was a boy were now warehouses and storage facilities. One lot was piled twenty feet high with scrap metal—thousands of bed frames, boilers, pans, paint buckets, etc.—waiting to be transported down the coast where it would all be melted down for bombs and bullets.

As he passed East Boston Works, a guy stepped out from a side street. He had a bag over his shoulder and a gray lunchbox in his hand. Realizing who it was, Thomas sped up and pulled over, rolling down his window.

"Didn't you hear the whistle?"

The man looked over but didn't flinch.

"Nolan," he grumbled.

Vin Labadini was more of a low-life than a criminal. Stocky with big ears, he always looked angry or aggravated. Thomas had only known him for two years, but they had already clashed twice. The first was when he worked as a guard at the shipyard and then again when George was dating Labadini's sister Angela.

As someone who had stayed out of trouble, Thomas should have hated Labadini. Either incident would have been enough for a lifetime grudge. But after joining the force, he realized he needed contacts on the streets to get anything done. Or, as a lieutenant once put it, sometimes it was good to know bad people.

"How was that tip?" Labadini asked.

"Which tip?"

"The factory on Border Street."

"A few gas ration books, not much," Thomas said, which was a lie.

"You know what they make in there?"

"Raggedy Ann dolls?"

"Body bags."

Labadini seemed to get a sinister thrill out of it.

"Who's selling oil?" Thomas asked.

"Oil?"

"There might be a shortage this winter. I figured people were stockpiling already. Hedging a bit."

"It wouldn't be a bad investment if it's true."

"At the expense of poor families freezing to death."

Labadini snickered.

"I ain't heard nothing yet. Ask me in December."

Thomas slipped him a book of gas stamps, and he shoved them in his pocket.

"I got something for you too," Labadini said.

Opening his lunchbox, he took out a paper bag and opened it. Thomas peered in to see freshly ground coffee, something so scarce even restaurants were buying it on the black market.

"Smells good," he said.

"Top shelf. You won't find any chicory in there."

Thomas had been trading favors with him for months, but he never assumed anything was for free.

"What do I owe you?"

"It's on the house. But I need some help."

"What kinda help?"

"It's my pop. He's trying to get on the picket patrol—"

"Ain't he too old?"

"They'll take anyone."

The Coast Guard had formed a civilian fleet to patrol at night, watching for U-boats or enemy planes. There were ads in the newspapers and posters at train stations. Anyone with boating experience could join, and its members ranged from lowly sailors to seasoned yachtsmen.

"Why doesn't he stick with fishing?"

"The money is better," Labadini said. "They get petty officer pay. But his ID still says, 'Enemy Alien.' He thinks they won't hire him."

"He can get that removed now."

"There's a little problem."

Thomas got the hint. Restrictions against Italians were over except for people with criminal records.

"What'd he do?"

Labadini shrugged his shoulders.

"It was a long time ago."

"What did he do?" Thomas repeated.

"He had a little racket. He was taking numbers. It was years ago, during the Depression."

"Let me see what I can do."

5

THE FIRE CAPTAIN WALKED UP AND DOWN THE ROW WHILE THREE OF HIS men watched. Tall and handsome, he wore a navy coat with brass buttons and a dress uniform hat. Each time he spoke, all the girls nodded, their eyes wide and beaming.

"If you find yourself in a smoke-filled room," he said, "stay low."

"How low?" someone asked.

"On your belly. Slither like a snake if you have to."

Abby tried to listen, but she was distracted by shouting. On the far side of the field, some men were practicing rugby. They weren't wearing the BU colors, so she assumed it was a local team.

"Before opening a door, put your hand to it," the captain went on. "If it's hot, don't open it."

"What if there's someone inside?" another girl asked.

"Wait for the Fire Department. When they bring in the hoses, get outta the way as fast as you can. One burst could send you flying like Daffy Duck."

The only person who didn't laugh was Ms. Stetson who stood stone-faced in her green uniform. Even for a college professor, she was stern. Abby thought it was because, as a woman, she couldn't get ahead at Boston University. Harold said she was just a frustrated lesbian.

"Remember this. Your jacket could save your life."

The captain opened his coat, tucked his head in, and took a deep breath. Then he looked up and blew it out.

"An old trick from firefighting lore. There's always one last bit of clean air inside your jacket, even those fancy petticoats."

Everyone looked at each other, impressed.

"Any other questions?" he asked, but no one raised their hand. "Good. Let's practice some resuscitation."

They had been standing in the cold for two hours, and Abby was shivering. She understood the need for fire defense training, but at this point in the war, no one expected an air raid or bombing attack.

She had joined the Massachusetts Women's Defense Corps out of a sense of duty. But the only thing they did that seemed important or useful was patrolling during blackouts. She was tired of serving tea at war bond luncheons and marching in victory parades. She had considered going into the Women's Signal Corps, which at least paid, but she couldn't take off the four weeks for basic training.

As they broke up into groups, Frances ran over, her lashes dark. She was the only girl who got made up for drills and exercises.

"Happy to be your victim."

"I'm flattered," Abby joked.

Over on the sidelines, Major Ward watched as her staff got blankets out of an MWDC ambulance, one of a half-dozen donated to their unit. A stout woman in her late fifties, she was married to a banker and had no children. Abby had once made the mistake of asking if she was related to her parish priest. As a Yankee from Needham, the major had been horrified. In her crowd, Catholicism was more of an accusation than an attribute.

The girls carried the blankets over and spread them out.

"Victims, take your places," the captain said.

Frances lay flat on her back, smoothing out her skirt. Abby knelt beside her on the damp grass.

"Once you've got your victim away from the fire," the captain instructed, "check for burns. If you have your kit, pour some sulfur on them. Cover the wound as quickly as possible to prevent infection…"

He had a confident swagger, but his words were mangled by his working-class accent.

"If a victim is pulled from rubble, check for broken bones…"

Abby leaned over Frances and felt her arms and legs, surprised at how toned they were. Not only was she on the volleyball team, but she played tennis all summer.

"The first sign someone is suffering from smoke inhalation is coughing or hacking…"

"Isn't he a regular Albert Einstein," Frances whispered.

"Shhh!"

"If your victim isn't breathing," the captain said, "you need to try to resuscitate him. Tilt his head back, pinch his nose. Take a deep breath…"

Abby watched him glance over mischievously at his men, who stood waiting to see thirty girls kiss each other.

"Okay, okay," Major Ward said, scrambling over. "We get the idea. They've already had first aid training."

Abby extended her hand and helped Frances up.

"Ladies," the major called out, and they circled around. "We've just been notified by the Committee on Public Safety that there'll be a blackout test two weeks from today. Please make all necessary arrangements. You're to report to your posts no later than six pm."

She relieved them all with a salute, and everyone dispersed. Abby and Frances walked over to the bleachers where Harold was waiting. He had on a long coat and a felt hat with a bow.

"How many lives did you save?"

"I wouldn't have minded that captain saving mine," Frances said.

As they got their bags, the rugby team was coming off the field too.

"Abigail?"

Abby turned to see Mr. Glynn.

"Oh, hello, Professor."

He had on a striped shirt and shorts, his legs covered in mud.

"The Women's Army Corps is it?" he asked, wiping his glasses with a towel.

"*Defense* Corps," she said, but she wasn't offended because everyone got it wrong. "This is Frances."

Frances smiled.

"I was in your class last year," she said, and he winced, "...but I had a conflict in my schedule."

"I'm sorry to hear."

"And this is Harold," Abby said.

When Harold tipped his hat, they eyed each other for a little too long, almost like they had met before.

"How goes the scrum?" he asked.

"Too muddy for my tastes. Do you play?"

"In high school."

"You should join us."

"Too kind, thank you," Harold said, a nervous excitement in his voice. "Perhaps, I will."

"Right, then," Glynn said. "A pleasure."

He smiled at Abby and Frances, gave Harold a second look, and walked away.

......

BY THE TIME Abby got off the streetcar, it was almost dark. As she approached Gittell's Tailor, she noticed the light was on. She had the urge to go in, but she didn't want to bother Arthur's father. She used to go in a lot, but he'd never had any news or updates about his son. Two people worrying about the same person only made it worse for each other. So she stared straight ahead and went right by.

She was almost at her house when she heard a voice and stopped. Looking over, she saw two figures standing behind the fence of the corner church, and they weren't big enough to be intimidating. She walked over and realized it was a boy and a girl, their hands gripped to the pickets. Even in the shadowy light, she could tell they were about twelve years old.

"*Allo?*" the girl said.

Abby was as surprised as she was curious. In a neighborhood of Irish, Italians, and other Catholics, there weren't many Congregationalists. When she was young, the building looked abandoned with its overgrown hedges and cracked shingles. Everyone said it was haunted, and on Halloween, Abby and her friends would dare each other to knock on the door.

"Where are you going?" the boy asked in the same accent.

"I'm going home."

They wore ragged coats and caps, their cheeks red from the cold. Like any kids, their faces were bright and eager, but Abby could sense some faint weariness or distress.

"Where're you from?" she asked.

"England," the girl said.

"Brixton," the boy added.

"So, which is it?"

The boy hesitated, biting his lip. Abby could tell he was shier than the girl.

"Brixton is in England."

"What brings you to East Boston?"

"A big boat," the boy said, although it wasn't what she meant.

"Our flat was blown to smithereens!" the girl exclaimed.

Abby's face dropped. She struggled not to look sad or shocked. Even to kids, who probably didn't understand the seriousness of it, she didn't know what to say. She had heard about the bombing of London but had never met anyone who was there.

"Children!"

Abby looked over and a woman was standing in the side door. She had on a blue dress, an apron, and her dark hair in a bun. She nodded to Abby and said to the children, "Get inside. Your dinner's getting cold."

"Yes, Miss!"

They peered up at Abby with a look of disappointment, even longing. Then they let go of the fence and ran inside.

Abby waved and continued up the sidewalk. Most of the houses were dark, but that didn't mean people weren't home. Anyone living within a quarter mile of the coast now had to have blackout shades.

When she walked up the front steps, her mother was sitting on the porch with a ball of yarn on her lap and needles in her hands. After her husband had died, she had taken to knitting to keep her busy.

"Aren't you cold?" Abby asked.

"I find it refreshing."

"I just saw some children…at the Protestant church. I think they might be orphans."

"It's about time those people did something for someone."

The remark was harsh, but Abby couldn't argue. Her mother had grown up at a time when Protestants ran the city, looking down on the Irish and other groups.

"How's Chickie?" Abby asked.

"She's upset. Connie's giving her a bath to calm her down."

"Why?"

"Some boy called her a mongoloid today at school."

Abby's temper flared, remembering how cruel kids were. At fourteen, Chickie was two years behind in school, and she should have been a freshman. She had always been picked on, but it seemed worse in adolescence.

"Who said it?" Abby asked.

Her mother looked up.

"Oh, Abby, who knows?"

"Little bastard."

"Mind your language—"

A roar sounded overhead.

Abby leaned over the railing, but the sky was too dark to see. Seconds later, a plane shot by toward the airport. It was low enough that the ground shook, and the windows rattled. She could tell by the sound it was a fighter, something Arthur had taught her.

Her mother didn't seem fazed or distracted, wrapping the thread and hooking the stitches with a slow concentration. By now, they were all used to the war, and to death. Matteo Nunzio, who lived one street over, had been killed the weekend before in the South Pacific. Tim Enright's brother was missing after his merchant ship got torpedoed near Iceland. Still, she seemed remarkably calm for a woman who would startle at the sound of church bells.

"What're you having?" Abby asked, looking at the glass on the table.

Her mother glanced up.

"Cream soda."

"In this weather?"

"Just like your father."

The response was snippy, but it was also true. After her father had quit drinking, he'd drank cream soda year-round.

There was a tense silence, and Abby felt guilty for being suspicious.

"What's that gonna be?" she asked.

So far, her mother had only made mitts and a shawl. Abby was surprised when she held up something that resembled a sweater.

"For George?"

In the four letters her brother had sent them, all he'd talked about was the wind, rain, and cold. The Aleutians had been quiet since the Japanese had attacked in June, but the weather sounded brutal. Abby worried more about him suffering frostbite than getting shot. But they could only guess how he was or what he was doing. And not knowing was like a long and slow torment that made their days hell.

"You think it'll fit him?" her mother asked.

Abby's lips twitched, and her eyes got watery. Overcome with emotion, all she could do was nod.

6

ACROSS THE PACIFIC WAS ABOUT A U.S. ARMY CAPTAIN TRYING TO GET to China to become a mercenary, only to get dragged into a spy ring. Thomas liked Humphrey Bogart, but now everything was about the war, and sometimes he didn't want to be reminded of it. The song "Praise the Lord and Pass the Ammunition" was all over the radio, and the latest Popeye cartoon was called *Scrap the Japs*.

As they left the theater, he took Connie's hand. She looked stunning in her long red dress, her hair in Victory Rolls.

"What a film!" DiMarco said. "Whaddya say we get a drink?"

"Where?" Thomas asked.

"Anywhere. I'm parched."

Holding his arm was Sarah, an old friend of Abby's from their summers on Point Shirley. DiMarco and Sarah had met at Thomas' wedding back in July. At some point during the reception, they had disappeared down to the beach, returning later covered in sand and burrs. Considering she had rosy lips, curvy hips, and big breasts, Thomas understood why DiMarco liked her, but he never thought it would last.

Scollay Square was busy. All the bars and restaurants were packed. It was Boston's version of Times Square, with giant billboards and flashing signs. It had a bad reputation, especially after dark, but there were enough respectable places to offset the gin joints, burlesques, and tattoo parlors.

They approached a man selling paper roses, and Sarah turned to DiMarco.

"Won't you buy me one, hon?" she asked, her hands clasped as if in prayer.

He looked at the guy.

"How much?"

"Ten cents."

"I'll give you five."

When DiMarco flipped him a nickel, the man didn't haggle. He handed her one of the flowers with a smile.

"How do I look?" she asked, putting it in her hair.

"Like Carmen Miranda."

They acted like teenagers with all their giddiness and playful flirting. Thomas didn't know if he was repulsed or just jealous. He and Connie never had had much of a courtship. With Chickie in their lives, he felt like he had been thrown into adulthood. But he wouldn't have given it up for anything.

"Would you look at those rocks?" Sarah said.

She took Connie's hand, and they walked over to the window of a jeweler while Thomas and DiMarco waited.

"That's some lady you got," DiMarco said.

"I know."

"If that don't work out, let me know."

Thomas raised his fists and threw a fake punch, joking around like they did in high school.

"I need a favor," he said.

"Name it."

"You know Vin Labadini?"

DiMarco frowned.

"Unfortunately."

"His father is trying to get on the picket patrol, but he's been in trouble—"

"That whole family is trouble," DiMarco said, which wasn't far from the truth.

"He can't get 'Enemy Alien' taken off his ID because he's got a record."

"That's the Coast Guard, Thomas."

"I figured you might know somebody."

DiMarco looked flattered, which was what Thomas intended.

"Why you wanna stick your neck out for that rat?"

"He helps me out. Gives me tips."

DiMarco got distracted, and his face beamed. When Thomas turned, he saw the girls coming back.

"Let me see what I can do," DiMarco said, and then he looked at Sarah. "See anything expensive?"

"Plenty."

"Too bad it's closed," he said, winking at Thomas. "How 'bout this joint?"

They looked over to the Waldorf Cafeteria. There was a line out front, and it was so crowded inside the windows were fogged up.

"It looks too busy—"

"Officers!" A fat maître 'di waved from the doorway. "Please, come in!"

Thomas didn't recognize him, but he had worked the downtown beat for months and met hundreds of people. Either way, everyone liked to be in good with cops.

As they walked over, a loud drone rang out across the city. For an instant, everything seemed to stop. The entire square went silent. People started to trickle out of the bars and nightclubs. Some waved for taxis or scurried down into the subway. But air raid sirens didn't create the same panic they used to.

"Was this planned?" Thomas asked.

DiMarco shook his head.

"The chief didn't say anything."

Thomas looked at Connie who stood still with her lips pressed together. As composed as she was, he could tell she was shaken.

Before she came to America, she had lived in Malta with her

late husband. When the Germans bombed the island, her mother-in-law had been killed along with many other civilians. He knew she was haunted by it, the way she startled, her fits of sudden gloom.

Walking over, he took her gently by the arm. She was stiff, not trembling, which didn't surprise him. She always responded to fear with coldness.

"We're gonna call it a night," he said.

DiMarco and Sarah looked disappointed, but neither tried to discourage them. Thomas knew they understood.

"Sure, Thomas, sure," DiMarco said.

Sarah stepped over to hug Connie.

"A lovely evening."

Connie nodded with an uneasy smile.

"Very much so."

......

BY THE TIME they got back to East Boston, Connie had calmed down. With the window cracked, she leaned against the door, smoking, her pocketbook on her lap.

"What time did you tell Abby we'd be back?" Thomas asked.

"I said eleven."

As they drove down Bennington Street, the streetlamps were dim from blackout shades, casting a shadowy haze over the road. While shops had to close early, barrooms were allowed to stay open. Most had no windows, so they weren't a risk. But it said a lot about what the government thought was more important.

"How 'bout a walk on the beach?" he asked.

"The beach?"

"I need to go to the cottage anyway. Ma wants me to check the icebox."

She hesitated, gazing ahead with a mysterious wonder. He could never tell what she was thinking, but he somehow knew what she felt.

Finally, she looked over.

"I'd like that."

He hit the gas, and they went past their street. They drove another mile and went over the bridge into Winthrop. Compared to East Boston, it felt like a coastal village. The streets were quieter, and the homes more spread out. The exhaust from cars, buses, and trolleys was replaced by the smell of the ocean.

As they crossed the strand, Point Shirley loomed in the distance like a dark mass. Summer cottages were always shuttered for winter, but now most of the year-round residents were gone too. Even with the Navy patrolling, people were scared to live so close to the water. Not a week went by without a U-boat being reported, although many were false alarms.

They turned down Bay View Avenue, a narrow lane of saltbox houses whose shingles were cracked and faded from the salt air. As a boy, Thomas roamed the neighborhood with friends, from the rocky shoreline of the harbor to the beaches on the north side.

In the offseason, Point Shirley always felt empty, but now it seemed desolate, almost forgotten. The trees were bare from the strong winds, and a layer of sand covered the road. Thomas didn't see a single light until he came around the bend to the Loughrans'. Originally just summer residents, they had moved in full-time after retiring. They were some of the last holdouts in an area that, because of its location, was heavily restricted by the military. Houses on the coast were under a permanent blackout order, and the beaches were closed at night.

Thomas pulled in front of the family cottage, a small clapboard house his great-grandfather had built by hand fifty years before. It had two floors, a front porch, and was surrounded by a large yard. Facing Winthrop Harbor, it looked out to East Boston and the airport.

Thomas got out and gazed at the water. In the distance, the lights of the city were dimmer due to regulations, making it look like an ailing version of what it once was.

Connie walked over and stood beside him.

"So beautiful," she said.

Standing in the solemn quiet, he couldn't deny there was something romantic about wartime. They were thousands of miles from the fighting, yet he experienced some of the same excitement, fear, and urgency. If it didn't lessen his guilt over not enlisting, it at least made him feel more a part of the struggle.

"I'll go check the icebox," he said.

When he held out his hand, she just stared at it.

"Let's walk first," she said with a mischievous smile.

They both knew why they had come out there. Although they were married, intimacy at home was difficult. The walls were thick, but the floor creaked, and Chickie, who always had trouble sleeping, was in the next bedroom. Beyond that, Thomas was still uncomfortable having sex in Mrs. Ciarlone's house. He wasn't a prude, so it was more out of respect, especially with her son Sal away in the Navy.

"Meet you over at the rocks," he said.

As she walked off, he watched her, her figure swaying in the darkness. He crossed the lawn and went up to the front porch, which was covered in dead leaves. Kneeling down, he pulled one of the loose shingles, and a key fell out. He opened the door and walked inside. The air was dank, reeking of mildew, and he could still smell ash from the fireplace.

He walked into the kitchen, opened the icebox, and winced at a horrific stench. He took out a milk bottle and poured it into the sink, holding his breath as the thick rotten syrup streamed out.

"Thomas?" he heard.

The front door opened, and Connie burst in.

"I saw something!"

"What?"

"I don't know. A ship. But just the top."

Thomas put the bottle on the counter and grabbed her arm. They ran out of the house, across the street, and down to the shore, a steep barrier of rocks.

"Over there," she said, pointing toward the horizon.

All he saw was blackness and one or two tiny flickers of light, morse code from Navy or Coast Guard ships. Early in the war, their signals had caused panic, but now everyone knew what they were.

"I don't see anything," he said, but he knew her eyesight was better.

"Is that you, Thomas?"

When he turned, Mr. Loughran was standing at the top of the bluff. In his robe and slippers, he almost looked elderly, a thin wisp of hair fluttering at the top of his bald head.

"Mr. Loughran," Thomas said.

"Is everything alright?"

"Connie thinks she saw something...in the water."

"Like what?"

"A ship," she said. "But very low on the water."

Mr. Loughran stepped closer but didn't try to come down. After thirty years as a cop, his knees were bad, and he had arthritis.

"I doubt it," he said. "The Army's got all the channels mined. Winthrop harbor is too shallow for German U-boats."

"It was far out," Connie said.

"Like a silhouette?"

She nodded, but Thomas didn't think she knew what the word meant.

"Could be a sandbar. The tide's out."

In her face, Thomas saw the same quiet despondency she had when the sirens went off downtown. But even if she was paranoid, she was still a sensible girl. He owed it to her to believe her.

"We'll go over to the base and report it."

"It wouldn't hurt," Mr. Loughran said.

With a wave, he turned to go but stopped.

"Have you heard from George?"

Thomas hesitated.

"Not in a few weeks," he said, which was an understatement. It had been almost two months.

"Say hello to your mother, would ya?"

"I will. Thanks."

After he walked away, Thomas and Connie climbed up the rocks and went back to the road. He opened the door for her and then got in. Starting the engine, he pulled out and continued down the dark road.

"You think I'm crazy."

When he looked over, Connie sat hunched against the door with her arms crossed.

"No. Not at all."

"Maybe I see things. Maybe it's my imagination."

"Or maybe there was really something out there."

At the end, they turned right and headed toward Deer Island, a windswept stretch of barren land at the end of the peninsula. For years, the only thing out there was the state prison, a huge granite building surrounded by a barbed wire fence. But a year before, the Army had rebuilt Fort Dawes, a former Great War gun battery that had fallen into disrepair. Now part of the harbor defenses, it had two 90mm cannons and other artillery. Thomas hadn't been out there in years, but all summer, he watched as military trucks rumbled through Point Shirley, bringing troops and supplies.

They passed the prison, which looked even eerier with all the lights blocked out. As they continued, the road got bumpier, a mix of sand and asphalt. The coastline was dark, but the sky was clear, reflecting off the calm water. Anytime Thomas looked out, he couldn't help but think that a few thousand miles beyond, there was a war.

"Thomas?" Connie said, touching his arm.

Seeing a flashlight ahead, he slowed down. He pulled up to a checkpoint where two soldiers with rifles stood at a barricade, one on either side. As Thomas rolled down his window, he took out his badge, more as a courtesy than some attempt to influence or impress them. Civilian cops had no authority over the military.

A young private swaggered over, his chinstrap loose.

"Evenin' officer," he said. "I'm sorry. This area is restricted."

"My wife thinks she saw something out in the harbor."

The young man knelt slightly, leaning in the window.

"What do you think you saw, ma'am?"

"It was like a shape. Like a *sill-wet*," she said, but he seemed to understand what she meant.

"Hang on."

He went over to a guard post made of sandbags, and Thomas saw him reach for a field telephone. A minute later, the soldier came back.

"The CO said it was probably just a barge."

Thomas was relieved, although not surprised. He hadn't thought it was anything suspicious.

"Thanks."

Suddenly, headlights came up the road.

"Mind pulling over?" the young man asked.

Cutting the wheel, Thomas drove onto the grass, and the soldiers waved an Army truck through. The back was full of men, all in dirty work clothes, their faces scruffy. He knew the prison supplied workers for the military, but these men didn't look like inmates.

As he watched, they all stared back with hollow eyes. He was struck by an uneasy feeling, and he knew Connie had it too. When he looked over, she seemed almost frightened. Once the truck passed, he put his car into gear, turned around, and sped off.

7

ABBY STOOD ON THE COURT, HER KNEES BENT AND READY. AFTER A LONG day of work and classes, she was tired. Going home, she always had to worry about falling asleep on the streetcar, but in the moments she spent on the court, she felt energized. Practice revived her.

Waiting for the serve, she looked over to Frances who stood in a crisp white skirt, her hair in a ponytail. With the cool autumn nights, most of the girls had started wearing gym pants, but Frances was more concerned with style than comfort. For someone so athletic, she wasn't good at volleyball, or maybe the sport was too common for her to care. Sometimes Abby wondered if Ms. Stetson kept her on the team just so she could look at her legs.

The ball came flying over the net, and Abby knocked it back. It returned, this time faster, and the setter blocked it. They went back and forth a few more times. Abby's heart pounded, and her body tingled from the adrenaline.

Someone knocked the ball high in the air, and it came down over Frances. Jumping to hit it, she lost her balance, and a teammate caught her. It went by her and bounced out of bounds. When the whistle blew, the whole team moaned. No one liked to lose, even when it was only a scrimmage.

"That's all for tonight, ladies," Ms. Stetson said, standing on the sidelines with a clipboard. "We've a game with Babson on Thursday evening. Arrive no later than a half-hour beforehand."

Abby staggered off the court, her head slumped and out of breath.

"You can't win 'em all," Frances said, running to catch up.

Abby stopped and turned to her.

"Were you even trying?" she asked.

"I felt a little faint. It must be the lights."

"You seemed distracted."

"To be honest, love, I am. Mother has decided to move into the city."

"Where to?"

"Beacon Hill, most likely. She can't be around that lout anymore."

Abby regretted being snippy with her. While Frances' life looked glamorous from the outside, she knew the truth. Mr. Farrington, who worked for the Office of Civilian Defense, had been having an affair with a girl in the Women's Army Auxiliary Corps. Frances never complained about it, but Abby knew it must have been humiliating for her and her mother.

"What will you do for Thanksgiving?"

"Probably the Parker House or something."

They walked into the locker room, and Abby felt the warm steam. She used to shower after practice, but she didn't like carrying her makeup kit around all day. And with the cold, she worried her hair would freeze.

They got their bags, and as they left, Ms. Stetson was standing by the door.

"Goodnight, Miss," Frances said.

"Goodnight, ladies."

They crossed the court and went out the gymnasium doors into a dark corridor. As they walked, the floor creaked, and Abby felt a draft coming from the rooms. Situated behind Copley Square, the old building was out of place on the street of elegant brick townhouses. It was far enough away from campus to be inconvenient, and she assumed it had been donated to the university.

"Done so soon?"

Abby smiled when she saw Harold. He always showed up to their events whether it was volleyball practice or an MWDC meeting.

"Five minutes too late," Frances said.

"My life story."

Beneath his coat, he had on a striped shirt, and his hair was a mess. It was the first time Abby had ever seen him not in a suit.

"You're sweating," Frances said, reaching to push his bangs aside.

"And sore," he said, then he looked at Abby. "I took your friend up on his invitation."

It took her a moment to realize he meant Mr. Glynn.

"Rugby?"

"A game for barbarians, played by gentlemen."

"And which are you?" Frances joked.

"A bit of both."

They all laughed and walked toward the exit.

"Should you be fraternizing with professors?" Abby asked.

"It's all above board. I'm not in any of his classes."

"You should be glad you aren't," Abby said. "That man's got a grudge against the world."

"Just the British, something I would expect you, of all people to sympathize with, *Ms. Nolan*."

She understood what he meant, but she didn't agree. Even though her father had come from Ireland, she never felt a connection to the place. Her neighborhood used to be Irish, and now it was mostly Italian. She had gone to school with kids of many nationalities. They had all been taught that they were Americans.

He opened the door, and they went out into the brisk night air. The side streets of Back Bay were quiet, the only sounds the hiss of gas lamps and the rustle of dead leaves.

They followed the brick sidewalk for two blocks and came out to Huntington Avenue. Cars and taxis sped by, and the bars and lounges were all open. But Copley Square had none of the energy and excitement of before the war.

"How's about some tea to revive us all?" Harold asked.

"I've gotta get home," Frances said. "Mother is coming up tomorrow to look at an apartment."

"How about you?" he asked Abby.

"I...can't. I have work in the morning."

"We don't cavort like we used to."

While he said it lightheartedly, Abby could sense a tinge of disappointment, even longing.

In their freshmen year, they went out a lot, but now they were all too busy. Harold didn't have much family around, so Abby knew he was lonely. His mother was deceased, and his only brother had taken his own life six months before. He wasn't close with his father, who lived in Bermuda and was remarried.

"Are you going to your father's for Thanksgiving?" Frances asked.

"As it happens, probably not."

"Good. If Sal is in town, we'll all go out and have a time of it!"

Harold closed his eyes and smiled.

"I'd expect nothing less."

......

Abby trudged up the front steps and dropped her bookbag on the porch. With work, school, volleyball, and the MWDC, she was exhausted by the end of the week.

When she walked in, her mother was sitting in the recliner with a book, a cup of tea beside her.

"You're late," she said, but it wasn't an accusation.

"The subway broke down at Scollay Square."

As Abby hung up her coat, the rack looked empty, another sign of their dwindling family. She remembered the days when there were more jackets, scarves, and mittens than it could hold.

"I made stew," her mother said.

"Thanks. Any mail?"

Her mother looked up.

"Not today."

Sometimes it was a relief to hear nothing. Abby had had nightmares of getting a letter from the War Department saying George had been injured or worse.

She walked into the kitchen, and there was a cast iron pot on the stove. Reaching for a spoon, she lifted the cover and looked in to see chunks of carrots, potatoes, and leeks in brown gravy. When she tasted some, she winced from the salt. Then she noticed a box of Steero on the counter and realized it was just vegetables and bouillon cubes. With beef scarce, everyone had to get creative. Some shops were even selling horse meat as a substitute.

She closed the lid and walked out to the foyer, turning to go upstairs.

"Not hungry?" her mother asked.

"Not now."

"It's not to your liking?"

Abby could tell she was insulted.

"Where'd you get beef?" she asked sarcastically.

Mrs. Nolan put down her book.

"Never mind about the beef. Maybe you can tell me where you got the sugar?"

"Whaddya mean?"

"Not *whah-dah-yah*," she said, mimicking her. "It's *what do you*."

Anytime they bickered, she would try to correct Abby's speech or manners.

"Ma, I don't need a grammar lesson."

"Where did you get the sugar?"

Abby hesitated. She thought about denying it, but she was too old to be lying to her mother.

"The bakery."

"You stole it."

"They have loads of it. I figured with Thanksgiving coming—"

"You stole it!"

"I took a little!"

Her mother stood up, almost losing her balance. She wasn't as stable as she used to be. Abby had tried to be more understanding since her breakdown, but she also wasn't going to be pushed around.

"You're to take it back first thing in the morning."

"I'll do no such thing!"

Her mother came toward her, and Abby didn't back away.

"Yes, you will!"

"Like hell!"

They were both startled when the door swung open. Thomas stormed in, still dressed in his uniform, and said, "I need band-aids!"

Abby could tell he was upset, which was almost a relief. His anger would be enough to calm both of theirs. Their attention would shift, and the argument would be over.

"What happened?" Mrs. Nolan asked.

"Some little bastard shoved Chickie in the schoolyard. Her knees are scraped up."

Mrs. Nolan was flustered, but not because of his language. She never scolded Thomas for swearing.

"Let me check the cupboard," she said, rushing into the kitchen.

As Thomas waited, he looked at Abby.

"What's wrong?" he asked.

She looked away, her teeth gritted.

"Nothing."

8

Thomas sat at his desk going through reports. He liked having an office, even if he had to share it with the other sergeants. The air was dank, and the steam radiator hissed. It was only the second week of November, but the days were getting cold. Outside it was raining, casting a gray haze over the city. Had it been five degrees cooler, it would have been snow.

He loved the winter, but he knew this year would be different. With the Petroleum Administration for War predicting a fuel shortage, everyone was worried. Half the homes were rundown, with drafty windows and old furnaces. There was sure to be hoarding and theft, and people would suffer. Any time something got scarce, a black market would emerge, and all the crime and infighting that went along with it. Watching how society adapted to the struggles of wartime was like a crash course in human nature.

The phone rang. Thomas got up and went over to answer it.

"Hello?"

"Sergeant, there's a major here. He wants to speak with someone," the secretary said.

"A *major*?"

"That's right."

"Have him see Captain Vitti."

"He's out. Can I send him down to you?"

Thomas hesitated.

"Sure, I guess."

He hung up, and moments later, he heard footsteps. When he leaned out the door, he saw a tall man in a military uniform coming down the hallway. Even as a major, he was older than Thomas expected, with graying hair and a wrinkled brow. He held his hat under his arm, his olive jacket covered in bars and medals.

"Sergeant?" he asked with a curious look.

"Yes. Sergeant Nolan."

Thomas extended his hand, and they shook.

"Major Holdsworth," the man said. "I didn't expect someone so young."

Thomas grinned. It was something he heard a lot.

"Promotions have been quick. We're losing a lot of guys to the service."

"And I think I'm getting them."

Thomas led him into the office and shut the door. Looking around, he was embarrassed by the mess, a half-dozen desks and mismatched chairs. The walls were bare except for a corkboard with shift schedules and wanted photos.

"Please, sit," he said, but the major put up his hand.

"I'll only be a couple of minutes. I just wanted to stop by and introduce myself. Nothing formal or official."

"Of course."

"As you know, we've got a company over at Wood Island Park."

"The base?"

"Not a base, per se. Barracks and a storehouse," Holdsworth said, and then his tone changed. "We've got a negro unit down there. Part of the Signal Corps. You might see some of the boys around town."

Thomas nodded, not sure how to respond. He knew about prejudice, but East Boston had no blacks, so it was never a problem.

"I'll let the patrolmen know."

"We're also going to need to restrict parking on Neptune Road so the trucks can get through. Just during daylight hours."

"I'll get some signs posted."

"Good," the major said, straining to think. "Oh, I'm told some Red Cross girls have been using the park for training?"

"That's the Massachusetts Women's Defense Corps."

Holdsworth's expression soured. A lot of men, especially military officers, didn't respect any of the female volunteer services.

"Right. Well, they'll have to find somewhere else."

"I'll let my sister know."

"Your sister?"

"She's in the local unit."

The major hesitated.

"If that's the case, I suppose they could stay," he said. "As they say, one hand washes the other."

Thomas appreciated the courtesy.

"They meet there before blackouts. They're air raid wardens."

"Everyone has a part to play," Holdsworth said. "Thanks for your time, Sergeant."

"My pleasure."

"I'll see myself out."

The major shifted his hat from under one arm to the other, and they shook hands again. As he turned to leave, he stopped, looking around the office. The station wasn't glamorous, and to an Army major, it probably seemed like an administrative backwater.

"How're things on the home front?" he asked.

"Depends on the day."

"We're grateful for what you boys do. You're critical to the war effort."

Since joining the force, it was one of the kindest compliments Thomas had ever received. But for some reason, he felt ashamed.

"My brother's in the Army," he said.

"And where is he?"

"The...Aleutians...last we heard."

The major smiled.

"God bless him."

With that, he nodded and walked out.

......

THOMAS DROVE THROUGH THE STREETS, squinting in the late afternoon sun. He could've brought another officer out when he patrolled—most sergeants did. But he liked being alone. It gave him time to think.

With school out, there were kids everywhere, hanging on corners and in doorways, playing stickball in abandoned lots. When he passed a group of teenagers, one of them flicked his hand under his chin, an Italian insult. He hit the sirens, but none of the boys flinched. It took a lot more to intimidate people in the rougher neighborhoods.

He continued along the waterfront past a dozen dockyards and the annex of the Charlestown Navy Yard. Except for the ferry, everything in port was a military vessel, including a hospital ship, a Navy destroyer, and a Dutch frigate that had been stranded since the war started.

Soon he approached Jeffries Point, a sprawling neighborhood that overlooked downtown on the other side of the harbor. The streets were narrow, and the houses were shabby. It was mostly Italian, a mix of dockworkers, fishermen, and tradesmen.

Waiting at a light, Thomas saw three men in front of a bakery. He waited for it to turn and then raced across, stopping short at an angle.

"Nolan?" Labadini said, walking over. "You looking to get clobbered?"

He still had on his work clothes, his teeth stained from cigarettes.

"I'd like to see someone try."

As they talked, the other two men just glared.

"Any luck with my pops?"

"I talked with the lieutenant. He's working on it."

"Thanks."

"Got anything for me?"

"You need steaks?"

Thomas frowned.

"No contraband," he said like he hadn't accepted any before. "How 'bout a tip?"

Glancing around, Labadini leaned in the window and lowered his voice.

"You know the garage on Chelsea Street across from Jeveli's?"

"What about it?"

"I'm told they got more tires than Goodyear. And they're getting top dollar."

"A racket?"

Labadini cocked his neck, giving Thomas a sharp look.

"I ain't saying that," he said. "But they're definitely selling them over the price cap."

"Good. I need some new tires."

When Labadini grinned, Thomas revved the engine and sped away. Their conversations always ended like that. From a distance, they probably looked like an argument or spat. Thomas still didn't like Labadini, but he trusted him and more importantly, he relied on him. With Labadini's help, he had broken up a card game at the VFW Post and caught the gang of kids who were robbing old ladies in Day Square. He had gotten steaks for their Columbus Day party, and stockings for Connie, which had both been out of stock because of war shortages.

When Thomas got home, he went up his mother's steps and stopped. His first instinct was always to go into his childhood house. He turned around and walked next door, where Connie was waiting for him on the front porch.

"I went by the bakery," Thomas said.

"I left work early. Chickie was sick at school today."

"She was sick on Monday."

Connie gave him a skeptical look, and they walked in together.

"Where is she?" he asked, and she glanced up.

They went upstairs, and when Thomas opened Chickie's door, she was on the bed with her legs crossed, combing her doll's hair in long, steady strokes.

"Hi, honey," he said, sitting next to her. "You didn't feel well today?"

Chickie shook her head, staring down, her hair still damp from the bath.

"Belly ache," she said.

"How is it now?"

She shrugged her shoulders.

"Better now."

"How about we go see the boats this weekend?"

She looked up, her face beaming.

Adults were no longer impressed by all the ships in the harbor, but kids still were.

"Good. Now get some rest."

"Get some rest," she repeated.

Leaning over, he kissed her on the forehead, and she went back to her doll.

Thomas and Connie went back downstairs. He took off his coat and handed her his holster. She carried it into the living room, and he could hear her locking it in the cabinet. When she came back, she had a white box.

"What's this?" he asked.

"For your mother. From the bakery."

Opening it, he saw a half dozen shortbread cookies, all sprinkled with pink sugar. He reached for one, and she smacked his hand.

"For your mother," she repeated.

"I'll take them over. What's for dinner?"

"Macaroni."

Thomas didn't scoff, but they had already had it twice that week. Before he met her, he had never eaten pasta, which his mother used to call peasant food. But it was cheaper than meat and easier to get, and Chickie loved it.

"Be right back," he said.

He left and went over to his mother's house. When he walked in, she was in the kitchen doing the dishes, the kettle on the stove. Abby was at volleyball practice, so he knew she had eaten alone.

"Thomas," she said.

She took off her apron and had a nice dress on underneath. Her hair was in curls, and she even wore some light makeup.

"Don't you look fancy?"

"We had a meeting about the Victory Fund."

After losing her husband, volunteering had saved her life. Her church group was involved in everything from selling war bonds to knitting sweaters for soldiers. In a vacant lot nearby, they had built a Victory Garden so amazing the mayor gave them an award for it.

"Connie got these for you," he said, giving her the box. "Shortbread cookies."

"Oh, my favorite. Won't you have one?"

"No, thanks. I haven't eaten yet."

The kettle whistled, and she poured some tea. Thomas followed her out to the living room and stayed standing while she sat.

"Chickie came home early again from school today," he said. "Said she had a belly ache."

"Do you think she's sick?"

"I think it's nerves."

His mother sighed, and they both knew why.

"It's probably that boy, Clarence," she said.

"You know his name?"

"Chickie told me."

"Little bully," he sneered.

"He's probably just acting out. With the war, everybody's scared."

While Thomas trusted her wisdom, there was no excuse for taunting a troubled young girl.

"He's gonna be scared alright."

"Now who's the bully?" she said, and he scoffed. "Don't do anything rash. Besides, Chickie has to learn to stick up for herself."

Thomas nodded, but he didn't agree. As a young police officer and a middle-aged housewife, they would always have different ways of handling conflict.

"Did any mail come today?" he asked.

Blowing on her tea, she peered up. It was the simplest question, but the one he always dreaded to ask.

"Not today."

9

"Get another tray!"

Angela went out to the front, returning almost a minute later.

"Not that kind," Abby said. "That's for the bread."

"How can you tell?"

"The pastry ones are longer."

Angela never moved fast enough, which was probably why Eve had taken her off the counter. Mornings were frantic, especially with Thanksgiving approaching. The girls scurried around making boxes, getting things out of the cases, slicing bread. The only person who didn't rush was Eve, who took her role as manager as an excuse to do less work.

But working in the kitchen required the same if not more coordination. Each time Carlo took a hot pan out of the oven, he would place it on the rack. The pastries had to be iced or topped, depending on what they were. Then they had to be moved to a tray and taken out to the front.

Abby had been training Angela for over a week, and she still couldn't get it right. On Monday, she had dusted a tray of donuts with nutmeg instead of cinnamon, and they had to throw them out. The day before, she had used her hands instead of a spatula for the croissants and had torn them all apart.

"Abby," someone called.

When she turned, Connie was in the doorway. Even in a hairnet, she was beautiful, and Abby was proud to have her as a sister-in-law.

"There's no powdered sugar on those Bomboloni."

Abby glanced at Angela, who squirmed and looked away.

"I'll be right out."

She grabbed the shaker, and it was almost empty. Walking back to the storeroom, she went up to the cabinet with the sugar. A chill went up her back when she saw it had a padlock on it.

"I'll open it."

Startled, she turned to see Eve behind her.

"It's locked?" she said, somewhere between a question and a statement.

"Rita says somebody's been skimming off the top," she said, then she lowered her voice. "I bet it's that Labadini girl."

Abby forced a smile, struck by a private shame. Her mother scorned people like the Labadinis, and yet she was no different.

Eve took out a key and unlocked it. Abby filled the shaker, the powder dust going everywhere. As she went back through the kitchen, she looked at the clock and worried she would be late for class.

"Angie," she said. "Bring out those tarts, would you?"

The moment she walked out to the front, she stopped. Standing at the counter were two black soldiers, their service uniforms pressed and caps on tight. They were young, speaking quietly to each other and pointing at pastries through the glass.

A subtle tension filled the shop, or maybe it was just Abby's imagination. A couple of men in the corner were staring, but no one else seemed to care. While East Boston had lots of prejudice, it also never had any negroes. The only one Abby ever knew was a boy from high school, and he was half-Portuguese. If anyone was offended, they probably didn't know how to show it.

"'Scuse me," one of the men said. "What's this?"

"Bomboloni," Abby said, sliding the tray in.

"How 'bout them?"

She leaned over the glass.

"Um...those are cornetti."

Both men winced, which made Abby giggle. Of all the cases in the bakery, they had picked the Italian one.

"They good?"

"Delicious."

Angela came out with the tarts, and she seemed equally struck by the soldiers. When the shorter one looked at her, she smiled. Abby took the tray from her and put it in the case. Looking across the room, she saw that Connie and the other girls were busy boxing some pies.

"I gotta go," she said to Angela. "Mind helping these gentlemen?"

"I'd be happy to."

......

BY THE TIME Abby got off the streetcar, her first class was almost over. She didn't want to walk in late. So she skipped it, which made her feel a little guilty. She was on a scholarship and felt an obligation to take her studies seriously. But skipping also gave her a mischievous thrill, reminding her of the days when she and her friends would play hooky and take the train into town.

When she got to the cafeteria, Frances was at the corner table, which wasn't a surprise. Much like Harold, she never seemed to be in class, yet still passed all her courses. Abby attributed it to their private education and all the other advantages of wealth and sophistication. Until she met them, she had never heard anyone use the word "tutor" or "extracurricular."

Abby took a tray and got in line, reaching for an apple from the bin. Behind the counter, a stout woman stood grilling omelets and French toast. At the register, a soldier was paying for his breakfast. With his buzzed hair and clear skin, he reminded her of Arthur. Even so, she felt a mix of longing and bitterness. She couldn't understand why the troops were on campus and not overseas fighting like her brother and boyfriend.

"Abigail, dear," she heard, and Frances scurried over. "Order me some toast, won't you?"

She pressed a dollar bill into Abby's hand, which made it impossible to refuse.

"Anything else?"

"Just whatever you'd like, too."

Whenever they went out, either she or Harold would always pay. Abby knew they did it out of friendship, but sometimes it felt humiliating. Her mother had taught her to never take charity.

By the time she got their food and brought it over, Harold had shown up. Unlike his usual three-piece suits, he had on a tweed sportscoat and white cotton shirt. At his feet was a leather duffle bag.

"Aren't you casual?" she said.

She handed Frances her plate and sat down.

"We've a scrimmage today. I find this getup easier with all the changing and unchanging."

Abby bit into her toast, surprised to taste real butter. The week before, the cafeteria had only had margarine.

"I never knew you for such a sportsman," she said.

"It's not sport he's interested in," Frances said.

Harold just grinned and took a puff of his cigarette. Growing up in East Boston, Abby had been taught to be direct. She was still getting used to their side remarks and innuendoes. But before she could ask him to explain, he got distracted. Abby looked over and cringed when she saw Mr. Glynn walking toward them. He had a funny stride, his arms tight to his side, his small steps more like a shuffle. He wore a brown suit with a cream-colored shirt and silk tie. His hair was neatly combed, short on the sides and fuller on top.

"Good morning, Harold."

"Richie," Harold said, which was strangely informal. "This is Frances."

Glynn made a slight bow.

"How do you do?"

"And Abigail, of course," Harold added.

She put her hand to her mouth, still chewing.

"Yes, Miss Nolan," the professor said. "I didn't see you in class this morning."

"Sorry. My train was late."

"Sadly, you missed my talk about The Easter Rising."

"Sounds like a bake sale," Harold joked.

"My father was Irish," Abby said.

It was neither a good response nor an excuse for not going to class, but Mr. Glynn seemed curious.

"Was?"

"He passed away last year."

"Then I'm very sorry."

The mention of his death always caused an awkward pause.

"Well, I should be going. Nice to see you all," the professor said and then turned to Harold. "I'll see *you* on the field."

"I'll be there with bells on."

"More than that, I should hope."

As they all laughed, he looked at Harold with a subtle but simmering grin. Then he nodded and walked away.

"He's sweet," Frances said.

"A bit hard up on Irish politics, but a good egg nonetheless."

"I think you make a dazzling pair."

Abby froze.

"Oh, didn't you know?" Frances said. "Harold never played rugby. It was all a ruse."

"Not a *ruse*. And I did play junior year until I pulled my Achilles."

"After how many games was that?"

"Three, I believe."

Abby chuckled and took a sip of her tea.

"Consider it a redux of my athletic career," he went on.

"More like redux of your libido."

"Trust me, darling, that has never gone dormant."

As they spoke, Abby sank in the chair, glancing around. It never bothered her that Harold was queer. She once had a great-uncle from NYC who had been rumored to be that way. But she didn't like them talking about it out in the open, more for his sake than hers.

"Invite him to Cocoanut Grove with us next Saturday," Frances said eagerly. "He can meet Sal—"

"Sal?" Abby asked.

"His ship is stopping in Boston. I told you so."

"You said it was a rumor."

Frances tilted her head as if considering the misunderstanding. Despite all her good qualities, she never liked to admit when she was wrong or mistaken.

"Well, either way, he called me two nights ago. His ship is due in port next Wednesday."

"Just in time for Thanksgiving!" Harold said.

"Why the hell didn't he call Connie?" Abby blurted out before remembering the Ciarlones didn't have a phone.

They both looked at her.

"Because he wants it to be a surprise."

"At ease, Abigail," Harold joked, trying to soften the tension. "It's good news all around."

Abby felt bad for snapping. Even as close friends, none of them had ever argued. She was glad Sal was coming home, as much for Frances as for Chickie. But with Arthur away, some part of her was envious too.

"I'm sorry."

Frances smiled.

"Not at all," she said. "But hush hush, please. He doesn't want anyone to know."

10

As Thomas walked, he tried to hold Chickie's hand, but she kept pulling away to look at things. In an alleyway, she saw two cats fighting. Under a car, she found a pinecone, which was strange because there were no pine trees in East Boston. He loved her curiosity. It reminded him of his own at her age.

In middle school, Thomas, Abby, and their brother had taken the same route to school each morning, down Saratoga Street and turning at Moore Street. It was only two blocks from their house, but it felt like miles. The thrill of being free and independent had never gotten old. He remembered seeing the milkman go by, his wagon pulled by two horses. One time, George had thrown a snowball at a car, and the driver had gotten out and chased them.

When Thomas and Chickie got to the school, the schoolyard was busy. Younger kids were on one side, and the upper grades on the other. Over in the corner beside the dumpster was a giant pile of scrap, the metal and rubber that students had been collecting. Thomas wondered why the flag was at half-staff until he remembered it was Armistice Day, which seemed celebrated more in the past than now. With the country at war, people didn't want to be reminded of the last one.

As they walked toward the front doors, Thomas looked around, especially at the boys.

"Which one is Clarence?"

Chickie looked up with a scowl. The question wasn't fair, and he knew she wouldn't tell him anyway. Everyone scorned snitching.

"My friends," Chickie said.

Over at the fence, two kids were standing alone. The boy wore knickers that had been out of style for a decade. The girl had on a ragged petticoat that was two sizes too big.

"Are those your friends?" he asked.

Chickie nodded.

"Olive. Alfie."

"I think they're waiting for you," he said, then he kissed her on the forehead. "Have a good day."

"Good day."

She skipped over, swinging her lunchbox, and Thomas continued into the building.

The old school hadn't changed since he went there, with its high ceilings, scuffed-up floors, and dark hallways. As he went toward the office, he passed a memorial to students who had died in the Great War, including Mark Swiggins, his mother's first boyfriend. While he always found the plaque moving, he didn't have time for sentiment. He was angry.

"May I help you, officer?" the receptionist asked, and he whisked by her. "I'm sorry, you need an appoint—"

He stormed into the principal's office where Mrs. Giaconni was sitting at her desk.

"I beg your pardon," she said, standing up.

In her mid-forties, she wore a wool suit and pleated skirt, her hair in a pompadour.

"Someone's harassing my daughter. It needs to stop!"

Their eyes locked.

"And who is your daughter?"

"Chickie Ciarlone."

"Would you care to sit, Mr. Ciarlone?"

"It's Nolan."

"Nolan?" she asked, looking flustered.

Just the insinuation of a divorce or second marriage made most people uncomfortable.

"Thomas Nolan."

Her expression softened.

"Then you must be George Nolan's brother?"

Thomas felt the blood leave his face. He had entered in a rage, but the mention of his brother made him wilt.

"You know my brother?"

"Of course. He went to school with my son Paul."

Thomas tried but couldn't recall a Paul Giaconni. At East Boston High, there had been more Italian names than he could count.

"Now, who is bothering Chickie?" she asked.

"Clarence is his name."

"Clarence Morris," she said, rolling her eyes. "I'm not surprised. He's been discourteous to the English schoolchildren too."

"English schoolchildren?"

"We have some war refugees here at the school now. Four. Two are from London and two are from the North of England."

Thomas nodded, not sure how to respond.

"Clarence's older brother is with the Navy in the Pacific. It might explain why he's acting out."

While it wasn't an excuse, it was something Thomas could sympathize with.

"The war's been hard on everyone," he said.

"I'll have a talk with Clarence."

"I'd appreciate that."

She smiled, and he followed her out through the reception area, stopping at the doorway.

"Thank you again for bringing this matter to my attention, Mr. Nolan. Thank you, too, for keeping us all safe on the home front."

Thomas hesitated, struggling to respond.

"We do our best."

······

When Thomas walked into the station, DiMarco was at the counter talking to the young secretary. Lately, it seemed like he was in East Boston more than at headquarters. Lieutenants could move around, a freedom Thomas sometimes envied. But their job was also more administrative.

In high school, he and DiMarco had just been acquaintances. They had been on the boxing team and had fought in the same weight class. But the lieutenant was so much older that they had never socialized much. By the time Thomas was a senior, DiMarco was already on the police force. Now that they were adults, it was different. And with so many of their peers in the service, they had become good friends.

"Aren't you late, Sergeant?"

Thomas frowned and walked by, the lieutenant following him down the hallway.

"Since when do you keep track of time?"

"Did you hear we captured Casablanca?"

"Good. Maybe they'll make a film out of it."

But the war wasn't something to joke about. After almost a year of minor setbacks and small victories, things were finally looking up. The U.S. Army had landed in North Africa, the British had defeated Rommel in Egypt; the Soviets had the German army surrounded in Stalingrad, and the Japanese were getting clobbered in Guadalcanal and New Guinea. Somehow it felt like a turning point, although no one would say it. In a neighborhood of ethnic Catholics, people were superstitious.

When they got to the office, DiMarco shut the door. Thomas knew he had something to say.

"I went over to the Coast Guard station yesterday. Tell Mr. Labadini to re-register for his ID card. It's all set."

Thomas held out his hand, and they shook.

"Thanks," he said. "Now I'll feel safer with the picket patrol watching the coast."

The lieutenant chuckled.

"Don't underestimate them. They ain't just a bunch of crabbers. They tracked a German sub off Deer Island a couple weeks back."

Thomas felt a shiver go up his back.

"A U-boat?" he asked.

"Yeah. They think it was trying to lay mines."

Thomas had wanted to believe Connie saw something that night, and the news would be some vindication. But he also knew what fear could do to people. The constant threat of attack wore down everyone's nerves, often to the point of lunacy. The week before, a hysterical housewife had run into the station because she had heard a neighbor speaking German. And anytime a squadron flew by they would get a flood of calls from residents.

"What're you doing Thanksgiving weekend?"

"Um, working, I think," Thomas said, distracted.

"I want you and Connie to come out with us. We're going to Cocoanut Grove."

"I would but—"

"You already got the night off. I told the captain I need you for special duty."

Thomas gave an amused expression.

"Which is what exactly?" he asked.

"Celebrating my engagement. I asked Sarah to marry me."

11

Abby waited at the entrance to Wood Island Park with a dozen other girls. Some leaned against the trees; others sat on the grass smoking and talking, their bags at their sides. At the center stood Lieutenant Hastings, a middle-aged woman from Beacon Hill who kept her hair short and wore studded earrings. Despite her plain appearance, she had an upper-class sophistication. She had been assigned to East Boston by chance, and Abby was sure she had never been there before the war.

The park was separated from the neighborhood by a marsh, the last remnant of nature in a dense and overpopulated part of the city. As girls came across the road, their figures were silhouetted against the half-lit city in the background.

A frigid wind came off the harbor, sweeping up the hill and rustling through the trees. Even in a wool skirt, jacket, and overcoat, Abby shivered. She couldn't stand still for too long without getting cold, so she was eager to start moving. But the women in her unit never got there on time, the one breach of discipline the lieutenant overlooked. Many were local, but some were not. After a long day at work or being home with their children, they had to suit up and take trains and busses to get there.

In the distance, Abby saw flickers of light down at the new Army camp. Gossip about the black soldiers stationed there had been spreading. Even Carlo had mentioned it, although, with his broken English, it was hard to tell whether it was a complaint or just an observation.

Whatever the controversy, the military had taken over a place that, for many residents, was sacred. The barracks had been built on a clearing that used to be flooded for public skating. Abby remembered spending long winter afternoons there with her brothers. The officers' quarters, a large wooden structure, was on top of the former baseball diamond. The Army Corps of Engineers had even cut down a row of ancient elms to make a parking lot. Combined with all the military planes taking off and landing over at the airport, some days it felt like they were under siege.

"Abby!"

When she turned, Giannina DiMarco was walking toward her. Her parents called her Gia, but everyone else called her Nina. She had fat cheeks and a plain face. But like any girl, she could be pretty when she smiled. Abby had known her since high school where they were a grade apart. Now Thomas worked with her brother Nick.

"Did you hear the news?" Nina asked.

"What news?"

"Nick is getting married."

Abby blinked.

"To Sarah?"

"Of course. Who else?"

"I'm delighted," Abby said.

Abby had never been petty, but she hated hearing about people going on with their lives when her own was on hold.

"Maybe we'll be bridesmaids?"

"Maybe."

"Fall in!"

They circled Lieutenant Hastings who stood with her back arched, a clipboard in her hands. On the ground beside her was a large crate with their equipment. Before the base opened, they had used a public works shed for storage, but the Army had taken it down. Now everything had to be dropped off by staff from headquarters.

"The blackout is expected to begin promptly at twenty hours," the lieutenant went on, squinting to see her watch, "which is in approximately seven minutes."

Earlier in the war, the authorities didn't announce the time, wanting to train people for a real attack. But after several gruesome accidents, including a car that had driven off the Longfellow Bridge, they had changed their policy.

"As usual, you're to go to your assigned districts. If anyone is uncooperative or belligerent, you're not to argue. Go immediately to the nearest police alarm."

People everywhere were irritable, and blackouts only made it worse. Female air raid wardens had been harassed, and auxiliary police officers had been assaulted. So far, there had been no looting, but criminals always tried to take advantage of the blackout period.

"Now get your torches and get into formation," the lieutenant said.

Nina unlocked the crate, and everyone stepped over to get a flashlight. Then they made a line along the road, with Lieutenant Hastings standing at the front. Angela Labadini walked over and stood next to Abby.

The sirens rang out, their metallic hum thundering across the night sky. Lieutenant Hastings waved her arms, and they started to march. The noise lasted sixty seconds and then stopped, leaving a haunting silence. Slowly, the lights of the city went off, the tallest buildings first, spreading like a wildfire of blackness. It continued to the outer neighborhoods and then into the towns up and down the coast.

"How do you like the bakery?" Abby asked.

Angela shrugged her shoulders.

"Ain't bad, I suppose."

"Are you still helping your father?" Nina asked, and Abby hadn't realized she was behind them.

"He's not fishing now."

The war had been hard on small fishermen, even with the high price of seafood. With the threat of U-boats, insurance rates had gone up, and many owners couldn't afford it. The bigger companies had bargained with the government to get them to pay part of the premium, but independent workers hadn't been so lucky.

"He's with the picket patrol," Angela added.

"What's a picket patrol?"

Before Angela could answer, she dropped to the ground as if she had fallen through a trap door.

"You okay?" Abby said, leaping to help her.

"What's the problem back there?" the lieutenant shouted, and everyone stopped.

"She fell."

The road out to Wood Island Park had always been rough. But with the construction of the base, the trucks and bulldozers had torn it up. The ruts were treacherous in the dark.

Abby and Nina lifted Angela. Taking a step, she stumbled, and they quickly caught her.

"Shit! It might be broke," she said, wincing in pain.

Lieutenant Hastings stormed over, giving them all a haughty look.

"Can she walk?" she asked like Angela wasn't there.

"I don't think so," Abby said.

"Then take her back. When I get to Maverick Square, I'll call headquarters and have someone get her."

"Yes, Miss."

Without another word, the lieutenant walked back to the front.

"Forward, march!" she exclaimed, and the column began to move.

Angela put her arms around Abby's and Nina's shoulders, and they all turned around.

"It hurts like hell," she said.

"Don't put any pressure on it," Abby said.

"Did you see Hastings' face when you said 'shit'?" Nina asked, chuckling.

As they approached the clearing, a vehicle came speeding up

from the base. Worried they would get hit, Abby waved her arms. Moments later, a jeep rolled up with its headlights off.

"Y'all alright?" she heard.

Squinting, she saw two black soldiers. They were both young, no more than twenty. She recognized the driver as one of the men who had come into the bakery on Monday.

"She might've broken her ankle," Nina said.

"Can you walk, Miss?"

"Not without screaming."

While she wasn't joking, everyone laughed.

"We can take you down to the camp," the driver said. "They got splints and such."

Angela looked at Abby and Nina.

"Sure, I suppose," she said.

Getting out, the men walked over and took Angela from them. They lifted her into the passenger's seat, no small act of courtesy because the jeep was tiny and had only two seats. The driver got in, and his partner squeezed into the back.

"How will—" Nina went to ask.

"The sergeant will drive her home once we get her fixed up."

Abby was uneasy, and not because the men were black. She had been taught to never let friends leave with strange men. But Angela was an adult, and she was tough as well as street-smart. If anyone could take care of herself, it was her.

When the driver gave them a casual salute, Abby and Nina waved. The jeep turned around, and they watched as it headed back toward the barracks.

12

Driving around the next morning, Thomas could tell when there had been a blackout the night before. The streets were quieter, and after sitting in total darkness for hours, people looked groggy. The sudden return of power created problems with transformers and other electrical equipment, and in some cases, caused fires. Men from the Public Works Department went around checking streetlights and traffic signals. There were always a few bad car accidents.

"I'm thinking of joining up."

Thomas looked over at Officer Carroll. He was the only cop in the precinct who didn't smoke, which was why Thomas didn't mind taking him out on patrol.

"Yeah?"

"I just can't sit here while all our boys are over there."

Over there. It was the phrase people used to describe a war that seemed to be everywhere except America itself.

"You're needed here too. We're all needed."

Thomas said it as much to comfort himself as to convince his partner. The department was losing cops every week, and even auxiliary officers were hard to find. In the last blackout, the Boy Scouts had been called in to help.

But he understood Carroll's restlessness. He had it too. His only consolation was knowing that if he didn't have Connie and Chickie to take care of, he would have been in the Army.

"What if the Krauts come here?" he asked.

Carroll shrugged his shoulders. While earlier in the war, an invasion was a real concern, no one expected it now. Or if they did, they were tired of worrying about it.

"You got a brother in the Navy, right?" Thomas asked.

"He's in San Francisco," Carroll said, almost like he was ashamed.

"Then your family's doing their part."

Carroll hesitated, gazing out the window.

"It ain't the same," he said.

They cruised around the neighborhood in silence. Although only two years apart in age, they didn't have much to talk about. Carroll was single and lived with friends in the North End; Thomas was married with a daughter.

When they got to Day Square, Thomas slowed down in front of the bakery. He looked in but didn't see Connie. A milk truck beeped, so he sped across the intersection and turned onto Chelsea Street.

They passed the garage that was selling tires illegally. It was strange to think that charging above the government price cap was now worse than selling something that was stolen. Either way, they had enough evidence to make a bust. The captain just hadn't approved it yet because they were too busy.

"Is that what I think it is?"

Up ahead was a salvage dump, one of the largest in East Boston. Carroll pointed, and Thomas saw two kids carrying a radiator. He knew they weren't donating it.

He pulled over, and they both got out.

"Hey!" he shouted.

When the boys looked over, Thomas was sure one of them was Clarence Morris.

"Stop!"

Instantly, they dropped the radiator, and it smashed on the sidewalk, shaking the ground. They took off, and Thomas and Carroll ran after them. At the next crossroads, the boys split up, one going straight and the other turning up a side street.

"You get that one!" Thomas shouted.

He chased one down an alleyway, dodging barrels and ducking under empty clotheslines. When the boy hurdled a fence, Thomas did too, landing in a small backyard with a dead garden and a statue of the Virgin Mary. Out of instinct, he reached for his gun but stopped. Stealing scrap metal was a felony, but he wasn't going to shoot a twelve-year-old kid for it.

Finally, he ran down a narrow driveway and stumbled out onto the next street.

"Sarge!"

He turned and saw Carroll rushing toward him.

"You get him?" he asked.

"Little bastard got away. You see where the other one went?"

Thomas shook his head.

"I...I think I know who he is."

"Where the hell were they goin' with a radiator?"

"You know what pig iron is worth these days?"

Thomas stood with his hands on his hips, gasping for breath, his eyes teary from exertion. He wasn't as fit as he used to be, and it wasn't from domestic life. When he first got on the force, he was a beat cop, walking for hours each day. Now that he was a sergeant, he drove everywhere.

"What happened?" Carroll asked, nodding.

Thomas looked down and noticed a cut on his hand.

"The fence," he said.

"You should get a tetanus shot."

Thomas wiped the blood off.

"C'mon," he said. "Let's get back to the cruiser before someone steals *that*."

......

. . .

When Thomas walked in the door, he smelled something cooking. Chickie ran down the stairs with her doll in her arms.

"Toh-ma!," she said, reaching up for a hug.

Connie came in from the kitchen, her hair pulled back and wearing dark red lipstick.

"*Lavati le mani. È ora di mangiare,*" she said to Chickie, who seemed to respond better to Italian.

Chickie did a little dance and then scurried back upstairs.

"She seems happy," Thomas said, and they kissed.

"Her enemy wasn't in school today."

While enemy didn't seem like the right word, it confirmed for him that the boy he chased was Clarence Morris.

"I'm not surprised," he said. "I didn't see you at the bakery today."

Her expression sharpened.

"You came in?"

"I drove by."

Thomas took off his coat, and she helped him.

"I left early," she said, and then she exclaimed, "Your hand!"

She grabbed his wrist, squinting to inspect the wound.

"It looks worse than it is."

"You need to clean it. It will infect."

"After dinner."

"No. Now. Please."

Their eyes locked, and Thomas consented with a nod. Connie wasn't stubborn, but she was persistent. After only four months of marriage, he had learned it was easier not to argue.

"We have no more peroxide," she said.

"My mother should have some."

Thomas left and went next door. When he walked into the house, he felt a chill. His mother always kept the temperature low, some leftover habit from the Depression.

"Ma?"

"In here, darling," she said.

He went into the dining room to find her knitting at the table. There were dozens of spools of yarn around her, all different colors.

"Do you want me to put on more coal?" he asked.

"Don't bother. I'll be in bed in a couple of hours."

Her voice had a strange tone, her words slow, almost forced. He was concerned enough that he stepped closer to see if her eyes were glassy. In the low lamplight, it was hard to tell, so he assumed she was just tired.

"What's all this for?" he asked.

"Bundles for Britain."

"Bundles for Britain?"

She held up a small blanket.

"For all the families suffering over in England. We're having an event at St. Mary's on the twenty-eighth. I'd love for you and Connie to come and bring Chickie."

For a woman who had always scorned social clubs and service organizations, she was more passionate about the war effort than anyone. The spring before, she had started one of the largest war bond drives in East Boston. Over the summer, she and her friends from church had planted Victory Gardens throughout the community.

"We're busy that night," Thomas said. "I'm going to Cocoanut Grove. Nick DiMarco got engaged."

She stopped what she was doing and looked up.

"To Sarah?"

Thomas chuckled. It was the same reaction he got whenever he told anyone who knew them.

"They're in love," he snickered.

"Don't knock it. It's the only thing keeping this world together."

"Do you have any peroxide?" he asked.

"Peroxide?"

He held out his palm.

"What happened?"

"It looks worse than it is," he said, which he knew didn't answer the question.

She immediately put down her needles and rushed into the kitchen, returning with a brown bottle. Soaking a rag, she sat in front of him and took his hand. As she wiped away the dried blood, he got sentimental, remembering how she used to tend to his and his brother's wounds.

"Does that hurt?"

"Naw," he said, although he felt a little sting. "I think I chased that boy who's been bothering Chickie."

"How do you know who he is?"

"Because I went to see the principal last week."

She peered up, giving him a sharp look.

"Thomas, you really shouldn't."

"No one has a right to bully her. She's different."

She didn't argue.

"There," his mother said. Finished with his hand, she stood. "But you should really get a tetanus shot."

He wanted to scoff but didn't. She had lived through a time when there were no vaccines. As a girl, she had a cousin from Maine who had died from rabies. Her grandmother had died of diphtheria, a disease that was terrifying to even say.

"Maybe I'll do that."

13

The pans came out of the oven faster than Abby could keep up. Using a spatula, she moved the hot pastries onto trays to take to the front. With Thanksgiving only two days away, the bakery was busier than any other time of year, including Christmas. They had hired extra help, but even eight girls working at once wasn't enough.

"Abby!"

When she looked back, Eve was standing in the doorway holding a trash bin. Her hair was clipped up, her forehead glistening, and she looked out of breath. Abby hadn't seen her work so hard in months, but the holidays always made up for all her slacking.

"Take this out. Would ya?"

Abby rushed over with a fresh batch of lemon meringue tarts.

"I'll trade," she said.

She handed Eve the tray and took the bin. She went out the back door into the narrow alley behind the building. The air was frigid, the ground covered in dead leaves and litter. In the summer, none of the girls went out there because of the rats. In the winter, it was too cold, especially with the wind coming off the flats at Wood Island Park.

As she emptied the trash into the dumpster, she heard the squeak of brakes. Looking over, she watched a black soldier in a jeep stop on the side street beside the bakery. Angela got out of the passenger seat, waving before the young man sped off. She walked down the alleyway, still limping from her fall. While she hadn't broken her ankle, she had hurt herself bad enough that she had missed almost a week of work.

Somehow, the drop-off seemed scandalous, and Abby wished she hadn't seen it. She always stayed out of trouble by minding her own business. She wanted to dart back inside, but Angela had already seen her.

"How's the foot?" Abby asked.

"Better."

Angela wore lipstick and had on a pink headband, unusual for a girl who usually looked like she had just woken up. After an awkward moment, Abby smiled and got the door.

"Thanks," Angela said.

Abby took the bin out front and put it in the corner. The line was now twice as long, and people were waiting out on the sidewalk. Over at the register, Connie was ringing in an order, speaking in Italian to an elderly woman. Abby tried but couldn't get her attention. Sometimes they went a whole shift without talking.

She went back into the kitchen and took off her apron, reaching for a tissue on the shelf over the sink. Her nose seemed to run from November until April.

"Ab!" Eve said. "Can you help Angie with those before you leave?"

Over on the table, two pans of hot Danishes were waiting to be prepped. In the busy season, it didn't take much to stall the process. Even Carlo, who never complained, was standing by the oven with a look of mild frustration.

"Sure," Abby said, glancing at the clock.

She walked over and grabbed a can of icing. She worked quietly beside Angela, but she knew it wouldn't last.

"He was only giving me a lift, you know?" Angela said, her voice hushed but firm.

Abby wanted to ask *who?* but knew it would sound insincere.

"I'm sure you need it with that ankle."

They continued for another minute in silence.

"He's from Philadelphia."

Abby just nodded. She didn't know if Angela was looking for approval or advice, but she wasn't about to offer either. When it came to romance, everyone knew the risks and the taboos.

"He's nice," Angela went on, and Abby still didn't reply. "Don't you have anything to say?"

Abby lifted the tray and turned, giving her a pointed look.

"Nice men are hard to come by."

......

Mr. Glynn stood at the front of the classroom. He wore a checkered jacket with pinstriped pants, an outfit that would have clashed on most men. Considering how reserved he was, it seemed too flamboyant for his personality, and Abby wondered if it was an Irish thing. Europeans always had a better sense of fashion.

"During the Irish War of Independence," the professor said, "the British continued with their oppression of the Irish people by the introduction of the Black and Tans. Can anyone tell me who they were?"

A hand went up.

"Part of the Royal Irish Constabulary, the Irish police, sir," a young man said.

Glynn curled his lips like he wasn't satisfied.

"Technically, yes. But their significance is much greater. Can anyone elaborate?"

A girl in the back raised her hand.

"They were brought to Ireland by the British to maintain order during the Revolution."

This time, he frowned.

"If by 'maintain order,' you mean butchering people in the fields and burning down whole villages, perhaps."

Finally, Abby put up her hand, and the professor pointed.

"They were mostly veterans of the Great War, often men who had been out of work. In Ireland, they committed terrible atrocities against local civilians, so bad they were decried even in England."

For the first time that morning, the professor smiled.

"Bravo, Miss Nolan. And for these reasons, Irish resistance to British rule remains steadfast."

"The English are still our allies," someone said.

"America's, yes. Ireland remains a neutral country in this conflict."

"Sir?" someone asked, and Glynn pointed. "Weren't the Black and Tans there to stop the Irish Republican Army?"

"What's your point, Mr. Cutler?"

"Didn't the IRA exhibit the same violence and disregard for life that they accused the British of?"

"The IRA was formed to free Ireland from English tyranny. Considering your country's own history, I would imagine it's a struggle that every one of you can very much relate to."

Abby was relieved to hear students in the hallway because it meant class was over. While Mr. Glynn never hid his distaste for the British, the discussion was getting too controversial for even him.

"For next class, please read up through chapter eleven," he said, "the assassination of Michael Collins and the beginning of the Irish Civil War. Have a lovely Thanksgiving."

Abby put her notebook in her bag and got up.

"Miss Nolan?" the professor called.

She walked over to his desk.

"I applaud your understanding of the subject matter."

"I got it from my father."

"We'll make a Fenian out of you yet," he said, with a restrained smile.

"Terrific. Do they let women in?" she joked.

"I wanted to ask you something," he said, hesitating until the last student left. "I've been invited by Harold to come out this weekend—"

"To Cocoanut Grove."

"I understand you'll be joining us?"

"Frances, too."

"You see," he said, averting his eyes, "it sort of puts me in an awkward position."

She knew what he was going to say before he said it. As a professor, he wasn't supposed to socialize with students, an unwritten rule that many people broke. The semester before, Abby saw one of her classmates at a café with their biology professor. And she knew Ms. Stetson was having an affair with Mrs. Sears. Freshman year she had walked in on them hugging. At the time, she was horrified, which she attributed to being naïve. She soon learned the world wasn't as plain and conventional as she had been raised to believe.

"Richie!"

Abby turned and saw Harold in the doorway, a bag over his shoulder.

"Am I late?" he said, out of breath.

"Not at all. We start at noon."

Harold sighed, walking in with exaggerated relief. He moved differently around the professor, something Frances had noticed too. It was some little sashay that, while not quite feminine, had a hint of flirtation.

"I seemed to have forgotten my tennis shoes," Harold said.

"No bother. I've some to lend."

Harold put his hands together, bowing like a Yogi.

"Won't you come watch the match?" he asked Abby.

Even if she wasn't busy, she wouldn't have gone. She didn't like violent sports, and rugby seemed like a bunch of men wrestling in the mud.

"Thanks, but I have an MWDC meeting."

"The Ladies' Defense Corps is it?" the professor asked.

"Massachusetts Women's Defense Corps."

The name was clumsy to say, and she always had to correct people.

"That's unfortunate. We're playing the best team around. It should be quite a thrash."

"Break a leg," Abby said before realizing the irony.

"My dear," Harold said, "Let us hope your life-saving skills are better than your metaphors."

14

Thomas drove through Maverick Square traffic. Even with the heat on full, he was shivering. One of the hoses had a leak, but new ones weren't available, another consequence of the war. But staying warm was the least of his problems. The tires were so bald the car dragged, and he avoided trolley tracks because they were treacherous. He knew he would have to raid the garage on Chelsea Street if he wanted new ones anytime soon.

While it was his job to stop black markets, he was glad they had them. They used to be for things that were illegal or banned. Now they were for basic necessities. If he wanted meat, Labadini could get the best steaks around. If he wanted coffee or sugar, he knew a guy in Maverick Square who had buckets of it. Gasoline was never a problem. The station had stacks of the best ration coupons.

Sometimes he felt guilty taking things, but it never lasted. Times were tough, and all cops skimmed. It was a small benefit that made up for the low salary and long hours.

Stopped at a light, he saw Labadini standing in front of Sonny's bar with some guys. He could tell they had just left the shipyard. They had work clothes on under their coats and metal lunch boxes at their feet. As they talked, the steam from their breath mixed with cigarette smoke in a haze of gray.

Thomas tried not to make eye contact—he wasn't in the mood to talk. But the moment Labadini saw him, he shouted and stormed over, his arms flared. Thomas wasn't startled. Labadini always seemed angry, always looked like he was ready to lose his temper.

"Nolan," he grumbled. "I got a problem."

Thomas glanced up. With men like Labadini, it was best to just let them talk.

"I heard something 'bout my sister," he continued, his voice tense. "I don't like it."

"Angela?"

He nodded.

"Somebody seen her with a soldier."

"Plenty of those around."

Labadini scowled like he wasn't amused.

"You don't understand. He's a dirty—"

The slur stung. Thomas had witnessed a lot of petty prejudices growing up in East Boston, but his parents had never put up with racism in their home. The one time George had used that word, their father had smacked him so hard he had fallen back and broken a lamp.

"What the hell do you want me to do?" Thomas asked, almost insulted.

"Find out who he is, so I can break his fucking neck."

"You do that, and you'll be hanged."

"I'll take my chances."

Thomas was conflicted. He didn't want to do anything to jeopardize an American soldier. But he also understood the urge to protect a sibling, especially a sister.

"Let me see what I can find out."

......

. . .

THOMAS SAT on the couch while Chickie did her homework upstairs. The Ciarlones' living room was the same size as his mother's, with a fireplace and three windows. The décor was similar too, with floral wallpaper and dark furniture, mostly mahogany. When he first moved in, there had been a giant oval picture of Mrs. Ciarlone's deceased husband on the wall and some smaller photos of her Italian relatives. They had always made him uncomfortable, and Connie must have sensed it because she had removed them.

The longer he waited, the more his impatience turned to anger. On his way home, he had stopped at the bakery, and Connie hadn't been there. Eve Santangelo said she had left early but didn't know why. Now it was almost seven o'clock, and Chickie hadn't eaten.

Hearing footsteps, he got up and went to the door. It swung open, and Connie walked in.

"Where were you?" Thomas asked.

She brushed by him, the cold radiating off her body.

"I'm sorry I'm late. Where's Chickie?"

"Doing her homework. Where were you?" he repeated.

"Remember Marta from work?"

He always thought it was a strange name for an Italian, but he could never forget her friend from home. They were from the same village, and Marta had gotten Connie her first job when she came to America.

"I thought she moved to Providence."

"She lives in Pawtucket now," she said, sounding like *POO-tucket*. "She was in Boston today. We had lunch at Beachmont Café."

"And that took seven hours?"

"I left the bakery at two."

"I wish you had told me."

"*Conn-ah*," Chickie called from her bedroom.

"Be right there, honey," Connie said, hanging up her coat.

"You left early last week too."

"I went to the—"

"And Monday."

"I had important things to do."

"More important than your family?"

Connie spun around.

"God dammit, Thomas! Can I live my own life?"

Her face was tense, her eyes focused. But even in all her rage, she was beautiful. Thomas was no less furious, but he understood her frustration. Outside of their small circle, they didn't socialize much. She had arrived right before America got into the war and had never had time to make any friends. Now she was married with a child and a job.

"I'm sorry."

Before Thomas could respond, there was a knock at the door.

They looked at each other. Thomas stepped forward and grabbed the knob. When he opened the door, he froze.

"*Mamma Mia!*" Connie cried.

Standing on the porch was Sal, dressed in a peacoat and white cap. Connie lunged to hug him, letting out a flurry of Italian.

"You're back," Thomas said.

"My ship's in town till Sunday," he said, peeling Connie's arms off him. "Then we're headed to Europe. I wanted to surprise everyone."

"You sure did."

"Sal, Sal, Sal!"

Chickie ran down the stairs and jumped into her brother's arms, and he smothered her with kisses.

"Are you hungry?" Connie asked, wiping her eyes.

"Famished. The mess grub is awful."

"We have leftover meatloaf and potatoes," she said. "I'll heat it up."

"I'd take it cold."

Connie helped him take off his coat and then hurried into the kitchen. Thomas thought Chickie had gone with her until he heard her doing something upstairs.

Sal walked into the living room, looking around with a sentimental wonder. He had only been gone since September, but two months was an eternity in wartime.

"You hear what the Russians did at Stalingrad?"

Thomas stood leaning against the wall, his arms crossed.

"Fifteen-thousand Krauts dead," he said.

"Probably even more. And MacArthur's got the Japs cornered in New Guinea."

Conversations used to start with small talk about the weather or the Red Sox. Now they were all about the war. Thomas didn't mind, it kept them from discussing more serious things.

Sal had left for the Navy only a few days after his mother's death, and they hadn't had time to talk about the house or Chickie. While Connie insisted Sal would agree to the adoption, Thomas felt uneasy that it wasn't finalized. Beyond that, it was still Sal's home, and he felt like an intruder.

"You took down the picture of my pops," Sal said.

"They're in the guestroom now," Connie called out. "It's better. Photographs should not be over a fireplace."

The guestroom seemed like a stretch for a space that could barely fit a single bed and dresser, but Sal didn't seem offended.

"Have you heard from George?"

Thomas shook his head. The easiest way to cope with his brother being gone was to ignore or downplay it.

"Any idea where you're going?" he asked.

"Probably England, maybe Africa. They don't tell us nuttin'."

"Sal, Sal, Sal."

Chickie came back down waving a sheet of paper. She handed it to her brother, and he stared at it. Like Thomas, Sal had been raised to never show much emotion other than anger, laughter, or excitement over a homerun or a touchdown. For any kid in East Boston, the word "sissy" was the worst insult possible. But when Thomas saw Sal's face twitch, his eyes got watery, and he choked up.

Connie walked in, and Sal held up the paper. It was a crayon sketch of Sal and their mother. Standing between them was Chickie, smiling with her hair in pigtails.

"Supper's almost ready," Connie said, her voice trembling. "Chickie, go wash up, please."

15

Abby knew Thanksgiving would never be the same without their father. Now with her brother and Arthur gone, she feared it would be grim. In the days leading up to it, she had none of the giddy anticipation she had gotten as a girl. If it wasn't for her mother and Chickie, she would have skipped it.

At least they knew where they were eating. For weeks, they had been arguing over which house to use. Connie had offered to host, but Mrs. Nolan insisted on it. The matter was settled by a coin toss, something Chickie had suggested.

Abby stepped out of the tub, dripping wet and shivering all over. She had put on more coal at breakfast, and the house was still cold, a legacy of her father's stubbornness. He had refused to switch to gas when the rest of the street did. At the time, he had given some scientific reason, but she knew it had been more out of nostalgia. The briskets reminded him of the turf they had burned back in Ireland.

Abby stood in front of the mirror and dried herself off. Any time she saw her naked body, she thought of Arthur. Somedays she felt beautiful and others like a Plain Jane. While her face was smooth, her hair looked stringy. One of her breasts sagged more than the other, a flaw her mother said ran in the family.

"Abigail!"

Abby flinched.

"Be right down!"

Wrapping a towel around her, she ran into the bedroom. She threw on a dress, a cardigan sweater, and a pair of wool stockings. She had painted her nails and curled her hair the night before, but she would need to put on makeup before dinner.

When she got downstairs, all she heard was the clank of pots and pans in the kitchen. With Sal home, her mother was eager to make everything perfect, trying to make up for the absence of her own son.

Abby went into the dining room where the table looked ready for a royal banquet. Her mother had put out their best plates, a set of China that had been in the family for over a century. The silverware had been polished, and the burgundy napkins had been washed and ironed.

Her mother rushed in with a serving bowl. Her forehead was damp, and her cheeks were flushed. While it could have been from cooking, Abby felt a twinge of suspicion.

"Does Sal eat turnips?"

"I don't know, Ma."

"How 'bout beets."

"Maybe you should ask *him*."

Her mother frowned.

"Isn't there anything I can do?" Abby asked.

"Go over and help Connie."

Abby went out to the foyer and got her coat. She was only going next door, but the temperature was close to freezing.

When she walked out, she heard voices. Chickie was on the sidewalk in her best outfit, a blue petticoat and white knit hat. With her were the boy and girl from the church at the corner.

"Alfie and Olive," Chickie said, pointing.

"From England, right?"

"Brixton," they said at the same time.

Although almost teenagers, they still had a childish innocence.

Olive was slightly crossed-eyed and had freckles. Alfred looked like Spanky from *Our Gang* except not as chubby.

"Are you siblings?"

Olive winced.

"He's my *bro-thah*," she said.

The Ciarlones' front door opened, and Abby saw Thomas carrying three heavy serving dishes. He looked like he was struggling, which wasn't unusual. He always took on more than he could handle.

"Happy Thanksgiving," Abby said.

"Thank you, ma'am."

Abby went over to help Thomas and noticed he had on his uniform pants.

"Are you working?" she asked.

"When aren't I?"

"Can I help?"

"Do you see Angela Labadini much?" he asked.

"Just at the bakery."

"Do you know if she has a boyfriend?"

Abby stiffened up.

"I hardly talk to the girl."

"That's not what I asked."

Their eyes locked. Abby had always avoided gossip, which spread like the flu in East Boston. It was obvious that word was getting around about Angela. She didn't know why Thomas had asked, but she couldn't lie to him.

"There might be somebody."

......

ABBY SAT SLUMPED in the living room chair, so full her stomach ached. Even at twenty, her body was getting soft in areas that were firm only a couple of years before. She always worried about gaining weight. Volleyball kept her active, but it was only a few practices and one game each week, nothing like the exercise she got running for the track team in high school.

The meal was delicious. Mrs. Nolan had made turkey, potatoes, squash, and corn. Connie had brought over baked cod in a garlic tomato sauce, an Italian dish from back home. Even their mother had tried it, which was impressive for a woman who thought pepper was strong.

In the dining room, Thomas and Sal sat talking while Mrs. Nolan and Connie washed the dishes. Chickie was in the backyard with the two British children. Mrs. Nolan had invited them to eat, but they had said they weren't allowed to. They had waited out front until Chickie was done.

Bob Hope and Red Skelton were on the radio, making Abby chuckle. Anything was a relief from the news.

"How's George doing?" Sal asked.

"We haven't heard from him since September. We think he's still in the Aleutians."

"It's been quiet up there lately."

"Why do we even care about a bunch of islands in the arctic?"

"Whoever controls the Aleutians controls the Pacific shipping lanes."

Curious, Abby sat up to listen. Sal had only finished basic training, but he sounded like a combat veteran. He knew more about the war than any of them.

"And don't forget," he added. "The Japs could use the airbase on Attu to bomb American cities."

Just the image gave Abby a chill. The conversation even got the attention of their mother, who walked in from the kitchen.

"Why hasn't he written?" she blurted.

She clutched a wet rag, her eyes glassy, her mouth twitching. As everyone waited for Sal to answer, the house filled with a quiet tension.

"Probably just a snafu, Mrs. Nolan. The Aleutians are remote. The Army probably can't get mail out. It happens all the time."

If Abby didn't hear a collective sigh, she certainly felt it. The explanation was only a hunch, but it gave them all hope.

Thomas finished his coffee and stood up.

"Time to go," he said, and Connie walked in.

"When will you be home?"

"Hopefully by midnight."

They kissed, and he headed toward the door. When he opened it, the McNultys were standing outside.

"Off to work, Thomas?" Mrs. McNulty asked.

"As always."

"It could be worse." Mr. McNulty said with a wink. "You could be in the Solomons."

He laughed with a snort, but Abby saw Thomas' expression go sour. With their brother overseas, the war wasn't something to joke about.

"We've got our own battles here," Thomas said, and he walked out.

Abby's mother came in from the kitchen, and Mrs. McNulty handed her a bottle of wine.

"Red?" Mrs. Nolan said.

"Just something for your guests."

"Won't you have some?"

"Maybe half a glass."

"I'll take a highball if you've got it," Mr. McNulty said.

When Sal walked over, the McNultys both looked stunned.

"Salvatore? You're home?"

"Did the war end?" Mr. McNulty said.

Everyone laughed, and they shook hands.

"My ship's in port for a few days."

"Doesn't he look marvelous?" Mrs. Nolan said, rubbing the shoulder of his uniform jacket.

All night, she had been fawning over him, and Abby could tell it bothered her brother.

Mrs. Nolan went into the kitchen, and the McNultys sat on the couch.

"So how's college?" Mr. McNulty asked Abby.

"Terrific, thank you."

"Have you considered a field yet?" his wife asked.

It was the first time anyone had ever asked her. She was in her second year and still didn't have a concentration. In those few, short seconds, she scrambled to make a choice.

"Um, teaching…"

"Lord knows we need more good teachers," Mr. McNulty said, looking at his wife.

Mrs. Nolan returned with two glasses on a tray, and she looked flustered. Abby didn't like that she still made drinks for people, worried it could be tempting.

"Did someone say something about teaching?"

"Abigail just told us she's considering it for a career," Mrs. McNulty said.

"Hmm," Mrs. Nolan said. "The first I've heard of it."

In her voice, Abby detected a snicker, some hint of doubt or skepticism. All her life, her mother had supported but not encouraged her. It was a difference Abby only understood now that she was an adult. The only reason she had even gone to college was that her father had urged her to apply.

"Would you go check on Chickie?" her mother asked.

Abby frowned and got up. When she walked out the back door, Connie was smoking on the porch. She had on a coat, hat, and gloves which, even with the cold, seemed too much for just a cigarette.

"You looked dressed for the tundra."

Connie took a drag and quickly blew it out.

"I have to take some food to the church," she said.

Abby glanced down and saw a box beside her feet.

"Can I help?"

"No!" she said before softening her tone. "But thank you."

16

Thomas and Officer Carroll pulled out of the station with a cruiser behind them. Considering the operation, four officers seemed excessive. But anytime they made a bust, they had to have backup, something Captain Vitti said was for protection. Thomas knew the real reason. The more men involved, the less likely there would be any abuse or corruption.

"You hear the Brits took back Mejez el Bab?" Carroll asked.

Thomas had read the news that morning too, but he wasn't sure if Carroll was pronouncing it right.

"You even know where that is?"

Carroll hesitated.

"Tunis?" he ventured, not sounding sure.

"Yep. And you know where that is?"

Carroll thought again.

"In Africa?"

It was accurate enough that Thomas stopped prodding him. Everyone was rattling off the names of places they knew nothing about these days.

"You know where the Aleutians are?"

Carroll shook his head.

"Not sure. Why?" he asked.

"Never mind—"

An Army truck had pulled out in front of him. He hit the brakes, and they shot forward in their seats.

"Jesus!"

The military drove recklessly through the streets of East Boston. Some people called the precinct to complain, but most accepted it as another inconvenience of war.

"Ain't they like fish outta water," Carroll snickered.

As the truck sped off, Thomas saw a dozen black soldiers sitting in the back. With the temperature close to freezing, it seemed cruel that they had to ride out in the open.

"They're as good as anyone," Thomas said.

They went through Day Square and pulled into the lot of the garage. The bay doors were down due to the cold, but the lights were on inside. Everyone got out, and Thomas waved for the other officers to follow. They stormed through the front door and into a small office. Sitting behind a cluttered desk was a man with a pot belly and sad eyes. He had on overalls streaked with grease.

"What the hell's this about?" he demanded, standing.

Thomas reached into his coat and took out the search warrant. Considering the lieutenant got it a week before, he was sure it had expired, but most suspects didn't read them anyway. He was surprised when he unfolded it and saw the last name.

"Are you Jack Morris?" he asked.

"Yes."

"Morris. Any kids?"

"What—?"

"Just answer the question!" Thomas snapped.

"One daughter and two boys."

"How old?"

The man frowned, and even the officers looked confused.

"My daughter is ten. My older son is eighteen. He's in the service. My younger son is twelve. Why?"

Thomas didn't have to ask their names. He knew this was

Clarence's father. They had the same shaped head and the same pug nose. But he couldn't mention the coincidence, knowing it would prejudice the case.

"We need to look around," he said.

"Go 'head."

Hearing the clank of wrenches, Thomas nodded and the other two cops ran out to the bays.

"You got tires?" he asked.

"We're a garage, ain't we?"

Thomas stepped forward and stared at him.

"You know what I mean."

"Just some old retreads in the back."

"Show me."

Morris led them through a door into a supply room filled with automobile parts. As they walked, they stepped around radiators, exhaust pipes, and engine blocks. Stacked along the back wall were a dozen used tires which, although worn, were still valuable.

"I heard you've been selling new ones over the OPA price cap."

The man shook his head.

"That's what we've got. I've got the ration receipts for everything we've sold."

Thomas pressed his lips in frustration. Labadini never misled him on purpose, but his information wasn't always good. Over the summer, his tip about a "gambling racket" in the basement of a hair salon turned out to be a ladies' card game.

"What's in there?" Carroll asked.

Behind a metal shelf and some boxes, Thomas saw a door, hidden in the shadows.

"More parts," Morris said.

"Show me."

"It's just—"

"Show me!"

They walked over and started to move everything out of the way. When the man hesitated, Thomas shoved the shelf, and it toppled over, sending bolts and screws everywhere.

"Open it!" he shouted.

Morris took out some keys, his hand shaking, and unlocked the door. Thomas peered in to see dozens of brand-new tires, all styles and treads.

"Parts?" he snickered.

Morris stood with his head slumped. Thomas could tell he was more of a scofflaw than a criminal. With the war, even honest people were taking part in small scams, anything to make the hardships a little easier.

The other patrolmen walked in.

"Nothing out there, sir."

"We found the stash," Thomas said. "Arrest him."

"C'mon," Morris pleaded. "Can't you cut a guy a little slack for Thanksgiving?"

Thomas stared him in the eye.

"Thanksgiving was yesterday."

The response was harsh. When the officers began to cuff the man, Thomas felt guilty.

"No need for that," he said.

"Should we call for a wagon, sir?"

"I'll do it. Just take him down to the station."

They took Morris by the arms and led him out. Once they were gone, Thomas stepped into the room and reached for a light switch. Gazing at the tires, smelling the new rubber, he almost got giddy.

"Need tires?" Thomas asked.

Carroll grinned like he wasn't sure if it was a joke.

"Sure. I guess I could use some."

"Then go open the trunk."

......

As Thomas crossed the bridge into Winthrop, the sun was setting over Boston. With their cottage only another mile up the road in

Point Shirley, it was a familiar view. Over at the airport, an Army plane was landing, and it looked like a troop carrier.

He turned into the service station and parked out front. When he walked into the office, a bell above the door jingled. An older Italian mechanic was sitting behind the counter in greasy coveralls. A cigar burned in the ashtray on the counter. A small radio was playing from the shelf behind him.

"Maybe I help?" the man said with an accent.

"Can you replace some tires?"

"Tires? We have no tires."

"I have them. Can you put them on?"

"I can do."

Thomas gave him the keys and then sat in a dirty chair by the windows. As he waited, he was anxious. He was outside of his jurisdiction but still afraid of being seen. His uniform showed under his coat, and it was hard to hide a holster and gun. But it was the end of the day, and by the time the mechanic returned, no one had come in.

"Where you find such beautiful tires?"

"That's my business."

Thomas didn't mean to be rude, but he had to be firm.

"Want headlights painted too?"

"Painted?"

"Half the lens. New rule."

"How long will it take?"

"Ten minutes."

"Yeah, sure, okay, thanks," Thomas said.

He could never keep track of all the war policies and regulations, which seemed to change every month. At first, only houses on the coast had to have blackout shades. Then in May, a "dim-out" had been ordered within a twelve-mile radius of Boston. Shop signs had to be turned off, and streetlamps had to be shaded. After a wave of automobile fatalities from the darkness, the speed limit had been reduced to thirty-five MPH, and there had been talk of lowering it again. To most people, none of the precautions made sense. If a German plane or U-boat could see one light, they could see them all.

On the radio, Thomas could hear the news. He usually didn't pay attention, but when he heard the words "Aleutians" and "casualty," he gasped. He rushed over behind the counter and knelt to turn it up. He got a bittersweet relief when he realized it was only a soldier from Cape Cod.

"Mister?"

Thomas turned around to see the mechanic.

"Sorry, I thought I heard something..." he said, stumbling.

"Six dollars, please."

With his heart still pounding, Thomas took out his wallet. He opened it wide enough that a book of gas rations showed. When the man noticed, he said, "Cash or *check*?"

Their eyes met, a look of mutual understanding.

"I take check."

Thomas glanced around and then handed him the stamps. While he hadn't counted them, he knew it was much more than the bill.

"Thanks," he said.

The man gave him the keys.

"Come back any time."

Thomas walked out and got into the car. As he started to drive, the tires felt good, but the rumble underneath was getting louder. He knew he would need a new muffler soon. The shortages were difficult for everyone, but he knew he could get anything he needed.

17

ABBY RAN THE SHAKER OVER THE CHIACCHIERE, STRIPS OF SWEET dough. The canister was almost empty, and the bakery wouldn't get any more sugar until Monday. They had already made enough breads and pastries for the day. The weekend after Thanksgiving was always slow. Aside from the regulars who came in for coffee, a muffin, and some gossip, most people were still eating leftovers. Only two girls were working at the counter, and it was so quiet that Carlo, who never took a break, was out in the alley having a cigarette.

With no one to help her, Abby carried the tray out front herself. As she slid it into the case, the bell over the door rang. She glanced up to see a soldier walk in with his arm around a girl. They were both young, with bright faces and giddy smiles. Abby didn't recognize her, but she was sure the guy was from one of the nearby bases, probably Wood Island Park. No one ended up in East Boston by accident.

Before she leaned up, she fixed her hair. While she was faithful to Arthur, she still wanted to look good. She turned to leave, but the young man asked, "What're them there things?"

He had a strong southern accent.

"Chiacchiere," she said.

"And how about them?"

As he pointed, she looked under the case.

"Those are Bomboloni."

He glanced at his girlfriend with a toothy smile.

"Is everything around here Italian?"

Abby just raised her eyebrows. It was the kind of remark her mother used to make when the Irish were getting outnumbered.

"I'll help them," Eve said, interrupting.

When Abby returned to the kitchen, Carlo was reaching into the oven with a brush, cleaning out the crumbs and burnt dough. Even in the cold weather, he wore only an undershirt because of the heat.

Abby finished the last pan, and when she walked out to the front, the couple was gone. Looking at the clock, she took off her apron and went to get her things.

"Can you work till close?" Eve asked, following her out to the back.

"I'm going out tonight. Isn't Angie coming in?"

"She doesn't work here anymore."

Abby stopped.

"She doesn't?"

"She's been let go. Rita heard about her and that soldier."

The owner didn't seem like a bigot, so Abby assumed she did it out of precaution, not prejudice. As a sixty-year-old widow, she probably didn't want the controversy.

"That's a shame," Abby said, tossing her apron in the bin.

"Maybe she'll think twice next time before cavorting with a negro."

Abby's expression sharpened.

"What?"

"Don't act surprised, Abby. Everyone knows Angie is a slut."

"You're a bitch!"

Eve's face went red.

"Watch it, Abby! I'm your boss."

With her temper up, Abby wanted to smack the grin off her face. But when she saw Carlo wagging his finger, she held back. In a workplace that was mostly hot-headed young women, his calm intervention prevented a lot of arguments and fights.

Abby grabbed her coat and looked at Eve, shaking her head in disgust. Then she stormed out the back door.

......

THE LINE outside Cocoanut Grove went around the corner. It was a cold, windless night, and the sky was clear. The temperature was close to freezing, but most people were too happy to care. Thanksgiving was over, and the spirit of Christmas was in the air. But the excitement wasn't just about the holidays. After a year of war, things were looking up for the Allies. The newspapers no longer talked about if there would be a victory, but when.

Abby never liked waiting alone, but she knew it wouldn't be for long. With her hair in Victory Rolls, she felt prettier than she had in ages. Behind her, five sailors stood passing around a pint. They kept trying to flirt with her, and she let them. When one asked if she had a boyfriend, she winked and said, "Maybe."

After months of work and school, she needed to get out and relax. Frances always said she was too serious and for once, Abby agreed. She was willing to wait for Arthur, but she couldn't put her life on hold for him.

"Toodle-loo!"

Abby looked up and saw Frances and Sal coming toward her.

"Dreadfully cold," Frances said, rubbing her arms.

Sal wore civilian clothing, a long black coat and hat.

"Have you been waiting long?" he asked.

"Not too long."

Sal and Frances had been out all day, and it wasn't just for lunch and shopping. With Frances' mother in Duxbury for the weekend, they had gone to her apartment. By their faces, Abby could tell they had made love, that look of drowsy contentment. She wasn't jealous, and she even got a little thrill in knowing.

"C'mon," Sal said. "Let's head in."

He took Frances' hand, and Abby followed them to the front of the line. Before he had joined the Navy, he had worked at the nightclub for years, rising to become the head waiter. Abby wasn't surprised when the doorman exclaimed, "Salvatore!"

"Hey, Pauli," Sal said, and they hugged.

"You're back?"

"Just a couple of days. Good crowd tonight?"

"We expected more, but Holy Cross beat BC today."

"Everyone's home sulking."

"Hey, at least they're warm. Right?"

Sal smiled.

"Good to see you, Pauli," he said.

"Stay safe, Sal."

The man patted his shoulder and waved them all in. They walked through the revolving door, one at a time, and in an instant, the air went from cold to stuffy. The lobby was packed with people rushing in all directions. There were a lot of soldiers, both officers and enlisted men, their jackets pressed and pins gleaming. Abby saw some girls in uniform too, members of the Women's Auxiliary Army Corps and the Naval Reserve.

Sal took their coats, and they waited while he checked them in.

"How was your day?" Abby asked.

"Lovely. We had lunch and went shopping—"

Abby got distracted when she saw Nick DiMarco and Sarah. Then she realized her brother and Connie were with them.

She called out, and they came over.

"Thomas? You didn't tell me you were coming here tonight," she said.

"And you didn't tell me."

Abby reached to hug Sarah, still too stunned to speak. While they had been friends for years, they only saw each other in the summer.

Abby knew she had been going steady with Nick DiMarco, but it was weird seeing her outside of Point Shirley.

"Look at this gang," Sal said, walking back over.

"You didn't tell me you were coming here tonight," Connie said, repeating what Thomas said.

Stumped, Sal opened his arms wide.

"And yet here we are."

They all laughed and followed him through the lobby. They went under an archway, and into a grand ballroom. A band was playing on the stage, and the dance floor was full of couples. Streamers hung from the ceilings, and all around there were fake palms, creating the impression of a tropical paradise. The smoke from cigarettes and cigars was thick, adding to the mystique.

"How long have you been here?" Abby asked Thomas, seeing they already had drinks.

"Twenty minutes. I saw your friend Howard."

"*Harold.*"

"The funny one," Thomas said, puckering his lips like a woman.

"Where is he?"

"In the ballroom."

Sal called to a maître di in a tuxedo, and the man led them over to a large round table. As they went to sit, Harold came down the ramp with Mr. Glynn, who was limping. They both looked sharp in their dark suits, and Harold had on a gold waistcoat chain.

"Mr. Glynn?" Frances noticed his limp.

"He injured his ankle at practice today."

"Sit, sit, sit," Abby said, pulling out a chair.

"Just a strain," the professor said, seeming embarrassed by the attention.

Abby introduced everyone, creating a confusing flurry of hellos, handshakes, and hugs.

"Is it true Holy Cross beat Boston College today?" Harold asked.

A waiter walked up behind him.

"Fifty-five to twelve," he said, and everyone groaned.

The game was one of the biggest of the year, the two best Catholic institutions in the area. Abby didn't follow football, but all the men did. Anyone from the city supported Boston College; people in the suburbs and beyond had wanted Holy Cross to win. It was a rivalry that had social implications. The loss was tough, and she understood the disappointment. Now more than ever, people needed something to root for.

The young man took out a notepad, and Abby asked for a Martini. Harold ordered soda water, and the rest were a mix of cocktails. Mr. Glynn asked for a white wine which, even in such an elegant place, seemed too fancy.

When the waiter left, Nick DiMarco stood up.

"Drinks are on me tonight folks," he said. "I've got an announcement to make."

He looked down at Sarah who smiled back, her face beaming.

"As some of you already know, I've asked Sarah to marry me."

"And what did she say?" Harold asked.

Everyone laughed.

"I know these are tough times," he went on. "I've already lost some close friends. I know you all have too."

Some passing couples stopped to listen.

"In times like this, we gotta stick together…"

As Abby listened, she got emotional. In high school, Nick DiMarco had been friendly, but he had also been cocky. He was handsome, smart, and a good boxer, a rare combination in East Boston. She never imagined he could be so sentimental.

"I'd like to ask everyone here tonight, old friends and new, to join us in May for our wedding—"

"Which is where, precisely?" Harold asked.

Only he could interrupt without sounding rude.

"Well," DiMarco said, blushing. "We haven't quite worked out the details yet."

The waiter came back with an assistant, and they handed out the drinks.

"I'd like to propose a toast. First, for my lovely bride-to-be. And second, for our boys overseas. May they clobber the Japs and Krauts and come home!"

Everyone cheered and clapped, including some people at the next table. Frances and Abby reached for a napkin at the same time, both choking up. The speech was tender, but there was no time to reflect on it. As if on cue, the band broke into a fast number. Harold jumped up and extended his hand to Abby.

"Whaddya say we cut the rug?"

......

When Abby finally left the dance floor, she was dizzy and out of breath. Since Harold had quit drinking, he had more energy than a child, and she couldn't keep up.

She reached for some water, smiling at Mr. Glynn across the table. Harold had come over between numbers, but the professor had been mostly sitting alone. He didn't seem bored or self-conscious. Abby even noticed him rocking his head to the music. She knew some people got enjoyment from watching others have fun.

"Have you been in America for long?" she asked.

The professor cleared his throat.

"I arrived in the spring of forty-one."

"From Ireland?"

"Actually, England. I was teaching at the University of Bristol."

"You were lucky to get out. They've had a hell of a time."

His polite smile seemed to conceal some stronger reaction.

"They could've avoided it," he said.

"You really think so?"

"Well, don't forget they declared war on Germany first. They watched for years as Hitler rose to power, and they did nothing to stop it. They're hardly innocent. England has a very active Nazi Party."

It seemed wrong to criticize an ally of the United States, especially during wartime. Mr. Glynn was more of an intellectual than a rebel and Abby wanted to understand his grievance. And after the Martini, she was feeling mischievous enough to ask.

"Tell me, professor," she said. "How did you come to hate the British so much?"

He looked as delighted as he was startled by the question. She could tell it interested him. But before he could reply, Harold came over, his jacket open and sweat running down his neck.

"Is that water?" he asked Abby, pointing at a glass.

"Yes, mine."

Without asking, he grabbed it and drank it down.

"Your...your brother's a hell of a guy," he said, panting. "And Concetta, what a peach!"

"Isn't she though?"

"How're you, Richie?"

"Quite well. Thank you, Harold."

Abby saw the way they looked at each other, that public restraint and private longing. It was when they seemed the most at ease together that she felt the worst for them.

"I need more water."

"I'll get some," Abby said, standing up. "I need to use the powder room anyway."

"You're a doll."

She took her pocketbook and left, skirting around groups of people. The club was sprawling with two bar areas, a lounge in the basement, and a newer lounge behind the ballroom. She had been there a dozen times and still got lost.

When she got back to the lobby, there was still a line outside. She turned into the ladies' room beside the coat check and went to the mirror. As she put on lipstick, Frances walked over from the toilets. She had been unusually quiet all night, so much so that even Thomas had remarked on it.

"What a night."

"Quite," Frances said coldly.

"What's wrong?"

Frances looked around and leaned in.

"I think I'm pregnant."

Abby's mouth fell open, but she didn't have time to be shocked. Suddenly, they heard a terrifying scream.

"What the hell was that?" someone said.

The room went silent, women looking around in confusion. Abby quickly put away her makeup and nodded to Frances. The moment they walked out, she knew something was wrong.

"Fire!"

People were moving calmly toward the doors, but Abby sensed an emerging panic. Suddenly, she smelled smoke. Then in the stairwell going down to the Melody Lounge, she saw a glow.

"We've gotta go!" Frances shrieked.

"We can't leave without them!"

Abby took her by the arm, and they ran toward the ballroom. But it was too late. A stampede was coming at them, and Abby was knocked to the ground. She reached for Frances, but her friend got swept up by the mob. Covering her head, she felt the blows of feet.

The lobby was filling up with smoke. The screaming was unbearable. When Abby started to feel heat, she knew she had to get out or she would die. She remembered what she had learned at fire training. Staying low to the ground, she started to move, breathing only when necessary. Somehow she made it to the exit, but the revolving door was jammed, arms and legs flailing.

Still, she continued to crawl. She felt a cool draft and went toward it. As she tried to stand, someone grabbed her and shoved her through an opening. She stumbled out and collapsed on the sidewalk, coughing and gasping for air.

"Miss!" a fireman yelled. "Can you walk?"

Abby nodded.

"Please, clear the area."

She got up and staggered across the street. Three fire trucks had already arrived, and she heard more coming. The shrieking had stopped, replaced by moans, sobs, and, even worse, an eerie quiet.

Her dress was torn and one of her heels had broken off. Looking across at the club, she saw smoke rising from the roof.

Headlights came racing around the corner. Abby felt a surge of pride when she realized it was an MWDC wagon. Six girls jumped out, but she didn't see anyone she knew—the organization had thousands of members. They got first aid kits and other equipment from the back and then ran toward the scene.

"Abigail Nolan?"

Abby looked over and saw Private McCarthy from headquarters.

"Lynn," she said, barely able to speak.

"You were inside?"

Abby went toward her, her broken shoe in her hand, limping.

"Yes."

The girl looked at the smoldering building and then back to Abby.

"Who were you with?"

"Everyone," she said, which wasn't far from the truth.

When McCarthy walked over with a blanket, Abby waved her away. She was numb from terror and shock.

"You'll freeze," she said.

"I'm fine."

More fire trucks showed up, lights flashing across the narrow city street. Men jumped out and set up hoses as their colleagues hacked at the walls with axes. The fire seemed under control, but they continued to extract people. Out front, the bodies were piling up.

"Abby!"

Looking over, she saw Frances knelt on the sidewalk. Any joy she got in seeing her friend alive was only temporary. Her heart sank when she saw dark brown hair and a familiar dress. As she got closer, she realized it was Sarah and not Connie, who had both worn similar outfits. Abby didn't have to ask. She knew she was dead.

Two paramedics ran over.

"Miss, you need to make room," one of them said, helping Frances up.

Abby put her arm around her, and they walked away from the scene.

"Where're the others?" Frances asked, her voice weak, her face wracked with tears.

Abby turned to her and shook her head.

"I don't know."

18

Thomas opened his eyes, squinting in the white lights. Each time he woke up, for a moment he forgot where he was. His thigh was wrapped in gauze, and he had a bump on his head. But nothing hurt, and he was comfortable, probably from the morphine.

While he could have slept more, the nightmares were tormenting. He had visions of running through the darkness, people screaming, flames, heat. They weren't much different from what he had experienced, but they were more vivid. His real memories were a blur, more like scattered images and sensations. Everything else he knew was from the news and conversations. Cocoanut Grove was all anyone was talking about.

It was the second deadliest fire in American history. Almost five hundred people had lost their lives. Some burned, but most had perished from smoke inhalation, which was why so many of the victims had looked untouched, almost like they were sleeping. They were old and young, soldiers and civilians, married and single. If Boston College had won that day, the mayor would have been there with his entourage, as well as many others. The upset had probably saved a few dozen lives.

The newspapers said it was caused by a busboy in the Melody Lounge who had been trying to fix a lightbulb. There were rumors that the owner, who had ties to organized crime, had used cheap construction materials and ignored safety inspections. Many of the emergency doors were locked or hidden to keep patrons from leaving without paying the bill. It was a scandal that shook the city and was the first time in months that the war wasn't on the front page.

The investigator who came to see Thomas said he had most likely broken out a side door because he was found unconscious in an alleyway. The fact that he was alone had only added to his guilt. Minutes before the fire, Connie had gone out for fresh air, something he didn't remember until she came to visit the next morning. When she walked into the hospital room with his mother, he gasped. Then he broke down in tears, the first time he had cried in years.

They still didn't know who had survived from their group. Sarah had died from trauma, not fumes, crushed in the panic. Harold and Mr. Glynn were still missing, which didn't mean they weren't alive. Victims were in hospitals all over the city, and many still hadn't been identified.

Already there were stories of heroism. One Coast Guard sailor had gone into the building four times for his girlfriend, receiving third-degree burns on over half his body. The actor Buck Jones was killed, as well as some well-known local entertainers. But fame or prestige meant little that night. In a blaze, everyone was equal, although not all were lucky.

"Thomas?"

He looked up and saw a nurse in the doorway. When she moved aside, Connie walked in. She had a long dress under her overcoat, curls pouring down from a felt beret. She always looked best in black, but the color now had a morbid significance.

"Hello," Thomas said, leaning up.

"I've got news."

Something about her tone told him it wasn't all good.

"The doctor said you can go home."

Thomas flashed a faint smile, feeling a mix of gratitude and dread. He was happy to be leaving, but he didn't know if he was ready to face the world again.

"What else?" he asked.

Connie looked away, her face tense. He could tell she was trying not to break down.

"Thomas," she said, stepping closer. "Sal didn't make it."

Their eyes locked.

"We found out yesterday," she added.

All at once, she started to sob. She leaned over the bed, and they hugged. As he patted her back, he felt her trembling.

Considering the scale of the tragedy, it was a miracle any of them were alive, and he was more angry than surprised. After all his family had been through, it was the final blow. Raised a Catholic, he had always believed in God. Now he wasn't so sure.

"Does Chickie know?" he asked.

She took the chair next to the bed, dabbing her eyes with a tissue.

"We told her."

"We?"

"Your...your mother and I," she said. "She's good at that sort of thing."

For all her quirks, his mother was calm in a crisis, which was why he wished she was there now. He dreaded the next question, but he knew he had to ask.

"How is Chickie?"

"At first, okay. Then she threw a tantrum. She wouldn't go to school today."

"I don't think she really understands—"

"She does," Connie said.

"And is that a good thing or bad?"

She sighed.

"I don't know."

......

. . .

With his leg still sore, Thomas let Connie drive. He was impressed. She didn't have an American license, but she had had one in Italy. Being married to a foreigner, he was always learning something new. She had never seen a car tunnel until she got to America, and as a little girl, she had rickets. They had been going steady for months before she told him she had been married. Before the war, she had lived with her husband in Malta, the small island in the Mediterranean where he was from. When the Germans attacked, they fled by boat to Sicily but were detained by soldiers. While she was let go, he was forced into the Italian army and later died in Greece. Thomas was hurt by the news, but he didn't hold it over her. She was a private person, and he knew the trauma and regret from her past made it even harder to talk about. She had come to America to start over.

They came out of the Sumner Tunnel into East Boston. It was only four-thirty and almost dark. The shops in Maverick Square had laurel and ornaments in the windows. A few homes had Christmas lights which ironically, couldn't be on at night because of the war regulations. It was the first of December, but it didn't feel like the holiday season.

They drove up Bennington Street, and the traffic was mild for Thursday evening. On the sidewalks, Thomas saw hunched old ladies carrying groceries and men in long coats with their pants tucked into their boots. It had snowed since he went into the hospital, although only a dusting. Still, the world had never seemed so cold and gray. It looked like the city itself was in mourning.

"We sank nine Japanese ships," Connie said.

Thomas looked over.

"Yeah?"

"In the Solomon Islands. It was in the newspaper."

When he grinned, it was more of a dark humor. She never talked about the war, and he understood why. But after the fire, any good news was a relief, wherever it came from.

"They say the war might be over in forty-three," Thomas said.

"Who did?"

"Someone in the British War Cabinet. I can't remember his name."

When they got home, Chickie was out front skipping rope with the two English kids.

"Looks like someone has new friends," Thomas said.

"They come by every day after school."

Thomas liked to see children playing. It reminded him of how the neighborhood was when he was young. Now everyone was grown up, and the street was mostly older people. Even the Braga twins were in high school. Except for families moving up from the poorer parts of East Boston, young people usually went to the suburbs.

Connie got the crutches from the backseat, but Thomas wouldn't take them. He hadn't broken any bones. His leg was bruised, and he had some cuts on his head and leg. He didn't know if something had fallen on him or if it was from getting knocked down. His worst injury was smoke inhalation, which left him with constant coughing and nausea. At times, he felt like he was choking.

He got out, and Chickie looked over. For a moment, they stared at each other, and she looked almost frightened. Then a smile broke across her face.

"Dada," she said.

The way she spoke, she sounded like a little girl. As they hugged, Olive came over, her brother trailing behind.

"You survived the inferno!" she said.

"I did."

"Our house burned too," her brother said. "Our auntie died. And Artemis."

"Who's Artemis?"

"Our cat."

Thomas hesitated, not sure what to say. With over forty thousand civilians dead, the London Blitz made Cocoanut Grove look like a campfire.

"We're all lucky to be alive," he said.

As he went to go in, he looked at both houses, not sure which one to go into.

"Go see your mother," Connie said. "I'll make dinner."

He no longer argued or disagreed, obeying her like she was his guardian or caregiver. Grabbing the handrail, he started up the steps. By the time he reached the porch, he had to stop. He got winded easily, something the doctor said would get better with time.

When he walked in, his mother was standing in the foyer with flowers.

"Thomas!" she exclaimed.

She gave him a bouquet of white roses, and they hugged. Any joy he felt was quickly dashed when he smelled alcohol.

"I'm sorry about Sal," he said, pulling away.

She glanced down, biting her lip, and then looked up.

"How're you feeling?"

"Good, Ma," he said, giving her a curious look.

For weeks, he had quietly suspected she was drinking again. It was more a sense than a certainty, that glow in her expression, the breathiness of her voice. While he hadn't caught her yet, he had checked some of her glasses and cups.

"I made your favorite meal," she said. "Pork chops."

They weren't his favorite—she was confusing him with George.

"Connie's cooking, Ma."

"No, no, no," she said, grabbing his hand. "Tell her to come over."

She tried to drag him into the kitchen, but Abby walked in the front door. When she turned to look, her foot hit the corner, and she stumbled. Thomas caught her, but the strain made his leg hurt.

"I'm sorry," she said, giggling.

Thomas glanced at Abby, who just shook her head. Her look was enough to confirm his hunch. But there was no time for criticism or condemnation. Thomas hadn't seen her since the fire. She ran over, and they hugged for the first time in months, maybe years.

"You look better," she said.

Her voice was scratchy, and her eyes looked tired.

"Yeah?"

"I came to see you in the hospital. You don't remember?"
Thomas went to speak but stopped, feeling a wave of emotion.
"I...I don't remember much."
"Then you're lucky."
"We're all lucky."

19

Abby stood on the frozen grass at Holy Cross Cemetery, her arm around Frances. It was her third funeral in a year and a half, and she had to go to Quincy on Monday for Sarah's.

The only good news was that Harold's father had called that morning from Bermuda. Abby wasn't sure how he got her phone number, but he said his son had survived along with "a friend." It was a relief, although not a complete surprise. She and Frances searched the death notices every day and hadn't seen their names.

What made the service even harder for Abby was having to stare across the plot at the monument with her father's name, Bartholomew Francis Nolan. When Mrs. Ciarlone died, she had no close relatives in America, and her husband was buried in a municipal cemetery in Somerville. Abby had suggested putting her in their family plot, and no one objected. Now Sal and his mother would be together, which would make it easier for Chickie to visit them.

Attendance was small by East Boston standards, with a few dozen neighbors and some people from church. The Ciarlones had moved next door when Abby was in eighth grade and had never been very social. Sal was friendly, but they hadn't seen him much because he had worked all the time. Chickie had always been the most outgoing, winning the hearts of everyone she met. Abby could never have imagined their lives would become so intertwined.

A frigid breeze came up the hill, shaking the barren trees. Abby was too numb to feel the cold. Frances just stared off in a daze, seeming more bitter than sad. Her mother had come, but her father couldn't make it, saying he had been called to Washington on official business.

Once the priest finished the liturgy, he stepped away. Two soldiers from the honor guard lifted the American flag off the casket and folded it. One of them marched over and handed it to Mrs. Nolan. Knowing the deceased wasn't married, he probably assumed she was his mother.

Glancing over, Frances smirked, a moment of humor in an otherwise grim time. But the mistake seemed to emphasize all she had lost. Abby didn't know what it meant for her pregnancy—they hadn't had time to talk about it.

Turning away, the men raised their rifles and fired three shots into the air. The crack echoed across the cemetery. In the distance, Abby saw some birds scatter. The military ceremony was solemn, and the soldiers were experts at their job. After a year of war, they had had a lot of practice.

The service ended, and people slowly dispersed. Frances clutched Abby's arm as they walked back to the cars. Her mother was standing beside a Cadillac, a black driver holding open the door. Abby wondered if she owned or hired it. While she had only met Mrs. Farrington a few times, she knew she liked to show off.

As they got close, Abby stopped.

"See you there."

"No," Frances said. "Come with us, please."

Abby looked over to her brother who was waiting at the Ford with Connie, Chickie, and their mother. He had on his police uniform and hat and a long service coat with brass buttons. She thought he had worn it for display until he told her he had to work later. The department had given anyone involved in the fire time off —Thomas wasn't the only cop in the club that night. But he was never the type to sit around, and routine was always a good remedy for grief.

When she waved, he nodded. She followed Frances into the Cadillac, her coat sliding over the smooth leather. She had never been in such a fine car and wanted to look around. But instead, she put her purse on her lap and stared ahead, knowing it was the wrong time to snoop.

They made a U-turn on the narrow road. Although at the crest of a hill, the Nolan family plot was also on a dead end. Abby had always sensed something symbolic about the location but couldn't put it into words.

As they drove away, Frances stared at the gravesite. Everyone was gone, including the honor guard. The only people left were two cemetery employees, who stood waiting with their shovels.

......

THE RECEPTION WAS at the Statler Hotel downtown, one of the most elegant establishments in the city. Mrs. Farrington had rented an entire banquet room. The walls were lined with paintings in gilded frames. A row of chandeliers hung from the ceiling.

Frances sat with her mother and younger brother who was a senior at Boston College High School. There were lots of people Abby didn't recognize, women in fine dresses and jewelry. At the next table were Sal's friends, young men with buzzcuts and somber faces. Some of them Abby knew from East Boston, but the rest were coworkers from Cocoanut Grove or men from the Navy.

Abby sipped her lobster bisque, which had too much brandy and not enough salt. When the waiters brought around wine, she looked at Thomas. Instantly, he covered their mother's glass. Glancing around, Mrs. Nolan pushed his hand away with a look of quiet embarrassment.

Mrs. Farrington stood up, and the room went silent. She had on a black evening gown with pearl buttons. Abby hadn't noticed what she was wearing earlier, but she could have sworn she had changed.

"Friends," she said, her voice emotional. "I want to thank you all for joining us here today."

Frances sat with a tense pout, and Abby understood why. Her parents had never liked Sal. Her mother was always cordial, but her father once called him a "pot boy."

"In life, we often don't know why such terrible things happen. Last weekend, five hundred people lost their lives just a block from this hotel. By some miracle, many survived, including my daughter..."

She stooped to rub Frances' shoulder.

"This past summer, Salvatore made the decision to enlist in the United States Navy. He wanted to join his fellow countrymen in resisting the evils of Nazism and the Japanese Empire. And while he never got to realize those dreams, he will forever be a hero to us."

Everyone clapped, and a few guys cheered.

"So I'd like to propose a toast," she went on, and they all raised their glasses. "To Salvatore Ciarlone. Our hero. May he remain forever in our hearts."

The waiters came around with plates. Abby lifted the silver cover to see duck confit with potatoes and a pea puree. None of them were picky, but the meal was exotic by any standard. Mrs. Nolan had a look of hesitant curiosity, and Chickie just grinned, poking at the leg with her fork.

Abby ate some of it, but she wasn't very hungry. She wiped her mouth and got up to use the powder room. After crying on and off all day, she wanted to check her makeup and get a tissue.

As she approached the doors, they opened suddenly, and she froze.

"My god!" she exclaimed.

Everyone turned, and Harold came in pushing Mr. Glynn in a wheelchair. He walked straight up to Abby and kissed the top of her head.

"We made it, darling," he said softly.

She nodded, tears falling from her eyes. Frances ran over, and they hugged in a circle, shocked beyond words. The call that morning from Bermuda had been short and staticky. All Abby and Frances knew was that Harold and Mr. Glynn had survived, not the extent of their injuries. It was a relief to see they hadn't been scarred or disfigured.

"How are you?" Frances asked the professor.

"I...am...alive," he said, his voice jittery.

Before she could respond or ask more, Harold said, "There'll be plenty of time to discuss all the dirty details later."

He smoothed out his jacket and took out a cigarette. As he lit it, Abby noticed stitches on the back of his hand.

A small crowd gathered around them. As usual, Harold enjoyed the attention, but Mr. Glynn did not. Mrs. Farrington walked over with two women.

"Please come join us," she said. "We've made space at the head of the table."

"What's the fare?" he asked, and everyone laughed.

"Duck confit."

"*Avec pommes de terre à la sarladaise?*"

Mrs. Farrington smiled. Whether she spoke French or not didn't matter. Abby knew it was some sort of signal of upper-class affiliation.

"*Avec pommes de terre.*"

Harold took a bow and got behind the wheelchair.

"Lead the way, Madam."

20

Thomas closed the furnace door and put the shovel in the corner. It was the last of the coal, but he wasn't concerned. The shortage everyone feared was for fuel oil, not coal.

As he went back up the stairs, he had to crouch. The old basement was like a tomb. The floor was dirt, the walls made from the rocks his great-grandfather had dug up for the foundation. When Thomas was a boy, he and his brother would go down there to explore. Once George had found a piece of a Revolutionary War musket, which now sat under glass at the East Boston library. The only signs of life were ants in summertime and spiders year-round. It was so cold and dank that even rats stayed away.

Thomas came out to the kitchen, and his mother was cooking eggs on the stove.

"Won't you eat?" she asked.

"Not hungry."

"You have to eat—"

"Not hungry, Ma."

The night before, he had walked in to find her passed out in the living room chair. It could have been from exhaustion, but it was clear she was drinking again. While she tried to hide it, she was getting careless. On Monday, Abby had discovered an open bottle of gin on the counter.

Standing at the sink, Thomas washed his hands. As he turned to go, he said, "I'll have more coal delivered today."

She just nodded, not looking over. As disgusted as he was, he also had sympathy. With her husband gone, she was lonely, and they hadn't heard from George in months. But at a time when everyone was stressed, it seemed selfish to go back to something that had almost destroyed her.

Without another word, he grabbed his coat and left. He got in the Ford and pulled away.

Outside it was gray, almost gloomy. It was December 7th, one year since the attack on Pearl Harbor. Across the world, the Allies were winning on every front. American troops were in North Africa, the Japanese were retreating in New Guinea, and the Russians had the Germans surrounded at Stalingrad. Still, the war was far from over, and some days it was hard to feel good about anything.

After the Cocoanut Grove fire, Thomas wondered how much more people could take. There was a shortage in everything from meat to manpower. The government was talking about enforcing a 48-hour work week. Almost twenty thousand Americans were dead. Everywhere he went, he saw gold stars in the windows of homes. His mother used to tell him when someone from East Boston had been killed, but he no longer wanted to know.

He drove down Bennington Street with the window down. It was still hard to breathe, and he sometimes got the sensation that he was suffocating. The fresh air helped, but it was frigid. At night, the temperature had been in the twenties for a week straight. With meteorologists expecting a harsh winter, everyone was panicked about a kerosene shortage.

When Thomas got to the station, he found a spot in the back lot. He used to park on the street, which made it easier to come and go, but he wanted to avoid the front desk. Everyone at work now looked at him differently, and he didn't want their pity.

He walked up the rear stairwell and into the corridor. Turning into his office, he saw Lieutenant DiMarco standing by the window in a casual suit, his tie loose.

"Nick?" he said.

"Hey, Thomas."

They hadn't seen each other since Sarah's funeral on Monday. DiMarco had just gotten out of the hospital the day before. Aside from some scratches on his face, he looked fine. Like Thomas and the other survivors, his worst wounds were hidden, the private agony of smoke inhalation.

"How're you?"

The lieutenant shrugged his shoulders.

"Alright, I suppose," he said, but it didn't seem true.

"Have a seat," Thomas said.

"I won't be long. I just came by to tell you I've signed up."

Thomas thought he had misheard him.

"Pardon?"

"Enlisted. The Army. I'm heading out Monday."

"What about—?"

"I passed the physical with aces. I guess doctors don't check lungs."

Thomas paused.

"I wish I could join you," he said.

"Don't be silly. You've got a wife and kid to protect. I've got nothing keeping me here now."

The remark was as affirming for Thomas as it was unfortunate for DiMarco.

"Thanks."

They walked toward each other and shook hands. Then the lieutenant surprised him with a hug, patting his back.

"Kill a Kraut for me," Thomas said.

"I don't know where I'll be yet. I hear they need guys bad in the Pacific."

"Write me."

"What do I look like, a dame?" DiMarco said, putting up his fists.

He took a fake swipe, and Thomas dodged it.

"Too slow!"

They both laughed, the first real laugh Thomas had had in days.

"Whaddya say we grab a drink Friday night?" he asked.

"I can't. My mother's making a big dinner."

Thomas knew it was going to be a sad farewell. DiMarco had two older sisters, but he was the only boy in the family.

"How about Saturday?"

"Sure, Thomas. Maybe."

It sounded like a contradiction, but Thomas knew why he couldn't decide. Anyone leaving for the service had a lot to do.

"C'mon. We'll grab a quick dinner. I'll pay."

The lieutenant peered up with a sarcastic smile.

"Well, in that case."

"Good. Red Shutter Café?"

"Red Shutter Café."

"Six o'clock?"

"Six o'clock."

DiMarco patted Thomas' arm and put on his hat.

"See you then, pal," he said, and then he walked out the door.

......

THOMAS DROVE down Border Street along the water. In the distance, he saw a ferry coming across from Rowes Wharf. He could tell it was going fast by the wake. With so much boat traffic, small vessels had to be quick. Earlier in the month, a trawler had been cut in two by a troopship in the predawn darkness. No one was killed, but it was a reminder of how dangerous things had gotten.

Across the harbor, the city was shrouded in a misty haze, the tops of all the buildings white. It had snowed four inches the day before, the first big storm of the year. In the scramble for gasoline, plows were low on the list, and the streets were a mess. The new tires helped, but Thomas still had to go slow.

As he approached East Boston Works, there was a shift change. The men all wore bulky clothing, knit hats, and gloves. Some even had on face coverings. Working the docks was hard in the winter. The wind whipped off the water, and ice had to be chipped off gantry cranes and gangways. Thomas remembered his father coming home with red ears, his hands so chapped they bled.

But he hadn't come down to the shipyard to reminisce. When he tapped his horn, Labadini looked over from the crowd. He waved to his coworkers and walked over.

"Thomas," he said. "How you doin'?"

In all their interactions, it was the first time he ever sounded sincere or concerned.

"A little better each day."

"Yeah? Good. They're gonna hang the owner of the Grove."

"As they should."

"I heard about Nick DiMarco's girl."

"My wife's cousin died too."

Labadini took a drag on his cigarette.

"Terrible."

"Things busy down here?"

"There's a British frigate coming in tonight. Got whacked by a U-boat south of Greenland. They say it's leaking oil like a sieve."

"Speaking of it, who's selling oil?"

"What kinda oil?"

"Heating oil. That shortage is coming, and it's gonna get cold."

Labadini's expression changed.

"Tell me what you found out about my sister?"

Their conversations were always like that, a casual back and forth, each feeling out what the other could offer.

"She's been seeing a soldier from the Wood Island Park barracks."

Their eyes locked.

"Is that all?"

"A black guy."

Labadini clenched his fists and gritted his teeth like he was about to explode.

"I'm gonna fucking kill him!"

"Vin. This ain't a barfight."

"What do you expect me to do?"

"Maybe I could talk to the Major."

"You know him?"

"Yeah, I mean...he came into the station once."

Labadini flicked his cigarette and started to walk away.

"Hey, what about the oil?" Thomas asked.

"I'll ask around."

The moment he drove away, he regretted offering to talk to Major Holdsworth. Labadini was a hothead, and if he did anything stupid, Thomas could end up in trouble too. But they all made promises they couldn't keep, and he didn't owe Labadini anything.

He was halfway home when he got stuck behind a military convoy. A couple of the trucks turned right toward Wood Island Park, and the rest went straight, either to Fort Dawes or some base further north. By now, there were outposts and gun batteries up and down the coast.

Waiting at a light, he saw Connie step off the trolley. Once it passed, he sped across and pulled up beside her.

"You scared me," she said, getting in.

"Where were you?"

"I had to go to the tailor."

"Why didn't you go to Gittell's?"

"He doesn't do dry cleaning."

Thomas nodded and said no more. He knew it was the dress she had worn to Cocoanut Grove. All their clothes still reeked of fire, a lingering reminder of the horrors of that night. It was a bitter stench, like ash except far more pungent. Thomas had washed his trousers three times and couldn't get it out, so he had thrown them away.

"How was work?" she asked.

"Nick DiMarco is joining the Army."

He stopped in front of their house and turned off the engine.

"Do you wish you did?"

The question was blunt, although he knew she didn't mean it that way. Staring ahead, he just sighed.

"Sometimes."

They got out and headed to his mother's house first to get Chickie. When they walked in, he said, "I've gotta get a few things."

He went upstairs to his bedroom and opened the top drawer of his dresser, grabbing some wool socks. He had been living at the Ciarlones' now for almost three months and still had half his things next door.

Before he left, he stopped to look around. The room he had shared with his brother seemed to get smaller each year. It was tidy now, the floors clean and the tables clear. Over by the window, George's bed was made with an old blanket and a single pillow. On the wall next to it was the Red Sox pennant he had won in a Boy Scouts raffle. Thomas could never stand in there for too long without feeling sentimental.

When he came downstairs, Chickie was in the dining room, her schoolbooks spread out across the table. He couldn't tell if she was still doing her homework, but she wouldn't look up at Connie. She never wanted to go home, and tonight she was especially defiant.

"Thomas?"

He looked back and his mother was waving from the hallway. Anytime he saw her now, he looked for signs of drinking, red eyes or the faint smell of booze. He was relieved that she appeared to be sober.

"Hey, Ma."

"Chickie's upset," she whispered.

Thomas rolled his eyes. He wasn't insensitive, but she had been pampering her granddaughter since long before Sal's death.

"No, it's serious. You know that boy Morris from her school?"

"The bully."

"His brother was killed in the Pacific last week."

"Who told you that?"

"Delia Menzel."

He didn't recognize the name, so he assumed it was someone from church.

"That's a shame."

"It's worse than that. His father's in jail."

Thomas froze.

"Thomas?"

They were interrupted when Chickie walked over. Seeing she had her bag over her shoulder, Thomas knew Connie had finally convinced her to leave.

"Ready to go?" he asked, and she nodded.

She wore a turtleneck sweater and the plaid skirt that Connie had given her.

"Won't you stay for dinner?" Mrs. Nolan asked.

"Not tonight, Ma."

They had already been over twice that week. One of the problems with living so close was that everything was an invitation.

"Thank you, Catherine," Connie said.

They all drifted over to the door.

"Thomas," his mother said. "I need a Christmas tree. I can't find one anywhere."

With the labor shortage, farms in Maine and New Hampshire couldn't harvest their trees. Only six trainloads had come down to Boston compared with the one hundred and seventy-five of the previous year. Already there was a black market, and officers had been told to look out for price gouging.

"They're gonna be hard to find this season, Ma."

"But we need a Christmas tree," she said, pleading.

Thomas glanced at Connie and Chickie who stood wide-eyed and waiting for his response.

"I'll see what I can do."

21

After all that had happened, Abby was glad to finally be back at school. She had been out for over two weeks. She had gone back to work earlier, but only because she needed the money. And moving sheet pans and dressing pastries was easier than studying. Aside from headaches, she was feeling better. The bruises on her arms had faded; the scratches on her neck, which she had covered with her hair, were almost healed. She had survived one of the worst tragedies in American history with injuries she could have gotten from slipping on the rocks at the beach.

Still, she found it hard to focus, especially in Calculus. It was the only subject she had with a majority of men. She didn't even like math but had picked it after Harold dared her to take something brainy. Now she was behind, and the semester was almost over. The administration had been considerate, allowing her to skip the finals she wasn't prepared for and take the ones she was. They even let her decide which was which.

"Miss Nolan?"

The old professor stood at the chalkboard with a pointer in his hand. He had a mop of unkempt hair, thick white eyebrows that quivered when he spoke.

"What's the first step in determining the slope of a tangent line?" he asked.

Abby sat up and cleared her throat.

"Um, find the derivative to get the slope m at the point given."

The room went silent.

"Bravo, Miss Nolan."

When he smiled, she smiled back. She was proud she got it right, but she was also self-conscious. Anytime someone was kind to her now, she assumed it was out of pity. She hadn't told anyone at BU that she had been at the fire, but word had spread fast, and she had missed a lot of school.

The class ended, and she reached for her bag. Walking out, her heart began to race. The rush of students always brought back memories from that night. Overcome by a slight panic, she ran to the end of the corridor. The moment she turned the corner, she slammed into someone.

"Pardon," she said.

Standing in front of her was a young man in a service uniform. She could never see a soldier without thinking of Arthur, the agony of not knowing whether he was alive or dead.

"You alright, Miss?"

He knelt and picked up her books, handing them to her with a smile.

"Yes...sorry."

Their eyes locked, and she had trouble looking away. She continued through the lobby, staring straight ahead. She always got the feeling now that people were watching her.

"Abigail?"

Startled, she turned to see Frances in a small sitting area near the stairs.

"You're back?" she blurted.

"I am."

Frances' voice was quiet, her manner subdued. They hadn't seen each other since Sarah's funeral.

"How are you?" Abby asked, taking the chair beside her.

"As good as could be, I suppose."

Abby nodded, her nostrils flaring with emotion. For the first minute, they just stared at each other. Like any two people who had gone through a tragedy together, they didn't have to speak to communicate.

"Are you gonna take any of your finals?"

Frances shook her head and lit a cigarette. She always looked more sophisticated when she smoked.

"Maybe English Literature. Definitely not Chemistry. I was already failing."

Abby started to giggle, and all at once, they broke into laughter.

"My girls?"

They turned and Harold was coming down the hallway. He had a duffel bag over his shoulder, and his arms were open wide.

"What're you both doing in this drafty lobby?" he joked.

Abby and Frances got up, and they all hugged.

"Just like old times," he said.

"Won't you sit?" Frances asked.

"I can't, unfortunately. We've got a short practice at noon. It's Richard's first time on the pitch since..."

When he hesitated, Abby felt a strange anticipation.

"Since...*the fiasco*. Yes, that seems fitting."

Abby and Frances responded with grim smiles. Only Harold could make something as horrific as the Cocoanut Grove fire sound like a clerical mix-up.

"Who plays rugby in this weather?" Frances asked.

"The sport began in England, my dear."

"England doesn't get this cold."

"Mr. Glynn is back?" Abby asked.

"Since last week."

"He wasn't in class. We had a substitute."

"Playing hooky, I suppose," Harold said, looking mildly surprised. "Anyone for an early dinner? Maybe the Fairmont? It's on me."

"We've got patrol tonight."

Frances turned to Abby.

"Patrol?" she asked.

"For the blackout. We're meeting at Wood Island Park at six-thirty."

Frances waved her hand and looked away like a debutante who felt insulted.

"I'm done with the war," she said.

The statement warranted a witty reply—everyone wanted to be done with the war—but even Harold held back. Their friend had just lost her boyfriend, and they both knew she was heartbroken. Abby hadn't seen her in over a week, although they talked on the phone each day. But she had been through enough grief herself to know that sulking and cynicism wouldn't help it.

"Come tonight," she said cheerily. "We all need you."

She glanced at Harold who gave Frances an encouraging nod.

"Maybe."

......

ABBY GOT off the streetcar and ran down Neptune Road. Crossing the causeway over to Wood Island Park, she pulled her hat down and kept her hands in her pockets. The sun had just gone down, and it was below freezing. Looking ahead, she was relieved to see people. Girls in the MWDC weren't as reliable in the cold weather. At training the previous Friday, only half the unit had shown up.

But tonight was different. It was the first statewide blackout since the start of the war, and Major Ward had ordered everyone to be there. At a time when volunteer organizations needed all the help they could get, she had even threatened to expel anyone who wasn't.

Headlights flashed across the marsh, and Abby glanced back to see a taxi. It pulled up beside her, and the rear door swung open.

"Get in!"

She smiled when she realized it was Frances.

"You made it," she said, sliding into the backseat.

"Didn't I say I would?"

"You said *maybe*."

They continued toward the park and stopped at the clearing. Frances paid the driver, and they got out. As they walked over, everyone was quiet, and Abby knew why. They were the only ones from their unit who had been at the fire that night.

Standing in the middle was Lieutenant Hastings, leaning against her car wearing earmuffs and a heavy coat.

"Ladies," she said, acknowledging them with a smile.

Abby only felt guilty about surviving when people gave her special attention. Nick DiMarco's sister Nina was more sincere, walking over and hugging them.

As they waited, more unit members showed up. Some had walked, but many were dropped off by boyfriends and husbands. One girl had even ridden her bicycle.

"Fall in!"

Everyone gathered around the lieutenant, bundled up but shivering. The cold was brutal on Wood Island Park. Except for a few bare trees, there was nothing to stop the wind.

"Tonight is the first state-wide blackout," she began. "There will be no adjustments or exceptions. Even shipyards and factories will be expected to turn off all their lights..."

There was a chorus of *ohs* and *ahs*.

"Once the alarm sounds, you're to go directly to your posts. As usual, you're to look for any violations and report them immediately. The Army will be performing a flyover of the coast. Our success tonight will determine our ability to protect civilians in the event of an enemy attack."

After she finished, Sergeant DiMarco stepped over with a clipboard. With the lieutenant holding a flashlight, she started the roll call. She had only gotten through three names before she was interrupted by a noise. They all turned to see a jeep coming up the road from the barracks. It stopped in the shadows and a figure got out, scurrying toward them.

"Who's that?" the lieutenant yelled over.

"Private Angela Labadini."

Hastings paused.

"Very well, Private," she said, and Abby sighed in relief.

Angela ran up beside her, tucking her hair into her hat, fixing her coat. If Abby didn't know for certain why she was flustered, she had a good idea. She just hoped the other girls didn't have the same suspicions.

While they got into formation, Lieutenant Hastings stood at the front of the column, squinting to see her watch. Suddenly, the sirens rang out, echoing across the night. With the dim-out order, most buildings and homes were already dark. Across the city, some lights flickered off, but it was nowhere near as impressive as it used to be.

"Forward!" Hastings shouted, and they started to move.

The march used to be solemn, but now everyone rushed because they were cold. Once they got to Bennington Street, the unit began to disperse. At Day Square, Abby and Frances broke off with their group, which included Angela and two new members.

The streets were deserted, but after six months of blackout tests, people had gotten lazy. On one block alone, they had to knock on three doors, mostly elderly people who had left on a light or candle. On the train tracks, some vagrants had started a fire, but the Army had arrived before they could report it. Beyond the violations and oversights, it was sad to see East Boston without any Christmas lights.

This blackout was longer than any of the ones previous. They had patrolled their area several times, and the second siren still hadn't sounded. They weren't allowed to leave their posts until it did, and it was almost nine o'clock. Tired and cold, they stopped at a corner.

"I'm heading home," Angela said.

Frances sat on the curb and lit a cigarette.

"I won't say anything," she said.

Angela and the other girls looked at Abby. Somehow she had become the leader even though they were all privates. But she lived the closest and knew the streets.

"Go," she said.

Without a word, they walked off, leaving Abby alone with Frances.

"How're you getting home?" she asked.

Frances took a drag, blowing the smoke out her nose.

"I hadn't given it much thought, to be honest."

"Stay at my house."

"Could your brother give me a lift in the morning?"

"I'm sure," Abby said, although she didn't know. Thomas worked long hours, and she never knew his schedule.

"Thanks. I think I will."

"My mother's drinking again."

Frances glanced up, but she didn't seem as surprised as Abby expected.

"Who the hell isn't?"

Sometimes Abby admired her friend's indifference. Sitting beside her, she reached for the cigarette, and Frances gave it to her. She took a puff and tried not to cough.

"How're you feeling?" Abby asked, handing it back.

"Lost."

The response was poignant, but it wasn't what Abby meant.

"Are you pregnant?"

Frances scoffed.

"I already told you so."

"How do you know?"

"I just know."

"Have you seen a doctor?"

"Abby," she said, turning to her. "I haven't had my period since Sal left in September."

"What're you going to do?"

As Frances went to answer, they heard a noise. At first, it sounded like a faint rattle, but soon they realized it was the siren. They had been warned that the cold weather might impair the alarms. Slowly lights came on, mostly just streetlamps because the homes all had blackout shades.

Abby stood and then helped Frances up. As girly as her friend was, she didn't cry much. So Abby was startled to see tears rolling down her cheeks.

"This is awful," Frances said.

Abby didn't know if she meant the Cocoanut Grove fire, Sal's death, the pregnancy, or the war. Considering they were all traumatic in their own way, it was probably a combination. But she still had to ask.

"What is?"

"The whole bloody lot."

22

When Thomas walked into the station, Christmas music was playing on the radio. There was a wreath on the wall, a nativity scene on the counter, and some laurel on the tables in the waiting area. But all the decorations in the world couldn't make the dingy lobby look festive.

"Captain Vitti wants to see you," the secretary said.

"Okay, thanks."

Thomas continued down the hallway with a mild dread. The captain left his officers alone, and he was more of an administrator than a commander. If he wanted to talk, it usually meant something was wrong.

Thomas turned into the stairwell and went up to the third floor. When he reached the office, he knocked once and opened the door.

The room was small and cluttered. Along the walls were filing cabinets and shelves overflowing with documents and folders. It reeked of dust and cigar smoke.

"Thomas," the captain said.

"Morning, sir."

Captain Vitti was a hard man to read, and it wasn't his personality.

Half of his face had been paralyzed in the Great War. Some officers said it was from mustard gas, and others said it was shrapnel. Either way, one of his eyes drooped, and he spoke with a slight drawl. At one time, he had been a great athlete, his name memorialized on some plaque at East Boston High School. But like a lot of cops, especially the higher-ups, those glory days were gone. He had gotten fat and lazy.

"Have a seat. How goes the battle?"

He had been using military metaphors long before the war.

"Still in the trenches," Thomas said, sitting down.

"I hear the grand jury meets Friday."

Thomas shifted in the chair. Any mention of the fire made him anxious.

"Let's hope for an indictment."

"I've no doubt. That owner Welansky is a snake. Locked exit doors? Shoddy electrical work? Flammable decorations? The place was a tinder box."

Thomas hadn't told anyone he was at Cocoanut Grove because he didn't have to. The names of survivors had spread faster than the fire itself. While it made him a minor celebrity, it wasn't the kind of attention he wanted.

"So? How're you feeling?" the captain asked.

"Better each day."

It was something he had repeated so many times it felt meaningless.

"Happy to hear it."

Vitti put down his pen and leaned back in the chair.

"There's…something I wanted to talk to you about," he said, speaking low. "You know, everyone's struggling to get by."

"True."

With superiors, it was always better not to say too much.

"The Office of Price Administration is cracking down on anyone violating the ration regulations. That includes cops. The chief sent out a memo this morning."

Thomas wanted to scoff, but he didn't. OPA agents were more

corrupt than anybody. A week before, one was arrested for taking cash from a factory owner to overlook price controls.

"I'm not talking about the occasional pound of coffee or sugar," Vitti went on. "I think what they're mostly concerned about is gas and oil because of the shortage. We don't want any of our men caught up in it or the feds will be all over us."

Thomas glanced up.

"I thought they already were."

Since the start of the war, their department had been clashing with the FBI over everything from jurisdiction to oversight. Every officer resented the intrusion, regardless of rank.

"Just keep an eye on your men. And keep your nose clean."

"I will, sir."

Leaving the office, Thomas felt uneasy, even a little bitter. The captain's warning seemed aimed at him, although it could have been his own guilt or paranoia. The pay increase he got for making sergeant didn't make up for the long hours. He always saw those small gifts and kickbacks as some compensation for it.

He turned into his office and swiped some keys off the wall, not caring which cruiser it was. His agitation must have been obvious because the moment he walked out, Officer Carroll came around the corner and said, "Everything alright, Sarge?"

"What time are you on until?"

"Does it matter?"

Thomas frowned, but he understood the irony. A schedule meant little when the department could change it at any moment.

"Let's take a drive."

Carroll followed him down the stairwell, and they went out to the back lot. Thomas didn't say anything until they got in the car and pulled out to the street.

"Remember those guys we busted for making gas rations back in October?"

"The body bag factory?"

"Yeah."

"You took their stuff, gave them a warning."

Thomas glanced over, giving him a sharp look.

"Does anyone else know that?"

"No. That was ages ago."

Thomas smiled, as much out of relief as amusement. At their age, the days were like weeks, the weeks like years.

"Don't ever mention that."

"Never, Sarge."

At Day Square, Thomas cut the wheel, and they went down Neptune Road, a narrow street of triple-deckers. Some were well-kept, but many were rundown with trash barrels in the alleys, rusted jalopies in the driveways. A few of the homes were even abandoned. In a place as dense as East Boston, the slums mixed easily with the tidier, middle-class neighborhoods. Thomas only lived a half mile away but felt like he was in another world.

Once they reached the tracks, the dilapidation ended. They came out to a marsh where, on the other side, Wood Island Park loomed against the backdrop of the airport. When Thomas was a boy, it was a magical place, an escape from the congested city streets. In winter, kids from all over would come to build igloos, have snowball fights, and skate on the frozen pond. In summer, they would play baseball and swim at the beach.

As they drove across, a gust off the water shook the car. Thomas could see chimney smoke from the new Army barracks. They pulled into the park and followed the road along the shoreline. The footpaths were empty; the grass was covered in frost. The trees were all bare except for a row of firs that stood full and firm against the bitter harbor wind.

They approached a checkpoint where two soldiers stood beside a steel barricade. Both wore heavy wool coats and hats with earflaps, but it still seemed too cold not to have a guardhouse.

When Thomas stopped, one of the men walked over.

"Afternoon," he said, his face red and eyes watery.

"I need to talk to Major Holdsworth."

"He's at Fort Hawes."

Thomas stared across the bay to Winthrop, the water shimmering with whitecaps. While he couldn't see the fort, which was on the eastern end of Deer Island, he could see the faint outline of his family's cottage on Point Shirley.

"You know when he'll be back?"

The soldier called over to his partner who had to shout over the wind.

"Out there all week."

"Thanks."

Thomas made a U-turn, and they headed back. Once they were around the bend, he glanced over his shoulder. Then he pulled over and got out.

Opening the trunk, he searched through a box of tools and found a small hatchet, its blade corroded but sharp.

"What're you doing?" Carroll asked, walking over.

Thomas looked up at the cluster of fir trees on the hill.

"You need a Christmas tree?" he asked with a hint of mischief.

Carroll grinned.

"As a matter of fact, I do."

"Then c'mon."

......

BY THE TIME Thomas got home, it had started to snow. It was only flurries, nothing that would stick. He stepped out and reached into his back pocket for a penknife. When he cut the twine on the roof, the tree slid off into his arms. It was smaller than in years past, or maybe he was just getting older. But it was a fine Balsam fir with a straight trunk and thick, full branches. He was amazed it had survived on the windy plains of Wood Island Park.

He carried it up the front steps and stood it upright on the porch. With the blackout shades, he couldn't see inside, but he knew his mother was home. He knocked on the door and seconds later, she opened it.

Her face dropped—her eyes went wide.

"Thomas?"

"Merry Christmas, Ma."

She wore a long bathrobe over a sweater, her hair in rollers. He looked for signs that she had been drinking but didn't see any.

"It's beautiful," she said. "Where on earth did you find it?"

With a smile, he dragged it inside, the sweet smell of fir filling the house. He took it over to the living room where his mother had been reading by candlelight to save on electricity. The chair and table still had to be moved, so he leaned it against the wall. It was the same place they had always put it, the corner between the bookshelf and the window. Thomas remembered the excitement of coming down the stairs on Christmas morning with his two siblings to see piles of wrapped presents beneath.

"A Christmas tree?"

Abby stood at the bottom of the stairs in her MWDC uniform, her hair tied up. Thomas thought she was going out until he saw her bare feet and realized she had just gotten home. She scurried over, feeling the branches, picking off a few burrs. But the tree was clean, its needles shiny and pointed.

"The ornaments are in the shed," Mrs. Nolan said.

"Not now, Ma. I'll get them tomorrow."

The door opened, and Connie walked in with Chickie, who wore her best coat. They both looked stunned, Connie mumbling something in Italian. Chickie ran over and Thomas put his arm around her.

"Where you found it?" Connie asked.

"The McNultys' back yard."

She looked confused until she realized he was joking. He could have told them, but it would have been a bad example, especially for Chickie. With the shortage, people were stealing trees from streets, parks, and road embankments. A few nights before, the station got a call that some boys had run off with the tree from the nativity scene in Maverick Square.

"This calls for a celebration," Mrs. Nolan said, and she walked out to the kitchen.

Thomas glanced at Abby, hoping she didn't mean alcohol. Their mother hadn't lied about her drinking, but she had been hiding it, which in some ways was worse. Thomas felt the same tension he used to get before his father quit, remembering how it only took one insult, accusation, or snide remark to start a family blowout.

"Did you just get home?" he asked Connie.

"We were at her rehearsal practice."

"Rehearsal?"

"Christmas rehearsal," Chickie said.

"Friday night," Connie added.

Thomas looked at her and then Chickie.

"Right," he said.

While he acted like he hadn't forgotten, he could tell Connie knew with her look of quiet scorn. He was relieved when his mother returned with a tray of sugar cookies. She held them out to Chickie first, who smiled and took two.

"Where'd you get sugar?" Thomas asked, reaching for one.

"Abby got it."

Taking a bite, he looked over at his sister.

"Really? Which shop?"

"The same one that sells Christmas trees," she said.

At this point, all their misdeeds, indiscretions, and small sins were worth a laugh. Even their mother—who had scolded Abby a month before for stealing sugar—seemed willing to ignore any minor wrongdoings. After a year of war, people were overlooking things that, in the past, they would have been outraged by. Sometimes even morality had to adapt.

In the warm glow of the candlelight, they stood eating cookies in silence. Snowflakes tapped against the windows; the furnace rumbled in the basement. It was a moment of shared joy and contentment at a time when both were in short supply. Thomas rarely got sentimental. But looking around, he got choked up in the realization that, except for his brother, he was with everyone he loved in the world.

23

Abby sat in the waiting room at Mass General Hospital. Compared to the last time she was there, it was eerily quiet. The morning after the fire, when she, her mother, and Connie had come to see Thomas, it was chaos. All the benches had been full, and people had even been sitting on the floor, camping out in the hallways. While there hadn't been any panic, the tense whispers and muffled sobbing were almost worse. Now it felt empty.

Beside the reception desk, Abby saw a few notes and photographs taped to the wall, but nothing like before. By now, everyone from the Cocoanut Grove fire had been identified and accounted for. The morgues were no longer overflowing, and most victims had been buried. The public's attention had turned from sympathy to outrage over why the tragedy had happened.

Next to her someone had left a copy of yesterday's newspaper with the headline "STATE BLACKED OUT." Three hundred thousand civil defense workers had taken part in the exercise. Towns from Cape Cod to the Berkshires had gone dark. From Abby's small corner of East Boston, it didn't seem remarkable. They had been doing blackouts all year long.

When Ms. Stetson first asked her to join the MWDC, Abby was

afraid to say no. She knew nothing about the organization, but she saw it as just some other activity to juggle on top of work, school, and volleyball. Now with George in the service, she was proud to be part of the war effort.

The doors swung open, and Abby looked up. Frances strutted out with a nurse. She wore a pink petticoat and hat, a black purse hanging from her arm.

"Ready?" she said, and Abby stood up.

Frances thanked the nurse, and Abby followed her out. For the first few minutes, they didn't talk, which was unusual for Frances. But once they turned the corner, she said, "It's settled. I'm pregnant."

Abby didn't know whether to congratulate or console her.

"At least now you know."

They took the elevator down to the first floor. As they passed through the lobby, Abby kept her head down and didn't look around. They could have been there for a thousand reasons, but she worried about seeing someone she knew. Not only was having a child out of wedlock scorned, but it was a burden on the mother, a double curse for any young woman. She knew a girl in high school who had gotten pregnant. To avoid the shame, the family sent her back to Italy to have the child.

They walked out the main doors into the clear, cool morning. It had snowed again the night before, leaving a thin layer of white over the hospital grounds. Frances waved for a taxi, and they got in.

Even in the sun, the city looked dismal. As they passed the Boston Common, the fence was being dismantled for scrap. The brownstones along Beacon Street had no holiday lights, their elegant windows obstructed by dark shades. Cardinal O'Connell had banned decorations on churches, and the Fire Commissioner had done the same for stores and public buildings. Even caroling was forbidden, authorities worried that with the dim-out order, the streets were too dark and dangerous. The combination of the war and the Cocoanut Grove tragedy had turned Boston into a city besieged by safeguards and precautions. The only sign that it was Christmas was some streamers over the entrance to the Statehouse, although they could have been left over from Thanksgiving.

When they got to BU, the cabbie dropped them at Marsh Chapel. In warmer weather, the courtyard was often crowded. Now it was desolate, and not just because of the cold. Many students had already gone home for the holiday break, which had been extended by a week due to fuel and rationing problems. There were fewer soldiers too. Several hundred members of the Officers' Training Corps had left for Fort Devens the week before in a grand parade down Commonwealth Avenue.

Frances took out a cigarette, cupping her hands to light it. So far, Abby had been quiet, not asking any questions. She had gone to the appointment to support her friend, not to judge her. But ignoring problems didn't make them go away.

"What do you think you'll do?" she asked.

Frances blew out the smoke, her eyes flitting.

"Have a child, I suppose."

"Will you tell your mother?"

"I imagine I should."

I suppose. I imagine. Frances' apathy had always been part of her style, giving her an air of confidence. But Abby could tell she was confused and afraid. She had lost her boyfriend and had to deal with a pregnancy. Abby was sure Sal would have proposed to her, and maybe that night. It was sad to think that now there was nothing to commemorate their few short months together.

"Well, I guess I should be going," Frances said.

But neither of them cared, and there was no great urgency. It was the last day of the semester. Frances had one more final, and Abby just had to hand in a paper.

"I'll call you later?" Abby asked.

Frances dropped her cigarette and stamped it out.

"Please do."

Leaning up, she kissed Abby on the cheek and walked off. Abby watched her until she was out of sight and then headed in the other direction.

When she opened the side door of the College of Liberal Arts building, she got a burst of musty air. The hallway wasn't much warmer than outside. The university had been keeping the temperature as low as it could be without the pipes freezing.

As she approached Mr. Glynn's office, the lights were off. She turned the doorknob, and it was locked.

"Miss Nolan?"

Startled, Abby spun around.

"Ms. Stetson," she said.

"Mr. Glynn won't be back, I'm afraid."

"I have to hand in my essay."

"He's been released from his duties here at the university."

Abby blinked in confusion.

"Released from his duties?"

"Terminated, Miss Nolan," she said.

Considering Ms. Stetson was queer too, Abby would have expected more sympathy for her colleague. But loyalties were complicated, even for social outcasts. As the daughter of a Protestant minister from Canada, Ms. Stetson was a disciplined rule follower. The last person she would support was an Irish rebel like Glynn.

"I can get your paper to the dean if you'd like."

Abby reached into her bag and took out the essay, ten pages neatly typed on the typewriter she had borrowed from Mrs. McNulty. She gave it to Ms. Stetson who read the title with a restrained snicker, "*The American Revolution and the Struggle for Irish Independence.*"

Abby forced a smile. Nothing bothered a cynic more than kindness.

"Is there a Private Labadini in your unit?" Ms. Stetson asked.

"Angela. Yes."

"There're rumors she's been associating with a negro soldier. Do you know anything about it?"

Abby arched her back. It wasn't the first time she had clashed with the professor.

"Is that a crime?"

"Not in this state, perhaps. But in the Women's Defense Corps, we're held to certain standards."

"Which are what, precisely?"

Ms. Stetson stared, her eyes piercing and jaw tense. Whenever she got angry or offended, her underbite was more obvious. But Abby wouldn't look away. She was no longer the timid freshman she was a year before.

"Very well, Ms. Nolan," the professor said, and Abby felt a quiet relief. "Happy Christmas."

......

WHEN ABBY WALKED in the front door, the living room was a mess. The floor was covered with boxes of ornaments and strands of tinsel. In the corner, her mother was crouched by the tree in her nightgown and socks. Her legs were thin and pale, the varicose veins on her calves showing.

"Abby, dear," she said, glancing back. "Can you tighten these?"

Abby put down her bag and walked over. When her mother stood up, she could smell alcohol. She crouched and reached for the cast iron tree stand. Old and rusty, it had been in the family for generations.

"Wait," her mother said. "Let me straighten it first."

Once she did, Abby strained to turn the screws.

"How's that?" she asked.

"More to the left."

Abby loosened one side and tightened the other, the branches digging into her back.

"Better?"

Her mother stepped back, eyeing the tree like an architect.

"Just a tad more."

Abby frowned and tried again.

"Perfect!"

Abby sat up, picking pine needles off her coat.

"Isn't it marvelous?" her mother asked with a flair.

Abby hated the artificial cheerfulness of alcohol.

"Gorgeous, Ma."

Whenever her mother was drinking, she couldn't be around her for long without getting irritated or annoyed. But she knew she couldn't make her quit. Sometimes she was envious that her brother lived next door and didn't have to deal with her as much.

"Could you take the mittens I made down to St. Mary's?"

"Now?"

"Dinner will be ready when you get back."

When Abby hesitated, her mother gave her a pleading smile.

"Where do I put them?"

"There's a Bundles for Britain bin in the vestibule."

Before she could answer, her mother ran into the dining room and returned with a paper bag. Abby looked in to see a dozen pairs of mittens that were all shapes and sizes. She hadn't even had time to take off her coat, so she just fixed her scarf and turned to leave.

"Oh," her mother said, and Abby stopped. "See if any of the shops have sugar too, would you?"

Without answering, Abby walked out and slammed the door.

With the winter solstice just five days away, it was only four thirty and almost dark. The light snow that had melted in the sun was now starting to freeze.

As she passed the small church at the corner, someone said, "Abby?"

She looked over the fence and saw Olive and two other girls in the yard. One had a jump rope, but there was no place to use it on the icy, dead grass.

"Hello, Olive," Abby said.

"Where's Chickie?"

"Probably doing homework."

"Where's your brother?"

"He's in the quiet room."

"The quiet room?" Abby asked.

"When the boys are bad, they go in the quiet room."

The other two girls were shy, standing still and nodding. They were a couple of years younger than Olive. Knowing they were all refugees, Abby wondered if any of their parents had died in the Blitz. Either way, she pitied their situation. She had never been away for long enough to feel homesick, but she was sure it was awful.

Although the girls were dressed for the cold, their clothes were old and ragged. One of them had no gloves on. But the church took care of them, enrolling them in school and giving them a place to live. Even though Abby's mother disliked Protestants, she acknowledged their charity and good works.

"I've got something for you," Abby said.

She went into the bag and handed them each a pair of mittens. Their faces beamed as they took them and tried them on.

"Thank you, ma'am," they said.

"Merry Christmas."

"Merry Christmas, ma'am."

Abby waved and turned down Saratoga Street. St. Mary's was only two blocks from their house, a route she had walked hundreds of times in her life. Except for holidays, Connie and her mother were the only ones who went to mass now. Thomas was always working, and Abby was too lazy to get up on Sunday mornings.

The church was modest by Catholic standards. It was small and plain, only a step up from a meetinghouse. Once Irish, the parish was now mostly Italian with a smattering of Portuguese and Polish. But it held a special significance for their family. Her grandfather was one of the founders, and her mother had gone to the elementary school. Abby and her brothers had all been baptized and confirmed there. And finally, it was where they had held her father's funeral.

She went up the front stairs and into the arched entrance. When she opened the door, a service was in progress. She tiptoed over to the bin, dropped in the bag of mittens, and quickly left.

She ran toward Bennington Street, the temperature dropping by the minute. The shops looked strange at night with their neon signs off and their windows blacked out. But she could always spot some sliver of light that would let her know if they were still open.

She waited for a streetcar to go by and scurried across to the German market. Aside from the sugar, she wanted milk for tea. Her mother was the only one who drank it black.

When she walked in, Mr. Schultz was counting money at the register. She knew he was getting ready to close. Despite the new rules, some stores could stay open later if they offered critical services like pharmaceuticals or coal and heating oil. But for most owners, it was neither safe nor profitable. With fewer people on the streets after dark, criminals were bolder. Mr. Schultz had been robbed before. The last time, he had shot the assailant in the leg, so now everyone knew he had a gun.

Abby went down the aisle and saw that the shelf with the sugar was empty, which wasn't a surprise. With Christmas just a few days away, people were baking pies, cakes, and cookies.

"Pardon, Mr. Schultz," she called over. "By chance, would you have any sugar in the back?"

"I get more tomorrow but let me check."

He came around the counter and went into the storeroom. Moments later, he walked out holding a box of Domino Sugar.

"I kept for a customer. She didn't come to get it."

"Oh, that's terrific."

"The OPA just raised the price ceiling," he said, ringing it in. "But I give you the old price."

"Thank you."

"Six cents, please."

Opening her bag, she took out her purse and ration book. She gave him a dime and then carefully pulled off a sugar stamp.

"And how is your lovely mother?"

Abby stopped, looking up. She could have given him a polite reply. The hypocrisy of manners and etiquette was that whenever people greeted each other, they never expected an honest answer. She was tired of pretending things were fine.

"To be frank, she's damn lonely."

He stopped, his hand on the crank. For a moment, she thought she had been too blunt. Then she watched his expression soften. Emotion wasn't always as obvious in men, but she could tell he was moved.

"I know that feeling," he said, finally.

When his wife died, Abby was in first grade. Her father used to bring her into the store for candy: Turkish Taffy, Candy Buttons, and Red Hots. All she remembered was a tall blonde woman with a kind smile and a thick accent. The Schultzes had two sons who had worked there on and off over the years. But Abby never knew the family well, probably because they lived in Winthrop and were Lutherans. In the insular world of blue-collar Boston, geography and religion seemed to determine everything.

"These are difficult times..." he said, handing her the change.

She didn't know if he meant the war or the Christmas season.

"But we'll all get through it together."

24

As Thomas crossed the strand, he could see the family cottage. Situated at the bend in the road on the inner harbor, it was protected from the harsh winds of the coast. The trees around it were all barren; the rocky headland across the street was gray and windswept.

He didn't come out to the cottage much in the winter, and it felt like a different place. If he blinked, he could imagine his father sitting in his favorite chair on the lawn, his mother plucking roses off the bushes. As boys, he and George would stand on the rocks and watch the planes take off. At night, they would go down to the pier to drink beer and meet girls. Those summers felt like a lifetime ago, and he wanted to go back.

He was on duty and should've been in a police cruiser, but he had taken the Ford instead. He was leaving their jurisdiction without telling the captain, something that could've gotten him in trouble in the past. But everyone had been ignoring boundaries and borders. When he was with the harbor unit, they patrolled the Chelsea Navy Yard and other facilities outside of Boston. In the last blackout, the department had borrowed officers from Quincy and Everett.

He continued through Point Shirley past shuttered houses and empty side streets. The only shop open was Pulsifer's, which catered to fishermen and crabbers in the off-season. He drove to the neck that led to Deer Island, which had once been a separate landmass until The Hurricane of '38 had shifted the sands.

In the distance, the outer harbor was cluttered with ships, from tankers to ferries to Navy patrol boats. With U-boats prowling the coast, it was safest to travel in the daytime.

Over at the prison, dozens of men were in the yard. It seemed too cold to be out, even for convicts. The ground was covered in frost; the wind rattled the barbed wire fence. More unusual, however, was that they had on civilian clothes. As Thomas passed, they all stared at him.

He slowed down as he approached the Army checkpoint. A private walked over, pulling down his wool face mask.

"This area is restricted," he said.

Most soldiers Thomas had met were cordial, but he could tell this one wasn't.

"I was hoping to talk to Major Holdsworth."

"Is he expecting you?"

For a moment, Thomas considered lying, but he knew they would've found out.

"No."

"Then you can't see—"

Boom!

Thomas jumped in his seat.

"The hell was that?" he blurted.

The men looked at each other and laughed.

"We're testing the sixteen-inch guns."

Since the start of the war, Thomas had heard a lot of artillery blasts, but he had never been so close.

"I can call down to HQ, but I can't make any promises," the private said, surprising Thomas with his sudden courtesy.

"Please. If you don't mind."

"What's your name?"

"Sergeant Nolan."

The man walked over to a field telephone on top of a pile of sandbags. He made a call and came back, leaning against the car.

"You see that watchtower?" he asked, and Thomas nodded. "Beside it is the Battery Commander's station. The major is in there with Colonel Loring."

"Thanks."

"And stay on the road. Them fields are mined."

The private walked off with a smirk, and Thomas wasn't sure if he was kidding. He drove another hundred yards, pulling into a camp with a few small structures and some vehicles parked at different angles. Two soldiers were unloading oil barrels from a truck, but otherwise, it was quiet. The only sign of the test was black smoke hovering above the gun batteries down by the shore.

When Thomas got out, Major Holdsworth was already walking over to meet him. In the sunlight, he looked older than before.

"Sergeant Nolan," he said.

He peeled off one glove, and they shook hands.

"Afternoon, Major."

"What brings you to these parts?"

"I've got a little problem."

The major's expression tightened.

"Go on," he said.

"There's a local girl. Her family thinks she's been seeing a soldier from your barracks..."

With each word, Thomas looked for a reaction so he could stop before he went too far. When the major didn't scoff, he said, "A negro soldier."

Holdsworth nodded, pursing his lips. He thought for a moment and then cleared his throat.

"Sergeant, I don't tell my men who they can fraternize with on their own time...regardless of their *persuasion*."

Race was always a sensitive subject. Boston wasn't the Deep South, but people were prejudiced.

"I understand, sir," Thomas said.

"However, given the circumstances, I can see how this might be a distraction to the community," the major went on, then he lowered his voice. "That unit is headed to Northern Ireland in a week. They'll be attached to the 34th Infantry Division. That's not public knowledge."

Thomas felt a huge relief. The fact that the soldier would soon be gone solved the problem.

Holdsworth extended his hand, and they shook again.

"Keep up the good work on the home front."

"Thank you."

As they parted, Thomas remembered something.

"Sir," he said, and the major turned. "At the prison, the men in the yard...They don't look like inmates."

"That's because they aren't."

"No?"

"They're Italians."

The word sent a shiver up Thomas' spine, although he wasn't sure why. It had always been a strange contradiction that his neighborhood was full of people whose relatives and ancestors were from an enemy country.

"Prisoners of war," Holdsworth added. "They started arriving a few weeks ago."

In many ways, the war so far had just been a series of radio broadcasts, news stories, blackouts, and obituaries. The presence of POWs made it feel real and close.

"*That,*" the major emphasized, "is not public knowledge either."

......

THOMAS SAT at a table at the Red Shutter Café. It was quiet for a Saturday night. When the waitress came by, he ordered a beer, but what he really wanted was something hot. The temperature was expected to hit zero that night. The room was freezing, so he knew the owner had the thermostat down. Everyone was trying to conserve oil. The windows had heavy blackout curtains, but Thomas still felt a cold draft. Many people were eating with their coats on.

The restaurant wasn't a dive, but he would've preferred somewhere downtown, the Columbia Grill or even the Custom House. The only reason he had picked it was because DiMarco didn't have much time and it was close. It had shabby red carpeting, wobbly chairs, and stucco walls decorated with framed photographs of Boston. The décor hadn't been updated since the Twenties, which was ironic because it had once been a speakeasy. The ground floor was for dining, and upstairs had dancing after nine. When he was a boy, his mother and father had gone there for anniversaries and special occasions, but only when Jeveli's or the Beachmont Café were booked.

Finally, DiMarco walked in.

"Nick!" Thomas called out, waving.

"Sorry I'm late."

When they shook, his hands were stiff and cold.

"Chilly out there," Thomas said.

"Like goddamn Maine."

DiMarco took off his coat and scarf and hung them on the back of the chair. When the waitress came over, he gave her a second look. She was pretty, with dark hair and big eyes, but she was also missing a tooth.

She put down Thomas' glass of beer, and DiMarco stared at it.

"Whaddya wanna freeze to death?" he joked.

"Isn't alcohol supposed to warm you up?"

"Not a pilsner," he said, then he looked up. "Two Martinis, please. Dirty."

Thomas didn't know much about booze, other than his father had been a drunk. He could have a couple of beers or half a cocktail, but he had never really liked the feeling.

"The Brits invaded Burma," DiMarco said.

"I read that."

The news from abroad had been good all week. Rommel's Army was fleeing in North Africa, the Japanese were pinned down in New

Guinea, and Allied forces had started bombing Sicily. After the Cocoanut Grove fire, it was refreshing to start hearing about the war again.

"When do you ship out?" Thomas asked.

"I leave for basic next Thursday. Camp Belvoir."

"Where's that?"

"Some hick town in Virginia."

"And on Christmas Eve?"

"As good a time as any, right?"

Everything DiMarco said now was tinged with sarcasm or scorn. He was still striking enough that when he walked in, a few women had looked over. But his youthful glow was gone. Sarah's death had stunned him like no mortar or grenade ever would. While Thomas had no doubt he would kill some Krauts or Japs, he didn't know if his friend would ever love again.

The waitress came back with the drinks and gave them menus.

"Hungry?" Thomas asked.

"Famished. What're the specials?"

"We got meatballs and stuffed shells," the girl said, "and pork chops with roast potatoes."

DiMarco looked at Thomas who said, "You pick."

"We'll take the pork chops."

Thomas wasn't fussy, but it was the one he would have chosen. Connie made macaroni all the time, and although Chickie loved it, it was more about being frugal. With beef prices up, pasta was one of the cheapest foods around.

"How's Chickie doing?" DiMarco asked like he had read Thomas' mind.

"She's alright. It hasn't really sunk in yet."

"It ain't easy losing a brother."

Considering George was away, the remark stung. And Thomas didn't want to spend dinner talking about loss, death, and tragedy.

"Captain Vitti called me in the office today," he said, changing the subject.

"Oh yeah? How's Scarface doing?"

"He told me to keep an eye on my men. He said the OPA is cracking down on bribes."

"Bribes?"

"Like favors and stuff."

"You got something to worry about?"

Thomas took a sip of his drink, wincing from the vodka.

"I...I don't think so."

"Don't take it personally. The chief is just worried with all the government regulations. There's a lot of money being made off rationing..."

Like a lot of cops, Thomas never understood where that fine line between bending the rules and actual corruption was. The department was getting stricter, especially with anything that had to do with the war. An officer in Lowell had been kicked off the force for stealing gas coupons. In Springfield, a lieutenant was indicted for approving draft deferments in exchange for cash.

"Just keep your nose clean, that's all," DiMarco added.

Keep your nose clean. It was the same advice Captain Vitti had given him, which was no comfort.

By the time the food arrived, Thomas was a little woozy from the alcohol. The waitress put down the plates with a smile.

"To victory," DiMarco said, and they toasted.

As they ate, the music started upstairs, and couples started arriving to dance. Each time the front door opened, it sent a frigid breeze through the restaurant.

With the high price of meat, the portions were smaller than normal, and Thomas was done in minutes. Salt was plentiful, but he could tell they hadn't used enough butter. Either way, it didn't matter much because, with all the stress, his appetite wasn't what it used to be.

The waitress came back.

"Another round?"

"I'll have coffee," Thomas said.

"We won't have any more till next week."

Thomas looked across to DiMarco who wiped his chin with a napkin.

"I gotta get going, unfortunately. We'll take the check."

The moment the girl put the bill on the table, DiMarco swiped it up.

"Son of a bitch!" Thomas said.

"You get the next one."

Their eyes locked. Neither of them knew if there would be a next one.

"Deal."

DiMarco paid the bill, and they got up and put on their coats. As they headed toward the doors, people turned, especially the women. Thomas wanted to think it was their good looks, but it probably had more to do with how out of place they were here. With so many young men their age gone, they were a rare sight on a Saturday evening.

The moment they walked out, Thomas tensed up from the cold. Day Square was dark, and the streets were empty. They lingered in the doorway to stay out of the wind.

"Jesus," DiMarco said, pulling up his collar. "I hope they send me somewhere warm."

"Maybe you'll get posted to the Aleutians like my brother."

"Wouldn't that be ironic? Have you heard from him yet?"

Thomas shook his head.

"Not since September."

"Oh, I got these for you."

He reached into his pocket and took out a pile of stamps. Thomas didn't have to look any closer to know they were a mix of gas, butter, and sugar rations. He already had plenty, but after the warning DiMarco had just given him about shady behavior, he didn't want to admit it.

"Thanks."

"Do me a favor."

"Name it."

"Visit Sarah's parents. They're in Quincy. I can't remember the address—"

"I can get it from Abby."

For the first time that night, DiMarco smiled. Thomas felt a wave of emotion, although he didn't show it. He had known DiMarco for many years, and while they had never been close, he considered him a friend. As with a lot of people in his life, Thomas only realized how much he was going to miss him now that he was leaving. He could feel the same hollow angst he had gotten when his brother had left for the Army.

"Take care, Thomas."

DiMarco held out his hand, and when they shook, his grip was tight. It almost felt like he was clinging. Then Thomas leaned forward and hugged him. He wanted to say, "come back," but even in his head it sounded sappy, so instead he said, "Give 'em hell."

DiMarco shoved his hands in his pockets.

"You know I will."

With a casual nod, he walked off like they were parting after a game of sandlot baseball. And maybe DiMarco wanted it that way.

Thomas watched until he turned the corner, the sound of his footsteps fading. Standing alone, he could've gotten sad or sentimental. But what he felt was even deeper. It seemed like everyone in his life was being torn from him. Looking around the quiet square, he realized it wasn't the cold so much as it was the barrenness that bothered him.

25

Abby hurried down Tremont Street. She wore a scarf over her mouth; her hat was pulled down over her ears. She had on two sweaters and wool stockings and was still freezing.

It was the longest cold wave in Boston's history. For over two weeks, the temperature had been in the teens. The past three days, it had been below zero. It hadn't even been a month since one of the worst building fires in American history and now people had to worry about dying of hypothermia, an irony that wasn't lost on the newspaper columnists. The oil shortage everyone had dreaded had finally arrived. The War Production Board had ordered businesses, apartment buildings, and manufacturing plants to change their systems over to coal. Across the city, schools and public buildings were open around the clock for anyone who had no heat.

Despite all the struggles, it was starting to feel like Christmas in Boston. The sidewalks were crowded with shoppers; the bells of Salvation Army workers rang on street corners. Young boys were dressed in plaid coats and wool caps; girls wore red dresses and stockings.

Abby turned into the Howard Johnson's, a small diner with a long counter and parquet floors. Looking around, she saw Frances wave from a booth in the back. As she walked over, she passed three sailors at the soda fountain. They stared at her as she went by.

"Isn't it madness out there?" Frances said.

"'Tis the season."

Abby sat down and took off her scarf. Coming in from the cold, she was damp and sweaty. She reached for a napkin and patted her forehead.

"What happened to Richie?" she asked, and it still felt weird calling Mr. Glynn by his first name.

Before Frances could respond, a waitress came over. She was a young woman with dirty blonde hair and dark lipstick. Her checkered uniform didn't look warm, but she had on knit gloves.

"Can I get you a drink?" she asked.

"Just tea, please."

The moment she walked away, Abby looked at Frances.

"Well?"

"He was reported to the provost for 'unpatriotic activity.'"

Abby frowned.

"Unpatriotic? He's Irish."

"He's still in our country. Whatever he said violated their code of conduct."

Abby didn't like a university treating its professors like high school students. Mr. Glynn had strong views, but the problems between Ireland and Great Britain had started long before the war.

"I told my mother," Frances blurted.

"About?"

"Yes."

They were interrupted when the waitress came back.

"Will you be having lunch?" she asked.

"Yes, please."

A diner wasn't the best place to talk, but neither of them had much privacy. Abby still lived at home, and since the fire, Frances had left her dorm and moved into her mother's new apartment in Beacon Hill.

Abby ordered Chicken à la King and Frances got an egg salad sandwich. The woman wrote it down and walked away.

"How'd she take it?" Abby asked.

"Nothing a bottle and a half of wine didn't help."

Abby gave a sour smile, but sometimes she liked her friend's black humor.

"I've decided to keep it."

The word "it" seemed so impersonal it took Abby a second to realize what she had meant.

"Does your mother agree?"

Reaching into her purse, Frances took out a cigarette and lit it.

"I don't need her approval," she said. "I'm twenty-one years old."

When she took a drag, it must have been either too fast or too much. She broke into a fit of coughing so loud that people turned.

"Are you okay?" Abby asked, and the waitress ran over with a glass of water.

Frances nodded, blinking, gasping for air. She wiped her mouth with a napkin, and when she put it down, Abby noticed blood.

"There's—"

"I know," Frances said, looking embarrassed. "It happens sometimes."

"Did you tell the doctor?"

She shook her head, still out of breath.

"Dammit, Abby. I can only deal with one medical problem at a time."

......

AFTER LUNCH, they spent the rest of the afternoon shopping for gifts. They tried to go to Filene's, but the lines were too long, so they went to Conrad's. Abby got her mother a flannel robe and Thomas a pair of leather gloves, knowing he could use them for work too. Frances bought her mother a diamond bracelet and her father a new suit, which she had shipped to some address that wasn't her house in Duxbury. She was the only girl Abby knew who had a charge card, and she never seemed to worry about money.

They walked up Winter Street, a narrow lane lined with shops, all decorated for the holiday. On the sidewalks, street vendors sold everything from roasted peanuts to fudge. It had even snowed, just a few flurries but enough to add some festive charm to the cold afternoon. Except for soldiers, the only sign that there was even a war going on was a recruitment poster and a booth to buy bonds. Other than that, the world felt normal.

When they got to the corner, Frances stopped.

"Harold wants to have us over Wednesday night. Are you available?"

"Let me check my social calendar," Abby joked.

Frances smiled, and they kissed on the cheeks.

"A lovely day, dear. Thank you."

She raised her hand, and a taxi pulled over. While her mother's apartment was only on the other side of the Boston Common, she had on high heels, and it was frigid. Beyond that, she got winded easily. Abby didn't know if it was from the pregnancy or the fire, but she was worried now that her friend had coughed up blood.

The driver got out and opened the back door. He took her bags and put them in the trunk.

"Toodle-loo," Frances said.

Something about the words got Abby teary. Frances was far from her former self, but she didn't seem as depressed as before. She had only mentioned Sal once all day. When they had seen a mannequin in a tuxedo, she had said it reminded her of when he had worked at Cocoanut Grove.

The cab pulled away, and Abby crossed the street. She was about to go into Park Street Station when she heard children singing. She looked over to the Buddies' Club, a recreation center for servicemen that had a cafeteria, exercise facilities, and dance hall.

She stepped onto the damp grass of the Boston Common. Without a fence, it was as open as a prairie, and she wondered how many bullets and shell casings would be made from the metal. She followed the walkway to the club and saw a bandstand out front. Over the stage was a giant banner that read "United War Fund." The seats were filling up with soldiers and civilians, and more people were coming. A school choral group had just finished, and a brass band was setting up.

It was early enough that Abby was in no rush. She only needed to be home to help with dinner, which wasn't for another two hours. Her mother's drinking had gotten worse, or at least more frequent. She still tried to hide it, sometimes mixing vodka with her tea, but Abby could always tell when she was tipsy.

A man in a uniform walked out, and people clapped. Abby knew he was with the USO because their jackets had no bars or stripes. He introduced the band, which immediately broke into a fast number. In the brutal cold, there was no time for waltzes or tangos. A few brave couples walked out to a small dancing area in front of the stage.

As Abby stood watching, it felt good to have free time. For the past three months, she had gone from the bakery to the streetcar to class and then home. The only time she was outside was for MWDC exercises. There were social events at headquarters, luncheons and evening receptions. Anyone was invited, but it was mostly the leadership: pompous grande dames, society ladies, and lesbians.

The song ended with a drum roll, and when the crowd cheered, someone caught Abby's attention. Looking closer, she realized it was Angela Labadini and the black soldier. They were huddled in the back row, close enough to be a couple but far enough away to be proper. Still, they seemed nervous, he more than her. But in their eyes, Abby saw the sparkle that only comes from love, or at least the hope for it. She recognized that look because she knew the feeling. As scorned as their relationship would be, she had to admire their courage. In an unfair world, sometimes dignity and hope were the only way to fight back.

26

THOMAS AND CARROLL DROVE THROUGH THE FROZEN STREETS. THE windows of the cruiser were fogged up, and there was ice on the hood. Their shift had just started, and Thomas hadn't had breakfast. Connie had used the last of the coffee, and all the shops were out. They hadn't had any butter in a week, a shortage that the dairy farmers were blaming on the truckers and the truckers were blaming on the government because of gasoline rationing.

But at least they were warm. With the extreme temperatures, the chief had made an exception to the dress code. Thomas wore a thick scarf and a wool hat under his police cap. Carroll had on a turtleneck and mittens. Even if cops could afford cold weather gear, it was impossible to find. The factories that had made it now had contracts with the military. So men had to improvise, enhancing their regular uniforms with hand-knit sweaters and trapper hats. The day before, Thomas had seen an officer doing a traffic detail in a fur parka.

"The Brits bombed Munich yesterday," Carroll said.

"That's the Nazi's home turf."

"They say we're gonna invade France soon."

Following the war was like following the Red Sox by reading only the highlights and statistics. It had some of the satisfaction but none of the excitement or emotion. But even when the news was good, it didn't make up for the challenges at home. Unlike his mother who used coal, Thomas had to worry about oil. They had run out the night before and all had to sleep by the fireplace.

Soon they approached the waterfront, the sign "East Boston Works" looming over the buildings.

"Holy shit!"

When Carroll pointed, Thomas gasped. Across the harbor, he saw giant plumes of black smoke.

"That's South Boston," he said.

He punched the gas and raced toward Jeffries Point to get a better view. As they came to the end of Marginal Street, the fire looked even worse. The entire pier was engulfed, a giant cloud of smoke floating across the channel toward the airport. Just offshore, two Coast Guard boats and a tug were dowsing the flames with water cannons.

Thomas stopped in front of Bethlehem Steel, and they jumped out. The noise of alarms and sirens echoed across the harbor. They ran over to the shoreline where, six feet below, waves lapped against the breakwater.

"Sabotage?" Carroll asked.

"Doubt it."

A few yards away, two MPs stood by the rear gate of the shipyard. With bulky coats and face coverings, they looked like Arctic explorers.

"Any idea what happened?" Thomas yelled over.

One of the soldiers pulled down his mask.

"A coal wharf caught fire earlier this morning. They couldn't get to it because the hydrants were frozen."

The industrial flatlands of the seaport were far enough away from downtown that they weren't a threat. And Boston wasn't the tinderbox it had once been. When Thomas was young, a fire that had started in a barn two streets away had burned for almost twenty-four hours and destroyed five houses. His mother remembered the Chelsea Fire of 1908, and his grandfather had been alive for the Great Boston Fire of 1872.

"Ain't that something?" Carroll said.

They watched in amazement.

"Probably what war is like."

Even as Thomas said it, he knew it sounded naïve, something a child would say.

"I'll know soon."

Thomas glanced over.

"You'll know what?" he asked.

"I'll know what war is like."

Carroll had a mischievous grin.

"I enlisted yesterday, Sarge. I leave for the Army next week."

......

WHEN THOMAS GOT HOME, he went up the steps to his mother's house. Sometimes he wondered if he could ever get used to living at the Ciarlones'. He and Connie had talked about moving out of East Boston, which he knew would break his mother's heart. But if they did, it would only be after the war was over.

He walked in the door as Abby was coming down the stairs. She had on her MWDC uniform, her tie loose and no shoes on.

"Is Chickie here?"

"No," Abby said. "And thankfully so."

She nodded toward the kitchen.

"Thomas? Is that you?" their mother called.

In her voice, he heard some slight drawl or delay. He knew she had been drinking.

"Yeah, Ma."

"Chickie's down at the Protestant church with the refugee children."

Everything she said seemed to reveal some deeper meaning or

opinion. She could have just said the "corner" church, and "refugee" was harsh for two kids who were always over the house.

"Thanks, Ma. I'll get her."

Turning back to Abby, Thomas noticed a faint odor.

"You smell like smoke," he said.

"I was at the wharf fire in South Boston today."

"What were you doing there?"

"We were called up to help. We brought over a mobile canteen to serve coffee and donuts," she said with a sarcastic frown.

"We watched it from Bethlehem Steel. It looked enormous."

"Everyone thought the Germans had bombed us."

Thomas snickered, but it wasn't something to laugh about. People were on edge, and the sight of black smoke over the city was enough to make anyone panic.

"Can you blame them? We got some calls at the station."

"Abby?" their mother said. "Can you get the baking soda? I can't reach it."

"Yes, Ma."

"Good luck," Thomas whispered.

When Abby went to help, Thomas quickly left before their mother could ask him to stay for dinner. Outside, he saw someone coming up the street. He waited on the sidewalk and moments later, Chickie burst from the shadows with her arms out. She had on a black dress, patent leather shoes, and a bow in her hair.

"Don't you look snazzy?" he said, hugging her.

"It's so cold."

"It's gonna get even colder."

They walked up to their house, and the front door opened. Connie stepped out in a blue dress, her hair in curls. She even had on the pearl necklace she had inherited from Mrs. Ciarlone.

"Are you ready?" Connie asked.

"Ready for what?"

"Dada..." Chickie moaned.

Hearing her call him daddy was touching, but he was still confused.

"Her Christmas rehearsal. It's tonight."

Thomas cringed.

"Shouldn't we invite my mother?" he asked, deflecting the fact that he had forgotten.

Connie gave him a look that was kind but firm. He knew she needed a break from her mother-in-law.

"Perhaps some other time."

They walked over to the car, and Thomas opened the rear door, gesturing for them to enter.

"My ladies," he said.

They both sat in the back, which wasn't what he had intended, and they drove away.

They got to the school in minutes and parked out front. The neighborhood was dark except for a few glints escaping from the edges of windows and doorways. As they got out, Thomas saw flashing lights at the fuel depot on Chelsea River, either Morse Code or some other military signals. With temperatures expected to hit zero, no one was out, and the streets were desolate.

As they walked toward the entrance, the gate was still standing, but most of the fence around the property was gone. Thomas wondered how much more they could tear down for scrap before the city was just open lots and steps without handrails.

Inside, Mrs. Giaconni stood in the lobby greeting parents. Thomas took off his glove and shook her hand, embarrassed that his was so cold. They continued down the hallway, and when they got to the auditorium, Chickie waved goodbye and followed some students through a door that said "Backstage."

The room was only half full, and Thomas and Connie found spots near the front. The moment they sat down, the curtains opened. Thomas checked his watch, and it was exactly seven. Considering how cold the room was, he assumed the administration didn't want to waste any time. The building took a lot to heat. No one took off their coats, and men kept their hats on. One woman even had a blanket over her legs.

The stage was a curious mix of religious and popular symbols, including a nativity scene, Santa Claus, a Christmas tree, and an American GI holding a present. The backdrop had cut-out stars and a crescent moon. The decorations were impressive for a small school, and Thomas was sure they had used them before.

A teacher sat at the piano, and the students came out. They got into rows, and Thomas could tell it wasn't by height. Chickie was in the back, and she wasn't very tall.

Mrs. Giaconni walked up, her hands clasped.

"We'd like to welcome parents to our annual Christmas choral performance," she said, steam shooting from her breath. "First, we'd like to apologize for the temperature. We've been instructed by the school department to keep our thermostats down to conserve oil. As such, this year's Christmas show will be shorter than years past, although no less joyous. Thank you for coming, and may God bless our troops!"

Everyone clapped, and the music started. It opened with some fast numbers, "Rudolph the Red-nosed Reindeer" and "Jingle Bells." People tapped their feet, and many sang along. The choir continued through the whole repertoire of carols, including some Thomas hadn't heard in years. Finally, the students sang "O Holy Night" holding lighted candles which, after the Cocoanut Grove fire, had an eerie significance.

The show was over in a half hour, even quicker than Thomas had expected. As they got up, he looked around, nodding to people he knew. They were mostly neighbors and acquaintances, including a guy he always saw at the butcher shop. Most of his friends from high school were gone, either away in the service or living somewhere else.

The students poured out the side doors into the auditorium, and Chickie ran over.

"Good job," Thomas said.

"I love Christmas songs."

"Yeah? What's your favorite?"

"*Tu scendi dalle stelle!*"

Connie smiled and said something to her in Italian.

"I didn't hear that one tonight," he joked.

A couple of her classmates came over, young girls in dresses. They hugged Chickie, wished her a happy Christmas, and scurried away.

"Where're your British friends?"

Chickie made a sad face.

"Couldn't come."

As they walked up the aisle, Thomas saw a woman in the back row. She had a tense expression and dark circles under her eyes. Her daughter had just come off stage, and her son was standing beside her in a ragged suit and flat cap, a snarl on his face. When Thomas looked closer, he realized it was Clarence Morris. He didn't usually have much sympathy for bullies, but they looked troubled. And he never liked to see a family suffer.

He felt a tug on his coat.

"Dada," Chickie said. "You coming?"

Thomas looked down at her, smiling but distracted.

"Yes, darling."

27

THE DOORS OPENED, AND ABBY HOPPED OFF THE TROLLEY. THE BAKERY was only a few blocks from her house, but it was too cold to walk anywhere. Despite the temperature, there was a line out front of people waiting to buy bread and pastries for Christmas.

She passed by the crowd, saying hello to familiar customers and ladies she knew, and headed to the back of the building. When she turned into the alleyway, Connie was smoking beside the dumpster. Her coat was unbuttoned, and she had no gloves on. She looked too pretty for such a dingy place. Sometimes Abby thought she was too good to work there. With Thomas' sergeant's pay, Connie should have been home with Chickie who, more than other girls her age, needed a full-time mother.

"You'll catch a death of cold," Abby said, skirting by.

Connie just smiled.

Abby went in the back door, and Carlo was standing by the mixer. It might have been the first time she saw him wearing a long-sleeved shirt in the kitchen. Even the combination of the radiators and the oven wasn't enough to keep the shop warm.

Over in the corner, his nephew Jimmy was cutting dough to twist into croissants. He had worked at the bakery in high school and had gone steady with Loretta. Now a welder at East Boston Works, he sometimes came in to help.

Abby hung up her coat and scarf and put her pocketbook in a free cubby. As she reached for an apron, Eve ran over, and Abby couldn't tell if she looked frantic or mad. Maybe both.

Abby was ten minutes late on the busiest day of the year. But she didn't care. She had worked there longer than Eve, and the owner Rita liked her more. Eve didn't have the authority to fire or reprimand anyone. If she did, it would have been a risk at a time when it was impossible to find help.

"Could you help out front?" Eve asked, and Abby realized it wasn't about her. "I've gotta get more boxes."

"Sure thing."

Abby put the work apron back and got a decorative one instead. She grabbed a bonnet off the shelf and put it on, tucking her hair into the sides.

When she walked out to the front, there were no lines, just a mob of people. Half a dozen girls were working, but it wasn't enough. Abby pointed at the first customer, an old lady she knew from church.

"Yes, Mrs. Devers," she said with a smile.

"Four loaves of bread, please, Abigail. Two sweet Rye. Two plain."

"Sliced?"

"No, thank you."

As Abby reached for a paper bag, she stopped. Angela came in the front door, pushing through the crowd. Her black coat and hat seemed to highlight some darkness in her mood. She never looked happy, even when she smiled, but Abby could tell she was angry.

"Where's Eve?" she asked.

"She went down to the basement."

Angela stomped around the counter and walked to the back. When one of the younger girls looked over, Abby felt a sudden panic. She held her finger up to the customer and then went after Angela.

"Angela!" she called.

When she got to the kitchen, Angela was standing face-to-face with Eve in the hallway.

"Where's my check!" she barked.

"It was mailed to you."

Holding a stack of boxes, Eve tried to get by, but Angela wouldn't let her.

"You said that last week."

"You'll have to talk to Rita."

"I want my money!"

Eve looked up with a scowl.

"And I said, 'you'll have to talk to'—"

Angela shoved her with both hands. The boxes fell, and Eve stumbled back into the shelf, knocking over cans of syrup and fruit. Getting her balance, she lunged at Angela, and in an instant, they were fighting.

"Stop!" Abby shouted.

As she tried to separate them, she felt the blows of punches.

"Whore!" Eve said.

"Bitch!"

"Go to hell!"

Connie ran in from the front, waving her arms and shouting in Italian. Carlo grabbed Eve and his nephew grabbed Angela, and they tore them apart. As enraged as both girls were, they were no match for two grown men.

Everyone stood around in quiet exasperation, gasping and out of breath. Abby glanced over and the whole staff was watching from the doorway. Angela and Eve had calmed down, but Carlo was furious. His jaw was clenched; the veins in his forehead were throbbing. Because he was the oldest, everyone seemed to look to him for what to do next.

With one hand on his hip, he looked at Angela and wagged his finger.

"Out!" he shouted.

Her hair was a mess, and she had welts on her cheeks. She stared at Eve with a vile pout. Then she turned around and stormed out, slamming the back door.

......

ABBY TIPTOED UP THE NARROW, winding staircase. In her hand, she had two gifts, both in red wrapping paper with silver bows. When she got to the top and heard Charlie Parker playing, she knew she was at the right address.

Harold had moved since last semester, although only a block down the street. After he had quit drinking, he was superstitious about living in the same place. It didn't explain why it was his third apartment in two years, but he had always been a nomad. He had been born in Paris while his father had been working as a diplomat. He and his brother had spent some time in suburban New York until they had been shipped off to prep schools. As someone who had never left East Boston, Abby was always fascinated by his exotic life.

The door swung open before she could knock.

"Darling!" Harold said.

He wore a black pinstripe suit with a white rose in his lapel. His hair glistened with Brylcreem, the first time she had seen it combed back.

"How'd you know I was out here?"

He looked at his watch, a gold Hamilton he always wore loose.

"Because you're always a model of punctuality."

They kissed, and she could smell Chantilly, the same cologne she had bought Arthur for his birthday.

As she handed him the presents, his expression changed.

"Darling, what happened?" he asked.

Abby touched her cheek, feeling the scratch she got from either Eve or Angela. She had tried to cover it with makeup, but it still showed.

"A little mishap."

"A mishap?"

"I'll tell you about it later."

"*Entrez*," he said in a French accent.

When she walked in, she heard quiet weeping, and Harold gave her a cringing look. Frances was sitting on the couch with her head in her hands. There was a half-full Martini on the table and a cigarette smoldering in the ashtray.

"Frances?"

"Abigail," Frances said.

"What's wrong?"

"She's just drunk."

"I'm not drunk!" Frances said, but just by her voice, Abby could tell she was. "He's leaving us."

It was then Abby realized how empty the apartment was. The walls were bare, and all the rugs were gone. Aside from the furniture, the only décor was the Victrola on the buffet and a thin Christmas tree by the window. In the hallway to the bedroom, Abby noticed two suitcases and a trunk.

"It's true," he said.

Her mouth fell open.

"What?"

"Come," he said, taking her by the arm and patting her hand.

He led her into the living room, and she sat down beside Frances.

"Can I get you a drink?" Harold asked.

"Just water."

"No one drinks 'just water.' I'll make you tea."

"Okay," Abby said, distracted. "Thank you."

Frances took a drag on her cigarette.

"Sorry to be such a fusspot," she said.

"It wouldn't be Christmas without tears."

Frances smiled, dabbing her eyes with a tissue. She hadn't cried since Sal's funeral, and for weeks, her mood had wavered between irritable and gloomy. Abby didn't like to see her upset, but any emotion was better than none.

When Harold brought over the tea, she saw he had ginger ale. It reminded her of her father's cream soda habit. Harold shook the ice in his glass like he was ready to give a speech. He never got flustered, but Abby could tell he was anxious because he was still standing.

"As you know, Richie has been expelled by the university," he said, although "expelled" didn't sound like the right word. "He's asked me to go to Ireland with him. I've accepted."

"Ireland?"

"To help him recuperate, as it were. He can't travel alone."

Abby took a sip of her tea, too stunned to respond.

Mr. Glynn's injuries were worse than anyone else she knew. He had third-degree burns on his legs and smoke inhalation so bad that he had been on a ventilator for two weeks. In the hospital, he had caught an infection that almost killed him. As heartless as the termination seemed, Harold told them Glynn had been expecting it long before the fire. With the country at war, the administration didn't want any political agitators on staff, especially someone who was anti-British.

"Are passenger ships even going to Ireland?"

"That's what I asked," Frances said.

"No. Richie's cousin works at a shipping firm in Halifax, Nova Scotia. The freight routes to neutral countries are still open. Each trip, they take a few dozen civilians. Fares are generally reserved for high-priority cases, diplomats and—"

"You should fit right in," Frances said.

Abby chuckled.

"Isn't it dangerous?" she asked.

"Isn't everything?"

"When will you be back?"

"Depends on Richie's recovery, really, and whether or not I can get a similar arrangement back. God knows this bloody war can't go on forever."

When he stopped short, it was a dramatic end to a hard conversation. He stood with his trademark smile, lips tight together and one eyebrow slightly raised. The expression was anything but ironic, and in it, Abby saw some mix of sadness, fear, and hope. He wasn't going into battle, but soldiers weren't the only casualties. Crossing the Atlantic was a big risk. But he had made his decision. Abby got the same vacant feeling she had gotten when her brother and Arthur had left.

Harold cleared his throat.

"Now. Shall we open gifts and all that?"

Frances made a sour face but didn't object. Harold knelt by the tree, read off the names, and passed around the presents.

Abby got him a gold-plated cigarette case with his initials inscribed on the front. Frances got him a towel set that looked expensive. Abby gave Frances a leather-bound scrapbook, knowing how she liked to collect things. Frances got her a silver bracelet with interwoven links. Finally, Harold bought them both identical cashmere hats and gloves.

"Now you can be twins," he said.

Abby glanced over at Frances, and she smiled back. But any joy or happiness was bittersweet. At least the room felt more festive. The wrapping paper strewn across the floor added some color, reminding Abby of Christmas mornings when she was a girl. But Harold still hadn't sat down.

"When do you leave?" Abby asked.

"Tuesday morning. Ferry service from Boston to Maine has been suspended. We have to take a train to Bar Harbor. From there, a boat to Halifax."

For Abby, it all sounded so exciting.

"You'll let us know when you've arrived safely," Frances said.

"Unfortunately, the War Department has banned all telegraphs through New Years."

"Then send a carrier pigeon."

The joke was corny, but Abby had to laugh.

"How about some music?"

"Do you have White Christmas?" Frances asked.

Abby watched Harold start to roll his eyes before restraining himself. As a music snob, he would never play something as ordinary as Bing Crosby.

"How about some Ella Fitzgerald?" he suggested, walking over to the Victrola. "That's the closest thing I have to anything *white*."

"Why do you always get to pick?" Frances asked.

"He who pays the piper calls the tune."

"And who's paying you?"

Hearing them bicker made Abby smile.

"It's just an expression," Harold said, lowering the needle onto the record.

After a couple of seconds of static, "All I Need Is You" began to play. Harold sashayed over, moving to the rhythm.

"C'mon," he said, extending his arm. "Let's dance like old times."

Frances put down her tissue and took his hand. As they slow-danced across the empty floor, Abby tapped her foot. If he had asked her next, she would have joined him, but she was just as content to watch.

28

Thomas sat at the corner table with a dozen men from the station. Some were wearing their uniforms, and others had on regular clothes. The lights were low, and the cigarette smoke was thick. The going away party for Carroll was quiet, and only half of the officers who had been invited had shown up. Except for Thomas and Sergeant Silva, it was all patrolmen. Thomas knew most of them from the precinct, and many had joined the force at the same time as him. In a department dominated by white ethnics, their last names read like a Boston phonebook: Coppola, McGrail, O'Hanlon, Scipioni, Stanton. The only Jewish cop was Kagan who was picking at the remaining crust of the four pizzas they had eaten.

It was Christmas Eve, but the barroom was still busy. Across the room, a dozen guys in leather jackets stood playing pool. Some glanced over, but Thomas knew it was more out of curiosity. Like most dive bars in Maverick Square, Sonny's was a mix of people, from truck drivers to loan sharks, and everyone got along.

Thomas had already had three beers, the most he had drunk in months. He was getting tipsy and had to work later. So he was a little worried when he stood up to go piss and felt dizzy.

He walked by the bar where a couple of sailors stood talking to some local girls. He was almost at the bathroom when he heard, "Nolan?" and stopped.

When he turned around, Labadini was coming toward him. He had on a dirty coat and boots. If Thomas felt any camaraderie for him, it was because they were both in jobs where they had to work all the time.

"Vin," he said.

"Merry Christmas."

"Same to you."

"Now did you tell that fuckin' soldier to stay away from my sister?"

Thomas gave him a cold stare. He didn't like being told what to do, and the slur was harsh.

"They're leaving anyway," he said.

"Who's leaving?"

"The black unit. They're headed to Northern Ireland."

Labadini's expression softened.

"Good. Now I don't have to kill him."

He let out a hearty laugh that Thomas knew was just bravado. Labadini was a street thug, not a murderer.

"That's classified," Thomas said, leaning in to whisper. "Not a word. You hear?"

He glared and turned to go, but Labadini kept talking.

"My father saw your girl out at Point Shirley."

"Your girl" was vague, but Thomas knew he didn't mean Chickie. "Connie?"

"He leaves from the dock out there. He saw her walking alone. He said she looked cold."

"How's he know my wife?"

"He doesn't. One of the guys on his crew does. He worked with her at General Electric."

Thomas nodded.

"Okay, thanks."

He went into the lavatory, a dank room with three urinals and an exposed toilet. The rusted metal sink didn't work but ironically, he could hear water leaking somewhere above.

When he got back to the table, everyone was singing "For He's a Jolly Good Fellow." While no song seemed right for a guy going off to war, it was better than "Johnny We Hardly Knew Ye."

Officer Carroll stood grinning over a white cake. Thomas didn't know what the six lit candles signified, but the wax was melting over the frosting. Officer Stanton went to make a toast, and they all raised their glasses.

"Here's to staying positive and testing negative!"

There was a burst of laughter, the sound of clinking glasses. A pretty blonde waitress came over with plates and cut the cake.

By six o'clock, everyone was ready to leave. Some men were going back to the station, and others had to get home to their families. Thomas was working his third nightshift in a row, and he wanted to spend a few hours at his mother's house before he went in. Chickie no longer believed in Santa Claus, but her excitement on Christmas was still a kind of magic of its own.

When Sergeant Silva tried to order another round, everyone grumbled and said no. Thomas reached for his coat and tossed a ten-dollar bill on the pile. Except for Carroll, they all pitched in.

As they headed out, the bartender waved, and the waitress ran over. She hugged Carroll, kissed him on the cheek, and then said some kind words that Thomas couldn't catch over the noise of the room. A couple of the men hooted, but her affection was more motherly than romantic. It was the most emotional moment of the entire night.

They walked out and were immediately hit by a frigid wind. When Thomas groaned, Carroll put his arm over his shoulder. He had never been so chummy before. But as of noon that day, he was no longer on the force. Rank didn't matter. Thomas was glad they could spend their last few hours together as equals.

"Everything alright, Sarge?"

"Yeah, why?"

"You seem a little uptight is all."

Thomas frowned, although he appreciated the concern. The encounter with Labadini had made him uneasy.

"I'm not too keen on going in tonight."

In normal times, Maverick Square would have been crowded on Christmas Eve. But the shops were closed, and the streets were quiet. People walked out of the train station carrying bags of gifts from downtown stores: Filene's, Hovey's, and Gilchrist's. A week before, the Governor had extended holiday shopping hours only to shorten them again to conserve oil.

Officer McGrail walked over and started his car, a two-door Willys that made Thomas' Ford look like a Rolls-Royce. Carroll had already given up his apartment in the North End and was staying with his parents, so he needed a ride home.

Someone held out a lighter, and a few of the guys lit cigarettes. But it was too cold to linger, and Thomas' face was getting numb.

They said goodbye in a flurry of handshakes and backslaps. Like any parting between men, it was more sarcastic than heartfelt. Thomas was waiting for someone to say, "I hope the Army sends you somewhere warm." But considering how bad the fighting had gotten in Southeast Asia, the joke wasn't funny anymore. Five boys from East Boston had died in the Solomon Islands, and two were missing.

Finally, Carroll turned to Thomas.

"Good working with you, Sarge."

"Likewise. Keep those bastards on their toes."

Not knowing where he was going, it was general enough to include all enemies.

"And you do the same on this side of the world."

Thomas smiled and held out his hand. As they shook, he choked up. But with everyone else coughing and sniffling from the weather, he knew it wasn't obvious.

When McGrail tapped the horn, Carroll looked torn. Like he didn't want to leave. He waved to everyone and got into the car. They pulled out and made a wide U-turn, the tires spinning on the icy ground.

The car sped down Maverick Street, and Thomas watched it until it disappeared in the darkness. Saying goodbye in wartime had all the drama of a wake, although with none of the finality. Thomas was reminded of when his father had left for work the day he had died. At the time, he never could have known what was coming. But looking back, everything his father had done that morning had now taken on some mystical significance, from the breakfast he ate to the boots he wore. Thomas could never see someone walk away without wondering if he would ever see them again.

As he turned back to the group, a bum stepped out of an alleyway. He had on so many layers of clothing he looked inflated. His beard was covered in frost, and he had no gloves on. Thomas could smell him from twenty feet away, a wretched combination of urine, alcohol, and body odor.

"Santa?" someone said.

"Dad? Where you been?" another joked.

In an instant, they were all heckling the man. But it was only lighthearted fun, and even Thomas grinned. Anybody wandering around when it was fifteen degrees out deserved a few digs.

As the laughter died down, the man walked toward them. In a move that stunned everyone, he threw up his arm and yelled, "*Heil Hitler!*"

Stanton lunged forward and grabbed the guy.

"You're going down the station, buddy," he said.

"Get off me!"

When the man tried to resist, Stanton yanked his arm up behind his back.

"You know what the penalty is for saying that?"

"Let 'em go, Paul," someone said.

"Let him go nuttin'!

"He's just a bum," one of the guys said, a remark that was humiliating and sympathetic at the same time.

Stiff from the cold, the man was slow to respond. But it was obvious he was getting angry.

"I was a pipefitter before the Depression!" he said.

"The Depression's been over for five years, pal."

"Did you fall asleep in a dumpster Rip Van Winkle?"

If saluting the leader of their enemy wasn't a crime, it was probably some misdemeanor buried deep within the fine print of treason laws. A year before, a cobbler in South Boston had been arrested for having a swastika in his window. The Italian-American Club on Meridian Street had once had a picture of Mussolini in its front hallway, although it was quickly taken down after Pearl Harbor. With so much confusion and uncertainty, people lashed out in strange ways and often for attention.

"What did I do?" the man asked.

"Disturbing the peace."

"What? For saying, '*heil Hitler*'?"

Stanton looked at Sergeant Silva who shrugged his shoulders.

"You're on duty, not me."

Thomas didn't blame Stanton for grabbing the vagrant. There wasn't a guy there who hadn't been affected by the war. Officer Scipioni had two brothers in the service. O'Hanlon had lost a cousin at Wake Island. They were all worried, agitated, and frustrated.

"Let him go!" Thomas said, finally.

He spoke with enough force that no one argued. Everyone there knew the difference between a suggestion and an order. When Stanton let go, the man shot forward and stumbled over the curb, catching himself before falling into a passing car. He mumbled something none of them could hear and then vanished back into the shadows of the alleyway.

......

WHEN THOMAS GOT HOME, there were more cars than usual, so he had to park down the street. Like every Christmas Eve, his mother had people over.

He braced himself and got out, the air so cold his eyes stung. He ran up to his house to change his shirt before going over to his mother's. One of the guys had spilled his drink on him, and he didn't want to go to work later smelling like stale beer.

When he opened the front door, Connie was walking out from the kitchen holding a serving tray. She had on a long black dress, her hair curled.

"You are home," she said.

"I am. What's that?"

"Cheese soufflé."

"Cheese *soufflé*?" he said, correcting her pronunciation.

He was surprised she had made something so traditional. Most of her dishes included macaroni, and she never cooked without garlic.

"Your mother gave me the recipe."

"Were you at Point Shirley?" he asked.

"When?"

"Any time."

When she hesitated, he felt a creeping tension. A month earlier, he had confronted her about leaving work early. Now he had heard she had been out at Point Shirley. They never argued like other couples, and he wanted it that way. Back when his father drank, his parents had fought all the time. He remembered sitting in his bedroom with George and Abby while they listened to the shouting, the foot-stomping, and the occasional throwing of plates or glasses. He had no reason to distrust Connie; she had always been honest. But her behavior over the past month made him wonder.

"I took the bus to the cottage last week," she said, finally.

"Why?"

"Your mother thought there might be some wool blankets in the closet."

"Blankets for what?"

"For the British children," she said.

Thomas nodded, feeling a twinge of guilt.

"And she asked you to go to the cottage?"

"I went of my own accord."

Sensing that the tray was getting heavy, he asked, "Want me to bring that over?"

"I don't need help."

He opened the door, and she darted out.

He went upstairs to their bedroom, which was in perfect order. The sheets were smooth, the pillows were straight, and there were fresh flowers on Connie's vanity. After Mrs. Ciarlone died, his only condition for moving in had been that they replace everything. The furniture had been old-fashioned, and the décor had been personal, including a framed illustration of the ship Mrs. Ciarlone and her husband had taken over from Italy. Thomas wasn't superstitious, but he hadn't wanted to sleep among the keepsakes and possessions of a person who had died.

He grabbed a clean shirt from the closet, quickly put it on, and ran back downstairs. When he opened the front door, it had started to snow, endless flakes falling in the darkness.

He walked next door, and the house was packed. Many people had to stand because there weren't enough chairs. The air was thick with cigarette smoke and the smell of food. Glenn Miller was playing on the radio. The tree was thin, but his mother had filled it out with tinsel and ornaments, including a set of hand-painted ceramic bulbs his aunt in Maine had made years before.

Thomas took off his hat but left his coat on. He wasn't staying long, and he didn't want his holster showing.

"Thomas?" his mother said, rushing over.

She had on a long dress, high-heeled shoes, and pearls around her neck. He hadn't seen her so dressed up in years.

"Don't you look snazzy?"

"We're low on coal," she whispered.

On top of all the other problems, everyone now had to worry about freezing to death too. Oil was scarce, and there were lines in every neighborhood. Governor Saltonstall had declared a state of emergency, and the chief put out a bulletin asking officers to watch for hoarding. Mrs. Nolan was lucky to have a coal furnace, but the fire in South Boston had caused a temporary shortage.

"I'll bring some home tonight."

"Oh, you're a doll."

"Connie said she went to the cottage to get blankets?"

"Yes, for the refugee children—"

His mother was distracted, and when Thomas followed her gaze, he was surprised to see Mr. Schultz walking in.

"Henry!" his mother exclaimed.

He had snow on his coat and was holding a bouquet. When he handed her the flowers, she beamed.

As Thomas stepped away, Chickie ran over in a collared dress and patent leather shoes. For a moment, he thought she had on makeup until he realized the darkness around her eyes was from fatigue. She never slept in the days leading up to Christmas.

"Alfie and Olive," she said, pointing.

In the corner, the two British children were sitting at a folding table Mrs. Nolan had set up. They both had on sweaters, the girl wearing a patchwork dress under hers that looked handmade. With their hands on their laps, they looked around with a timid curiosity.

"I bet they can't wait for Santa."

Chickie rolled her eyes.

"There's no Santa," she said, and then she touched his badge. "You have to work?"

"I do. But I'll be home before you wake up."

"Promise."

"I promise."

When she smiled, he hugged her, and she ran back over to her friends. Thomas weaved through the crowd, nodding and smiling. For such a modest home, it held a lot of people.

On the mantel, his mother had placed a framed picture of George in uniform. Beside it was a glass vase with a single white flower, a small shrine to her son.

"Thomas?" Mr. McNulty said, walking over. "How goes the battle?"

"It'll be better once we get more oil."

"I heard a fuel company was broken into in Charlestown."

"Not my district, fortunately."

"They got ten thousand gallons."

Mr. McNulty shook the ice in his glass.

"Any news from George?"

"Not since September," he said, repeating what Mr. McNulty and most of their friends and neighbors already knew. "But you how bad V-Mail is."

"Well, with the Germans on the run in Russia, hopefully, this goddamn war will be over soon, and all our boys will come home."

Thomas grinned. He admired the sentiment, but he also had never heard Mr. McNulty swear.

Noticing Abby waving from the stairs, he said, "'Scuse me," and walked over to her.

"Did you see who's here?" she asked.

Thomas followed her gaze to the dining room. Standing beside his mother was Mr. Schultz. With his hat still in his hands, he smiled while Mrs. Nolan introduced him to people.

"The Kraut, you mean?" he said.

Abby frowned.

"He's been in America longer than we've been alive."

"He just walked in. What about him?"

"I invited him. I thought she could use some company."

Looking over again, Thomas saw in his mother's eyes some sparkle or shine that, for the first time in weeks, wasn't from alcohol. He knew loneliness could kill. He was sure it was the reason she had started drinking again. As he watched them mingle, he sensed in their shared glances and subtle flirtations the possibility of something more. And he didn't feel threatened.

"They seem to get along," he said.

After his father's death, it was the closest he could get to acknowledging the possibility of companionship for his mother.

29

ABBY SAT IN THE PEW WITH HER MOTHER, THE CHURCH SO COLD SHE could see her breath. On her other side was Chickie and then Connie and Thomas, an order that felt symbolic. Now that her brother had a wife and family, Abby sometimes worried he would move away, leaving just her and her mother in East Boston.

When Thomas was younger, he often talked about going to Melrose or Danvers, which their mother took as an insult. Mrs. Nolan had lived in their house her whole life, the last heir of a family that had once owned all the land between Saratoga Street and Chelsea Creek. Despite her husband's years of violent drinking, the only time she had threatened to leave him was when he had mentioned moving to the suburbs. She spoke of legacy and tradition and had more heirlooms than a duchess. Abby had always chalked it up to fear, that false comfort of familiarity. But with so much change, so many people being torn from her life, she finally understood the need to cling to something that felt permanent.

"On this Christmas morning, let us remember the young men from our community who in recent weeks have lost their lives whilst fighting in the service of our county..."

Abby looked up to the altar, realizing she had daydreamed. Father

Ward began to read off the names of the local boys who had been killed in action.

"Neal Paul McDonald, Gabriel John Mecozzi, Jeffrey Antonio Cid, Edgar Peter Cabral, Stephen Michael Lynch…"

He spoke with a slow intensity. She didn't know any of them, but she recognized some of their last names. All around, she could hear quiet moans and soft weeping. She was so focused that when someone touched her hand, she jumped. It was only Chickie, looking up with a sad smile that was almost as sweet as the bonnet on her head.

When it came time for Communion, they went up together. Abby hadn't been to confession in months, a requirement for the sacrament. In the past, her mother would have scolded her, but Abby knew she was just happy that her children were even at mass.

They returned to their seats, and Abby knelt on the bench with her hands clasped. She said a silent prayer for Arthur's safety and an end to the war.

"Dear brothers and sisters," Father Ward said, "In this time of unbearable cold, I would ask that you consider your neighbors who might not have enough oil to heat their homes, enough food to feed their families…"

People looked around, many with a reluctant enthusiasm. The hardships of life in wartime were enough to put anyone's sense of Christian charity to the test. In shops, Abby had seen grown women argue over the last box of sugar, the last stick of butter. Oil supplies were so low that one of the biggest dealers in East Boston had shut down. The government had said there would be more shortages in the new year. While they lived far from the battlefields of Europe, Africa, and the Pacific, some days, it felt like they were under siege.

The mass ended, and everyone started to file out. The moment Abby got near the doors, she felt a chill that made her seize up as if from an electric shock. For once, she wished the service had been longer. She tightened her scarf, took her mother's arm, and proceeded out with a quiet dread.

It had started to snow, the world covered with a thin layer of white. People lingered to say hello and wish each other Merry Christmas, but with the bone-numbing cold, any socializing was short. At ten o'clock, the temperature was in the teens and was going to drop further. In a rare moment of humor, Father Ward had joked that it was enough to make Santa Claus consider staying in.

Thomas had offered to drive, but their mother had said no. So they started to walk, and he led the way. They turned the corner onto Saratoga Street, a familiar route home. Chickie giggled as she caught snowflakes in her mouth, but otherwise, they were silent. The neighborhood felt desolate. Smoke rose from the chimneys, adding to the grayness of the morning. Abby had lived through almost twenty winters, but she never remembered one so bleak.

When they got to their street, someone called out, "Chickie!"

They stopped, and Olive came running out the side door of the church. She wore so many layers she looked twice her size. She had on two coats, thick mittens, and a knit hat that covered half her face.

"Happy Christmas!" she exclaimed.

She walked up to the fence, clutching the pickets.

"You look like a fur trapper," Abby said with a smile.

"We've no coal."

Abby's expression soured.

"No coal?"

"Mistress Helen has called for some, but the man hasn't come."

"Where's your brother?"

Olive glanced back over her shoulder.

"Inside with the other children."

Abby looked over to Thomas, who was standing with Connie and their mother a few yards up the sidewalk.

"Thomas, they—"

"I heard her," he said.

Their eyes locked. As twins, neither had more authority than the other, the power of an older sibling or the vulnerability of a younger one. She needed her mother's help to persuade him.

"Mother?"

"Poor things," Mrs. Nolan said, turning to her son. "Thomas, they could freeze to death."

In past years, "freeze to death" would have been an exaggeration, but now it was a real possibility.

Everyone stared at Thomas, including his wife. Her expression was more insistent than pleading. It was his first day off in weeks, and Abby knew he didn't want to go out. But he was the only one who could help. They had stopped asking him where he got things, whether it was coal, beef, butter, or ration stamps. Now they relied on him.

"Okay, I'll get them some," he said.

......

ABBY LAY ON THE COUCH, a shawl spread across her legs. Even with the furnace on full blast, there was a chill in the air. They had done everything the Committee on Public Safety suggested to insulate, including closing off any spare rooms and stuffing felt into the cracks of doors and windows. Her mother had even tried to staple down the blackout curtains, but the fabric was too thick.

In the kitchen, Connie was heating leftover ham, vegetables, and appetizers from the night before. Christmas supper would be small this year, not just because George was away. Mrs. Nolan had considered inviting some neighbors over, but with the oil shortage, no one wanted to leave their homes.

A gust shook the house, and the lights flickered. When Abby looked toward the dining room, her mother was too busy setting the table to notice. As usual, she was frantic, although there was no urgency. Abby didn't know if her face was red from rushing around or from alcohol.

"Abigail," her mother said, not looking over. "Go tell the girls it's time to eat."

Abby went upstairs. She could have just called, but she knew

Chickie and Olive wouldn't hear her because they were in her mother's bedroom. It was the largest room in the house, with a heavy oak door and two windows that looked out to the street. Her father had once planned on putting a bathroom next to the closet until his wife said having a second bathroom was an extravagance.

When Abby walked in, the girls were sitting at the vanity, styling their hair. They had left their shoes in the foyer and only had on socks.

Chickie loved her grandmother's room, and Abby understood why. With its antique four-poster bed, mahogany dresser, shaded lamps, and oriental rug, it had a nostalgic charm. The walls were covered in faded floral wallpaper, and there were oil paintings and framed pictures, including one of Abby's great-grandfather who had come from Ireland. The room didn't just look old—it smelled old. But it was more the familiar odor of a timeless place.

"Supper's ready," Abby said.

The girls both looked back at her startled like they hadn't heard her come in.

Abby walked over and the vanity was covered in makeup, tubes of lipstick and jars of ointments. Chickie wasn't a girl anymore, and she had put on eyeliner with precision. They had taken out jewelry too, an assortment of plated gold rings. As Abby stared at the mess, Chickie and Olive looked up with guilty expressions.

"Go wash up," she said. "I'll clean it."

"Thank you, Miss," Olive said.

As they scurried off, Abby called to them, and they stopped at the door.

"Wipe that off," she said, pointing at her eyes.

Her mother wouldn't mind them exploring, but she would never tolerate cosmetics on a young girl.

Abby put the makeup back in the case and dusted the powder off the top. She collected all her mother's rings and bracelets. When she opened the drawer to put them back, she froze. Laying on top was a card, the word V-Mail written across it in red. The return address said, "APO 070, San Francisco," but she knew it was from overseas. She turned it over, and started to read:

DEAR ABIGAIL,

I AM sorry I have not written sooner. In October, I caught a severe case of dengue fever and spent ten days in a field hospital. After being released, I trained for two weeks for an important mission which, I am proud to say, was a walloping success.

I cannot tell you where I am stationed except to say that it is in the South Pacific. My squadron has been very active since September, and we are currently awaiting orders for our next assignment.

Please know that you are in my thoughts every moment of every day, and I hope we will be together soon. Tell your mother and Thomas I say hello.

WITH LOVE,

ARTHUR

SHE FELL BACK and sat stunned on the edge of the bed. The note was short, and the writing felt rushed. She knew everything went through censors, and V-Mail was just a postcard. At least it let her know he was alive, which was the most anyone could ask for in wartime. But it didn't explain why her mother had it.

Looking at the date stamp, she saw it was sent on November 16th. Even taking into account travel time, it was over a month ago. In an instant, her joy turned to outrage. She stormed out of the room, and when she got downstairs, her mother was coming out from the kitchen.

"Abby, can you check the linen closet for—"

"What's this!" Abby snapped, holding up the letter.

"What?"

Abby walked toward her, her teeth gritted. When she smelled alcohol, it only fueled her rage.

"It's from Arthur!"

Connie ran over with a spatula in her hand.

"Abby, please, calm down."

"No! I won't calm down," Abby shouted, then she turned back to her mother. "Why was this in your drawer?"

"Drawer?"

"Your vanity! It was in the top drawer."

Mrs. Nolan bit her lip, her face trembling. It was the same reaction Abby had seen a dozen times before. Whenever her mother was confronted, challenged, or threatened, she acted like she was having a nervous breakdown. Abby was tired of all her sulking and self-pity. Their father had died, George was away, and she and her brother had survived one of the worst fires in American history. They had all been through a lot. But there was no excuse for her erratic behavior, no excuse for hiding a letter.

"I don't know," Mrs. Nolan muttered.

"Yes, you do, you drunken bitch! Did you forget?"

"How dare you—"

Abby smacked her across the face. Her mother put up her arms, and Connie jumped between them, shouting, "Stop it, stop it, stop it!"

The door swung open.

"What the hell is going on?"

Thomas stepped in carrying a bag of coal, his coat and hat covered in snow. Abby stood with her arms crossed, fuming and out of breath, while Connie consoled her mother.

"She had a letter from Arthur. She didn't tell me!"

"It may have come in the mail," Mrs. Nolan said, hunched over with her hand over her cheek.

Thomas walked over to her, and when she looked up, her left eye was half shut. Abby knew the swelling would go down, but the sight of it made her shudder. She hadn't meant to hit her so hard.

"I didn't mean to—"

Thomas spun around.

"Go!" he shouted, pointing upstairs.

At other times, in other seasons, Abby would have flown out the front door. After fights with her father, she used to go stay with a friend or take the bus out to Point Shirley. Their cottage had always been a refuge from the chaos of family strife. But between the cold and the fuel shortage, she couldn't leave now. She knew smacking her mother was wrong, but she didn't regret it. Clutching Arthur's letter, she scowled at them all and then ran up to her bedroom.

30

Thomas was at his desk when the call came in. He could have sent a patrolman, but he wanted to get out. Staying in the station for too long was worse than being in the cold. The old building was musty, and the air was dry. Without warning, he would go into a fit of coughing, spitting up chunks of dark phlegm, the remnants of burned toxins. The doctors had told him to expect it and had offered him some liquid morphine, which he had declined. While it meant his lungs were healing, it was no consolation for the agony. At least he wasn't alone. Some nights, he could hear Abby hacking next door.

Driving out of the lot, he turned right onto Meridian Street and only had to go two blocks. Everything in East Boston was close, something he either loved or loathed depending on the hour.

He pulled up to a small market, one of the few that was open. Except for barrooms and pharmacies, most businesses shut down the week between Christmas and New Year's. The streets were empty, but there were children everywhere. They congregated on the stoops of three-deckers and tenements, bundled up in hand-me-down clothes.

Getting out, Thomas walked over and opened the door. He couldn't remember if he had been there before, but all corner stores looked the same. The floors were warped, and the walls had shelves covered with everything from Rinso detergent to raisin bran. Behind a glass case were blocks of cheese and cold meats: salami, pastrami, roast beef, and tongue.

He stepped over to the cooler in the corner and saw bottles of milk and cream, packages of sliced bacon.

"Can I help you, Officer?"

When Thomas turned around, a middle-aged man in a collared shirt and glasses was standing by the counter. He was thin with a mild hunch.

"Where's your butter?" Thomas asked.

"We keep it out back now."

"Why?"

"It's been getting stolen."

"Can I see it?"

The man nodded, but it was obvious he was reluctant. He waved, and Thomas followed him into the storeroom. He opened the door to the refrigerator, and Thomas looked in to see a wooden crate filled with one-pound boxes of butter.

Leaning over, he grabbed two and held them up.

"How much do you charge for these?" he asked.

"For both?"

"For one."

"Fifty-one cents."

The ceiling price set by the government was three cents more, which made him look generous. But Thomas knew he was lying.

"Why did I hear you were charging close to sixty?"

"Bullshit!"

"We've got witnesses."

They only had one complaint, but Thomas had to bluff him.

"I've got other employees. Maybe it was one of them."

"Then you better talk to them. If I tell the OPA about this, they'll shut you down."

It was more a warning than a threat. Agents didn't have time to crack down on every small shop owner, vendor, and merchant. They were looking for widespread corruption and black-market activity.

"I better not get another report," Thomas said.

He shoved the butter into his coat, one box in each pocket. Then he walked away, the owner watching with an expression of disdain.

Outside, some boys were standing on the corner, their clothes damp and dirty. As they stared, Thomas reached into his pocket. He flicked them a few pennies, and they scrambled for them like pigeons after breadcrumbs.

"Thanks, sir!"

Thomas got in the cruiser. He turned around and went back down Meridian Street, passing the precinct. With the car now warm, he didn't want to go back to the office. His shift was almost over, and he hadn't been out all day.

As he drove through Maverick Square, the grates of all the shops were down. Some dockworkers in hooded jackets and work boots stood smoking in front of Sonny's. Over by a market, two men were struggling to get a new radiator out of a van. A half-full trolley rolled out from the station, its passengers gazing out like in a trance. Thomas didn't know if it was the weather or the war, but the entire world seemed weary.

Stopped at a light on Bennington Street, he watched an Army convoy approach. The moment they passed, he glanced into the back of the trucks to see dark faces staring out. After months of gossip and griping, the negro unit was finally leaving the Wood Island Park barracks.

Thomas was relieved, but he also felt bad for the men. Even in their own country, they were in hostile territory. East Boston wasn't like the South, but in some ways, a cold tolerance was no better than contempt. Thomas had never known many black people, but he understood prejudice. For years, his mother resented Italians for taking over the neighborhood; his father always hated Republicans.

......

THOMAS HADN'T GOTTEN home before six o'clock in weeks. It was still light out, and he could tell the days were getting longer. With things slow at the station, he didn't have to work that night. The captain had even let two officers go early. One had gotten tickets to see the Bruins play the Rangers; the other had wanted to take his girlfriend to see Ethel Merman in *Something for the Boys*.

Thomas got out and realized someone had salted the sidewalks and front steps. When he walked into the house, the air was chilly, but not cold. He had checked that morning, and they had enough oil for three more days if they were careful.

Like a lot of people, he resented the fuel crisis, knowing it didn't affect everyone the same. The grand estates on Beacon Hill didn't need emergency relief, and no one in Back Bay was going into shelters. His only consolation was that he knew he could get more even if he had to shakedown every dealer from Winthrop to Maverick Square.

He went into the kitchen and saw a fresh loaf of bread on the stove. He opened the icebox and put the butter away.

"Thomas? Is that you?"

He quickly hung up his coat and went upstairs. The bathroom door was cracked, so he pushed it open and saw Connie lying in the tub under a heap of suds. Her hair was up in a clip; her skin was white and smooth.

"Where's Chickie?" he asked.

"Your mother took her and the British children bowling."

"They walked?"

"Yes. The German cleaned the sidewalk."

Thomas stopped.

"What German?"

"From the shop."

He went into the bedroom and undid his holster and took off his shirt. Connie walked in wearing a bathrobe and sat down at her vanity.

"I saw that you made bread," he said.

He got a sweater from the dresser and put it on.

"We ran out of kerosene."

"I can get more."

Facing the mirror, she gave him a sharp look. She always asked him how he was able to get things that were regulated, scarce, or out of stock. He never told her, but he also didn't make excuses. Like everyone in the family, she drank the coffee he got and ate the steaks he brought home. They all benefited from the gifts and small favors he got as a cop.

"Do you know when they'll be back from bowling?" Thomas asked.

"Perhaps an hour or so."

Feeling mischievous, he walked over and began to rub her shoulders. Her muscles were tense, and her skin was clammy from the bath. When he caressed her neck, she put down her brush, and they started to kiss. Her lips were dry, and her movements were stiff. It seemed more out of duty than arousal, but Thomas didn't care. With work and Chickie, they hadn't slept together in weeks.

He untied her robe, and it fell to the floor. Taking her hand, he led her over to the bed. He kicked off his pants and tore off his sweater and undershirt. They went under the blankets, and he got on top, fumbling to get inside her. Once he did, he moved his hips, and her small breasts jiggled. She moaned once or twice, but otherwise, she seemed distracted.

Finally, he felt a building sensation of a warm pleasure. In a single burst, his entire body seized up, and he groaned. He rolled off her and lay on his back, staring at the ceiling. It was over in seconds.

"What's wrong?" he asked, still panting.

She tried to cuddle beside him, but it felt insincere.

"I am sorry," she said. "I'm just so cold."

"Aren't we all—"

"I am back!"

Hearing Chickie's voice from downstairs, Thomas cringed. But he also had to chuckle. She never walked in without announcing her arrival.

"*Siamo di sopra. Scendo subito!*" Connie yelled.

Then she jumped out of bed and ran to the closet, throwing on a long dress and a sweater. Once she left, Thomas got up to get dressed. Neither was ashamed, but Chickie understood sex now, and they didn't want to get caught.

When he came downstairs, Chickie stood by the door while Connie untied her boots. Her coat was damp, and her cheeks were red. Before he could ask about her day, she exclaimed, "Olive and Alfie are going away!"

"Going away? Where?"

"*Ow-wa-wa.*"

Thomas looked at Connie to explain.

"Iowa," she said, standing up. "The church can't take care of them anymore. They'll be leaving next month."

31

ABBY SAT IN NORTH STATION, HER HANDS STUFFED INTO THE WOOL hand muffler her mother had made her for Christmas. The elegant granite building had high ceilings and arched glass windows. On one side was a row of ticket booths that sold fares to places as far away as Dayton, Ohio and Chattanooga, Tennessee. On the other, there was a cafeteria, a taxi counter, and a walkway leading out to the Boston Garden. Overhead, schedule boards flickered.

With people going in and out to the trains, the lobby was freezing. The revolving doors would have helped, but after the Cocoanut Grove fire, they weren't allowed to be used. So Abby took a bench near the heating vents to stay warm. Everyone else must have had the same idea because now there was a small crowd around them.

She had arrived late, but she knew her friends wouldn't be on time. Work that morning had been slow. In three hours, they had only had a dozen customers, including a homeless man who had tried to buy a donut and coffee with half a dollar bill. So she left early and went home to change. She was glad she had. Waiting for her in the mailbox was a letter from BU, her grades for the semester. After two years of struggle, she had finally made the Dean's List, some glimmer of hope in an otherwise dismal time.

"Utterly bone-chilling!"

Frances' shrill voice cut through all the noise. Looking over, Abby saw her standing with Harold and Mr. Glynn, who was no longer in a wheelchair. Their luggage was light, one suitcase each and shoulder bags. Traveling abroad in wartime was difficult enough, and they couldn't take much. Harold had put most of his things in storage.

The moment Abby got up, someone took her seat. She walked over, and Frances said, "There you are! How long have you been waiting?"

"Not long."

"My dear," Harold said. "What's with that insatiable grin?"

Abby waved the envelope she had been holding since she had opened it.

"I made the Dean's List."

Harold put his hands together and took a slight bow.

"A parting gift."

"Oh, Abby, that's terrific," Frances told her.

The three of them hugged, and when Abby turned to the professor, he raised his hat with a polite smile.

"Well done, Ms. Nolan," he said.

"Nice to see you back on your feet."

"He's a model of recovery," Harold said.

"How're you feeling?" Abby asked.

"Quite better, thank you—"

"This damn cold isn't helping," Harold said. "He's been ordered to stay away from people and no strenuous activities."

"Will you stop interrupting?" Frances said, swatting his arm.

"I'm not interrupting. I'm simply stating facts."

"No one can ever finish a sentence around you."

Mr. Glynn watched them bicker, his eyes going side to side. Abby could never tell if he was amused or appalled by their spastic conversations. Finally, they went quiet so he could speak.

"The staying away from people I can handle. No strenuous activities is another matter."

"Oh stop it, Richie," Harold said. "We'll be back on the pitch again in no time."

When he put his arm around the professor's back, Abby looked at Frances. A busy train station was no place for displays of affection, especially between two men. They were saved from any awkwardness when a voice came over the loudspeaker.

"Attention all passengers, train number four-zero-three-six to Montreal now boarding on track five."

With ferries to Nova Scotia closed, their plans had changed. They now had to take an inland route.

"*C'est nous!*" Harold said.

Despite his dramatic flair, it was obvious he was anxious. The trip across the Atlantic was dangerous. As a girl, Abby had never worried about bad things happening. Now she expected them to. She didn't know if she had lost her optimism or if the world had just gotten more unpredictable. Either way, when she hugged him again, she squeezed extra hard.

She wiped her eyes and then turned to Mr. Glynn.

"When will you arrive in Ireland?" she asked.

"The boat leaves Thursday evening," Harold said.

"New Year's Eve," Frances said.

"No fireworks for us, unfortunately. We leave under the cover of darkness."

"If all goes well," Mr. Glynn explained, "we should be in Belfast in about two weeks' time."

"Richie assures me all the rubble has been cleared."

While it sounded like a joke, Abby was confused, and she could tell Frances was too.

"My parent's block was damaged last year," the professor said, his voice trailing off as he added, "in an air raid."

"And to think he's got a soft spot for the Germans," Harold said.

Mr. Glynn glanced aside, seeming irritated.

"I don't have a 'soft spot' for the Germans. What I do have are serious concerns about British colonial policy and the historical injustices of the Empire."

"*Ja, wohl!*"

The professor frowned. He always got flustered by Harold's playful remarks, but he also seemed to enjoy them.

"The Germans were targeting the shipyards," he explained to Abby and Frances. "And they were accurate...mostly."

As he said it, he sounded conflicted, even embarrassed. It was the worst time to talk about politics, so Abby was relieved when she heard the final announcement.

Harold took his and Mr. Glynn's suitcases, and they all headed toward the doors. When they walked out, they cringed in unison from the cold.

On the platform, maintenance workers were shoveling snow and chipping icicles off the overhang. A dozen trains sat idling on the tracks, smoke rising from their locomotives.

A black porter came over to take their bags.

"Well," Harold said. "I'm not one for farewells, so this isn't goodbye. It's goodbye for now."

Abby swallowed, nodding, trying to hold back tears.

"For now."

They all hugged one last time while the professor waited a few feet away. Suddenly, there was a loud toot. Harold and Mr. Glynn stepped into the car, Harold lingering in the doorway.

"Be careful," Abby said.

He blew them both kisses.

"Write!" Frances said.

Slowly, the train started to move. Frances clutched Abby's arm, and they watched as Harold's figure grew dimmer and dimmer. He was going where he wanted with a man he wanted to be with. If anything ever happened to him, Abby would always remember him smiling and waving. In a world where partings were often abrupt and sometimes final, it was the best anyone could hope for.

······

THEY SAT in the diner across from North Station. Frances had ordered an omelet but had only picked at it, smoking one cigarette after another. Abby had bacon, eggs, and toast, the first thing she had eaten all day. While her father's decision to stick with coal had turned out to be fortunate, he had also not converted to gas for the oven. They had run out of kerosene that morning.

"Well, that's it," Abby said. "He's gone."

"You heard him. He's gone for now."

"He said 'goodbye for now.'"

Frances looked up, rolling her eyes.

"Isn't that the same thing?"

"I guess."

Abby took a sip of her coffee. Two booths away, a group of sailors were laughing and joking around. She wondered how they could be so cheerful. One kept looking over, but she didn't smile back, not wanting to give him the wrong idea.

"Should you really be doing that?"

Frances looked at the cigarette between her fingers.

"Doing what?" she asked.

"Smoking."

"And why not?"

"It could be bad for..."

Abby hesitated, looking down at Frances' midsection.

"Says who?"

"An article in *Woman's Day*."

"Rubbish," Frances said, flicking into the ashtray.

Abby didn't argue, knowing her friend had enough to worry about. They both had lived through a tragedy and for Frances, the emotional torment wasn't over.

Thinking back to the fire, Abby got chills, haunted by the memory of the shouting, screaming, and panic. If there was any upside, it was that coming so close to death had made her fear it less. Still, she wondered why she had lived while so many others died. But she didn't feel guilty. While her father had been a skeptic, her mother had given her enough faith to believe everything happened for a reason.

The waitress looked over, and Abby waved for the check. They had been there for almost two hours, and they couldn't mope in a restaurant all day.

As she reached for her purse, Frances blurted, "Mother insists I put it up for adoption."

Abby froze. Glancing up, she looked around. Pregnancy wasn't something people talked about in public, especially with a girl who had no wedding ring.

"Where?"

Frances shrugged her shoulders.

"There's a place," she said, lighting another cigarette, "in New Hampshire. For these types of...situations. I'll go stay there for the remainder of the time."

"What kind of place?"

She took a quick drag and blew out the smoke.

"A private institution. That's all I know."

Abby paused.

"Is that what you want?"

"It's not about what I want, Abigail. It's about what's practical."

"And that's practical?"

Their eyes met.

"Who knows? How the hell can I care for a child? I can't even take care of myself for chrissakes..."

Abby was relieved when the waitress came over with the check. She knew Frances was agitated, and she didn't want to make it worse.

Abby left two dollars on the table, and they got up and put on their coat, hats, and gloves. As they walked out, they passed the sailors, and one of them said, "Hello."

He was looking at Frances, who always seemed to get the most attention. But Abby smiled at him, causing his friends to all jeer. It was sad to think they were young enough to get giddy around girls, yet mature enough to go to war.

Outside, Causeway Street was like a wind tunnel. Trains rattled by on the overhead rail, sending chunks of snow and ice onto the street. In front of an Army recruitment center, two ragged-looking boys were hawking newspapers. On the corner, some homeless men stood smoking under an air raid shelter sign.

"Shall I hail a taxi?"

"No need," Frances said. "My mother's place is only a five-minute walk," she said, looking toward Beacon Hill. "Which reminds me. She wants to invite you and your mother to a United War Fund reception she's helped organize."

"United War Fund?"

"In two weeks...at Copley Plaza."

"Copley Plaza? Sounds fancy."

"All the big-wigs should be there," Frances said, not hiding her sarcasm.

For all her pretensions, she never liked the social circles and society events her parents were a part of.

"I'll ask her."

Frances leaned in, and they hugged.

"Do, please," she said.

32

The night before, there had been an ice storm. Towns across the state had lost power, and the streets were bad enough that school had been canceled in Boston. As Thomas drove, the tires of the cruiser were so bald he could barely control it. The captain had put in a request for new ones weeks ago. But with rubber scarce and money tight, even the department couldn't get them. They would have had better luck going to the black market.

He pulled into a lot between Sansone Coal and the giant General Electric plant where Connie used to work. He remembered picking her up when her shifts had ended, hundreds of women, mostly young immigrants, pouring out the side doors. After Pearl Harbor, Italians who weren't citizens had been fired, including Connie. At the time, Thomas had been outraged, but there wasn't much he could have done. A city cop's power was no match for a company like G.E.

He parked and jumped out, leaving the car running. He walked up the steps, watching for ice, and knocked on a rusted metal door. It opened, and a fat, middle-aged man peered out. The top of his head was bald; his teeth were yellow from cigars or bad hygiene.

"Sergeant? What can I do for you?"

"A few bags of coal if you got it."

"What'd you do with the stuff I gave you last week?"

Thomas could have said he had given it to a church that was housing British refugee children, but it would have sounded melodramatic.

"Nothing lasts long in this weather."

The man nodded and shut the door. As Thomas waited, he looked around. He always got nervous taking favors, but in the industrial backstreets of East Boston, most people kept to themselves.

For months, Sansone Coal had been fighting with its neighbor over the property line of the lot they shared. In November, G.E. had switched from making lamps to producing war materiel. Now their trucks pulled in and out all day. A judge had ordered them not to block the coal company, but it was up to the police to enforce it. Thomas always made sure they complied.

Moments later, the loading dock door lifted with a creak. A young black man came down the ramp pushing a two-wheeler with five brown bags. Thomas opened the trunk and helped load them in, but they wouldn't fit.

"Hold on," the guy said.

He ran back into the building, returning with a piece of wire. He tied the trunk down, and Thomas handed him two crumpled one-dollar bills.

"Happy New Year."

"Thank you kindly," the man said, tipping his hat.

Thomas got in and backed out to the street, tires spinning.

In front of G.E. workers were leaving, men from one set of doors and women from another. Thomas' shift was over too, but he still had to go in that night. Every officer was ordered on duty for New Year's Eve, something old-timers had never recalled happening before. With the oil shortage, people were already frustrated. Then the day before, the OPA had announced that two hundred more foods would be rationed, mostly canned fruits and vegetables. The chief was worried there could be hoarding or even riots.

Instead of going straight toward Bennington Street, Thomas went right to stay off the main roads. He didn't want to be spotted driving around with coal in the trunk.

As he approached Day Square, he saw a faint plume of smoke. He wouldn't have been concerned except it was near the train tracks. Sliding to a stop, he jumped out and squeezed through a hole in the fence. In the distance, he saw three teenagers standing around a barrel fire.

"Hey!" he yelled.

When they turned, he immediately recognized Clarence Morris. He moved toward them, and they ran. He could've chased them, but the embankment was a minefield of snow, ice, and litter. Nabbing three kids for vandalism or trespassing wasn't worth breaking an ankle.

He kicked the barrel over, sending glowing embers across the frozen ground. It looked like they had burned a tire, the remnants of treads smoldering in the ash. As he waited for it to go out, a train passed, an endless stretch of tank cars. Whether they had gasoline, kerosene, or something else, he didn't know. But in a city starved for fuel, anything would help. Wiping his hands, he turned around and headed back to the cruiser.

......

THOMAS TURNED onto his street and parked behind the Ford. As he got out, he saw Mrs. McNulty in the window across the street. Everyone knew he was a cop, but the sight of a police car still got attention. She had always been nosey, something even her own kids had complained about. But with his mother home alone a lot of the time, Thomas liked having someone watching out for her.

He lifted two bags of coal out of the trunk, the most he could take. As he walked up his mother's front steps, Abby opened the door. She had on her MWDC uniform with no hat, and her hair was combed out.

"Did you get oil?" she asked.

"Just coal."

"We need kerosene."

He walked by, and she followed him into the kitchen.

"We ran out last night," she went on. "We had cold egg salad for dinner."

Thomas put the bags down beside the pantry.

"Egg salad *is* cold."

"I called five places today."

"Not sure if you heard. The whole state's out."

She frowned at the sarcasm.

"Then what should we do?"

"You can start by taking those down to the basement," he said, "There's three more in the car."

"I can't. They're too heavy."

Thomas loved his sister, but somewhere between adolescence and adulthood, she had gone soft. As a girl, she could outwrestle many of the boys on the street. One summer in Point Shirley, she had pulled up a lobster trap with her bare hands. She had always been more stubborn than athletic, one of the few qualities she shared with George.

"What would you do if I wasn't here?" he said.

As he went to leave, she blocked the hallway.

"Don't say that."

He sidestepped, but she wouldn't let him by.

"Move, will ya?"

"Don't say that!"

They stared at each other in a quiet standoff. But it didn't last. They heard footsteps moving above them. Moments later, their mother came down the stairs and walked into the kitchen.

"I thought I heard you come in."

"Hi, Ma," he said.

In her wrinkled nightgown and slippers, she looked like a bag lady. The harsh weather was a good excuse to laze around inside. But he hadn't seen her dressed up since Christmas and worried she wasn't bathing.

She walked over to the cabinet and reached for a tin of aspirin. Taking out two tablets, she swallowed them dry, something she said made them work better.

"Everything alright?" Thomas asked.

"Just a cold, I think. I've had a blinding headache all day. Did you find any oil for the stove?"

"No, but I will. I got some coal. I'll put some on for tonight."

"Bless your heart," she said, leaning up and kissing him on the cheek. "You'll have to forgive me tonight."

"Of course, Ma."

"There's some egg salad in the icebox."

"Thanks. Go get some rest."

She staggered out, dragging her feet like the slippers were too heavy. Abby stood leaning against the wall, her arms crossed and a pout on her face. They waited until their mother was back upstairs, and when the bedroom door shut, Thomas asked, "Is it the booze?"

"I don't know. But she's not right in the head."

"You need to call Dr. Berman."

Abby's eyes narrowed.

"I do?" she said, her tone defensive.

"We don't have a phone in the house."

"And what do I say?"

"You can start by telling him she's drinking again."

Thomas walked out to the car to get the other bags. By the time Abby had gotten her shoes and coat on to help, he was done. He carried them all down to the basement, one at a time, ducking under the low ceiling. The only thing he didn't like about free coal was having to bring it in himself. Deliveries were done through the side window and went straight into the bunker.

He shoveled some into the furnace, dust flying into his eyes. Crouched in the dirt, he stared into the chamber, mesmerized by the flames. Then he slammed the hatch shut and went back upstairs.

Abby had gone to her bedroom, and the house was quiet. He

washed his hands in the sink, turned off some lights, and blew out the candle his mother had left burning in the living room. Then he headed over to the place which, at different times, he called "next door," "home," and "the Ciarlones'." It still felt strange to see his mother and Abby only to leave and go twenty feet away.

When he walked in, he smelled something good. He had met with Captain Vitti for most of the afternoon to go over scheduling and hadn't eaten. Everyone was overworked, and having enough officers for each shift was a delicate balance. Their station had lost another two men that week to the service, one to the Army and another to the Coast Guard. Headquarters said they wouldn't get replacements until the end of January.

With so many job openings, most people were employed, and crime was down. But things were getting added to the precinct's plate all the time. It had been announced that local police departments would soon have to help FBI agents arrest draft dodgers. The governor had ordered a ban on pleasure driving to save on gas. Any service stations caught violating the coupon regulations would have their licenses taken away.

Beyond that, the cold snap was fast becoming a crisis. Public buildings were open day and night to provide shelter for families. Across the city, people could be seen carrying jugs and looking for oil. It reminded Thomas of the stories his father used to tell him about the Famine in Ireland, starving skeletons scouring the countryside for food. He couldn't think of a worse time to be a city cop.

When he walked into the kitchen, Connie was at the stove. She had on the flowered apron Chickie had made her in Home Economics class. One of the straps was longer than the other, but neither one of them had said anything.

"Smells delicious," Thomas said.

"I made a chowder with the leftover cod. How was your day?"

She glanced over, and her face was red from the cold.

"Good," he said, distracted. "Were you out somewhere?"

"I went to the shop for salt."

"There's a whole box in the pantry."

"We needed onions too. The old ones were rotten."

She put the lid on the pot and walked over. Standing on her tiptoes, she kissed him, and her lips were dry and chapped.

"You smell like a fire?" she said.

"Remember that boy who was bothering Chickie?"

"Clarence?"

"I saw him—"

"He won't be bothering her anymore, unfortunately," she said.

Thomas frowned. Whatever she meant, it was a strange way to phrase it.

"No?"

"He was expelled from the school."

She reached up to get bowls from the cabinet.

"Is that so?" Thomas mumbled.

Chickie came running in, her hair in braids. As he hugged her, he got a sinking feeling. East Boston had always been full of young delinquents, a consequence of poverty and overcrowding. At one time, his own brother had been one of them. Much of Thomas' job, especially as a rookie, had been kicking kids off of street corners and out of alleyways, arresting them for petty theft and loitering. He used to resent them, but he had some sympathy for the boys he had seen out on the tracks, if only because he saw a little of his brother in them.

"Everything alright, Dada?"

Connie looked over too.

"Yeah. Of course."

33

THE SNOW HAD STARTED SOMETIME AFTER MIDNIGHT AND HADN'T stopped. By now there was half a foot, and Abby hadn't seen a single plow. With the gas restrictions and the storm, even people with cars had taken public transportation. The trolley was so packed that she had to stand. Clutching the handrail, she stared out into the white haze. By the time they got to Kenmore Square, they had passed three accidents, including a milk truck on its side.

Finally, they stopped at BU, and the doors opened. Abby held down her hat and stepped out into the storm. She scurried across the street and into the building where she collapsed on a bench out of breath. Reaching for a tissue, she wiped the moisture off her face, the frost off her eyelashes.

She peeled off her gloves, opened her bag, and took out her schedule. Irish History II had been removed from the curriculum, which was no surprise. Mr. Glynn had been the only one teaching it. He had complained that the administration had never respected the subject, seeing it as just an extension of British history. It wasn't the only class that had been canceled. Abby's Philosophy course was postponed until they could find someone to teach it, and Fine Arts had been pushed to the next semester. Courses in shorthand, typewriting, and secretarial administration were all available, probably because they were taught by women. Otherwise, there was a shortage of teachers across the state. Everyone was scrambling to make up for the thousands of men leaving or already gone.

For her language requirement, she had chosen French. Her mother had said she should've taken Italian, which she was more familiar with. But Abby had always been fascinated by France and its culture.

She looked at her watch and saw that she was a half hour early. In the week it was closed, the bakery had run out of heating oil. Eve had come in that morning to find the pipes frozen and had to send everybody home.

It was too cold to wait in the lobby, and the cafeteria wasn't open yet. So Abby grabbed her things, turned into the first stairwell, and walked up to the third floor. As she approached the classroom, the light was on. She opened the door, and the moment she walked in, she froze.

"Ms. Stetson?"

"Ms. Nolan," the professor said with a hint of irony.

"You're teaching this class?"

"I am now."

"You speak French?"

"My mother was Quebecois. I was raised in New Brunswick."

Abby didn't know enough about Canada to understand what it meant, so she assumed the answer was a "yes."

"You're quite early," the professor added, and it sounded like an accusation.

"I...wanted to get a head start on the new year."

Ms. Stetson made a tight smile.

"Indeed. Please, have a seat."

With no place to hide, Abby sat in the front row. The professor was always awkward to be around, especially alone. So Abby was surprised when she blurted, "I understand Harold Merrill has withdrawn from the college."

"Yes."

"And has gone to Ireland?"

Abby hesitated.

"That's correct."

"Quite risky for these times. And difficult. May I ask what business he has there?"

The question was forward enough that Abby was suspicious, thinking maybe Ms. Stetson already knew. Either way, she had no reason to lie.

"He's escorting Mr. Glynn back home."

The professor's eyes narrowed. Abby sensed some subtle apprehension she knew was probably envy. Harold was crossing the Atlantic in wartime with the man he admired, possibly loved. In the annals of secret affections and private devotion, there was nothing more romantic.

"Mr. Glynn has been through a lot," Ms. Stetson said, finally.

It sounded more like an observation than an expression of sympathy or understanding.

"Yes, he has."

Abby was relieved when some more students walked in. She got a new notebook out of her bag, and the professor got up to write on the chalkboard.

The conversation had been short and strange, but Abby had to accept Ms. Stetson despite her quirks. She wanted to play volleyball in the fall, and now she had her as a French teacher. And she couldn't deny that, at a time when everyone was leaving, it was nice to see a familiar face.

Once class was over, she put her things away and walked out. With the bakery closed that morning, she hadn't had anything to eat, so she went straight to the cafeteria. As she waited in line, she looked over to the corner table where, as reliable as the sun, Harold and Frances always used to be. Now it was empty.

"Abby?"

Abby spun around to see Frances.

"Fran!" she cried, elated by the sight of her.

As they hugged, she felt a slight bulge around her friend's midsection. At four months pregnant, Frances was starting to show.

"What can I get you?" Abby asked.

"Oh, Ab—"

"Just tell me!"

"Okay. Just tea. I already ate. Thank you."

Abby ordered two teas and toast for herself. She usually had coffee, but with shortages, a lot of it was cut with chicory, and she hated the taste.

When she walked over to the table and sat down, she realized that neither of them had taken the chair Harold used to sit in.

"Lovely," France said, taking her tea.

Someone had left a copy of the Globe, the headline "Reds Roll Nazis Back" printed in large, bold letters. Frances must have noticed Abby looking because she said, "How much farther can they roll back?"

The Russians had been crushing the Germans for weeks, and on Sunday, the Allies had finally beaten the Japanese in Indonesia. The news across the world had been good, but no one knew what it meant or when the war would end. Casualties continued to pour in, and at Mass on Sunday, Father Ward read out the names of two more local boys who had been killed. Like at Christmas, Abby didn't know them. But she feared it was only a matter of time before some old classmate or friend was on the list.

"They should be in Belfast by tomorrow," Abby said.

"With bells and fanfare, I suppose."

"We would've heard if there was any trouble. Don't you think?"

Frances shrugged her shoulders, clutching the bag on her lap. Abby noticed that she wasn't smoking.

"Maybe, maybe not."

"But I'm sure they made it."

"Time will tell."

Even for Frances, the remark was harsh. Before Sal's death, she could at least fake optimism. Now everything she said was tinged with bitterness and gloom. When Abby had told her about Arthur's letter, Frances said she should move on, not wait. Abby had been insulted, but she hadn't shown it, knowing how grief always sought out company.

"Well," Frances said, getting up. "Time for Psychology. The professor was a student of Freud's, so it should be interesting."

"Did I tell you Ms. Stetson is teaching my French class?"

"It suits her. She's from Canada, isn't she?"

"New Brunswick."

"So are we on for Saturday?" Frances asked.

"Saturday?"

"The United War Fund gala at Copley."

"Right. I look forward to it."

"And your mother?"

Abby hesitated, nodding.

"She'll be with me."

"Swell," Frances said. "Toodle-loo!"

......

BY LATE AFTERNOON, it was still snowing, everything buried under a thick layer of white. The plows had finally come out, and many of them were Army trucks.

As the train creaked under Sumner Tunnel, Abby couldn't wait to get off. She felt like she was suffocating and not just because it was crowded. With a shortage, people were scouring the city for oil. Passengers were carrying kerosene in everything from paint cans to milk bottles, creating a horrible stench.

Finally, they pulled into Maverick Station and the doors opened. Abby burst out and ran across the platform, trying to avoid the slushy water dripping from the ceiling. She was almost at the stairs when she heard her name and stopped.

Looking over, she saw someone waving from the corner. As she walked over, she realized who it was.

"Angela?"

"Hey, Abby."

Angela had on a bulky overcoat and a frayed knit hat; her cheeks had pimples, and she looked unkempt. The redness under her eyes could have been from tears, but it was probably from the cold.

"What're you doing here?" Abby asked.

"My father kicked me out."

"Where're you staying?"

"Different places."

"Can I...do anything?"

"A few dollars, if you can spare it."

"Of course," Abby said.

She opened her bag and flipped through her wallet, squinting in the low light.

"He's gone you know?"

Abby looked up, and their eyes met. She didn't have to ask who.

"I'm sorry," she said, her voice shaking.

It was a shame they could only talk about the soldier with hints and whispers. Thinking about Harold's situation, Abby wondered how the whole damn world could be so cruel. A war was no time to put limits and conditions on love.

Abby handed her five dollars, more than she made in a week. Angela looked stunned, so Abby was surprised when she just took it and asked, "Have you heard from George at all?"

Abby made a sad smile, remembering how they had dated before the war.

"Not since September."

Folding the bill, Angela stuffed it in her pocket. Abby saw that her nails were all dirty and chipped.

"There's shelters open," she said.

Hearing a bell, she looked back, and a streetcar was getting ready to leave.

"I gotta go."

Angela nodded.

"Thanks, Abby."

She walked away and disappeared back into the shadows. Abby ran for the trolley, catching it just before the doors closed.

When she got off at Bennington Street, she was damp with sweat. With freezing temperatures and a heating crisis, trains seemed the warmest places around, especially with all the people.

She waited for some cars to pass and then hurried over to the market. She walked in, and Mr. Schultz looked up from the register.

"Abigail," he said. "Quite a tempest out there."

"A blizzard is more like it."

"Can I help you?"

"A prescription from Dr. Berman, please," she said, loosening her scarf.

He walked over to the drug counter, which was separated by a half door.

"I was making deliveries all afternoon. Let me check to see if Anna prepared it."

He opened a drawer and looked through the bottles, squinting to read the labels. As Abby watched, she felt a nervous anticipation, but she was also captivated. For his age, he had a remarkably full head of hair, and he was handsome and kind, a rare combination. Knowing her mother had gone out with him a few times since Thanksgiving, she had dreaded coming in to get the drugs.

"Katherine Nolan," he said, finally. "Benzedrine?"

She listened for any signs of surprise, concern, or contempt. She was relieved there were none.

"That's her," Abby said.

He walked back over to the register.

"One per day in the morning. Never later. She won't sleep."

He rang it in, and Abby dropped three quarters into his hand. After seeing Angela, she was low on money and didn't get paid until Friday.

"Thank you," she said.

"Stay warm."

She left the shop and crossed Bennington Street, the wind whipping against her face. She didn't know if the storm had picked up or if she had just been out in it for too long. By the time she got home, she had snow up her sleeves and down her back.

When she walked in, her mother was reading a book in the living room. The lamp was on, but she had several candles going too. Although East Boston hadn't lost power in the ice storm the week before, everyone still wanted to be prepared.

"How was school?"

"Ms. Stetson is teaching my French class."

Her mother glanced over. For the first time in days, she wasn't in a nightgown and slippers. She looked like she had bathed, even done her hair.

"Stetson? Is she the queer one?"

Abby chuckled to herself, unbuttoning her coat.

"She's the odd one."

Kneeling down, she untied her boots, the laces swelled with water. She got the medicine from her bag and walked over.

"Here," she said, holding out the bottle.

Mrs. Nolan closed her book and put it down. Abby looked at the cup on the table, trying to see what was in it. Her mother didn't look drunk, but she had put rum in her tea before.

"What's this?"

"It's for you."

Squinting, she read the label and then groaned.

"Oh, Abigail, I can't—"

"Take them!"

Her mother flinched. After she left the psych ward the spring before, the doctor told her to take the drug when she was feeling "particularly morose." He only let her stop after she was off alcohol for six months.

"They'll help you," Abby added.

"I don't need pills. I just need to get out a little more."

"Good, because we're going to Copley Plaza Saturday night."

"Copley Plaza? What on earth would I be doing there?"

"Frances' mother has invited us to an event for the United War Fund."

Abby held out the medicine, her expression firm. She didn't like treating her mother like a child, but she knew sick people needed prodding.

"You know," Mrs. Nolan said, her voice low and shaky, "it's been hard not knowing if your brother is alive or dead."

Abby welled up with emotion.

"I know, Ma," she said.

But she was angry too. They all used George as an excuse for their own frustrations and grievances, and her mother was the worst.

"The United War Fund?"

She said it with a snicker, and Abby knew why. The group was mostly debutantes, society women, and local celebrities—anyone with wealth or status. They were people whose contributions to the war effort were far grander than her church bake sales and neighborhood bond drives.

Mrs. Nolan had always struggled to bridge the gaps between the world of the elite and the world of the ordinary. She scorned the rich for having too much and the poor for not doing enough to get more, which was an impossible way to live.

"So, you'll go?" Abby asked.

Her mother swiped the bottle from her hand.

"If you insist."

34

Thomas sat at the long table with eight of his patrolmen. The room at the back of the station used to be for storage until Captain Vitti turned it into a boardroom. It had low ceilings, no windows, and worst of all, no heat. When Thomas got up that morning, it was ten degrees out, and it hadn't gotten any warmer.

The cold spell was set to continue, and the city had less than two days' supply of kerosene. The governor had announced that the state would start evacuating families, and The Red Cross had been called in to help. The wealthy didn't have to worry. Already real estate agents were advertising homes in the country stocked with fuel and food. But in the poorer neighborhoods, the MWDC was going door to door handing out sweaters, blankets, and fresh water. Churches, town halls, libraries, and public buildings were all ordered to stay open. Everyone knew what the cold could do, but not what would happen if the region ran out of oil. At the least, there could be panic in the streets. At most, complete chaos.

"I need at least two cruisers in Maverick Square at all times. People might try to sleep in the station..."

Thomas read through the bulletin from the chief, two pages of guidelines and instructions.

"Families without heat should try to stay with relatives first. We'll provide the transportation. If they have nowhere to go, then take them to a shelter—"

"What if they don't wanna go?" an officer blurted.

"Try to persuade them."

Thomas still wasn't comfortable giving orders, especially to men his own age. But it was a good question, and something everyone wondered about. In the slums of Boston, people were as stubborn as they were proud. The more someone needed help, the less likely they were to take it. One mother in Roxbury had told the newspapers, "I'd let my kids freeze to death before taking them to a shelter!"

"Pleasure driving is now strictly forbidden," Thomas went on. "OPA agents will have checkpoints all over the state. If we catch anyone, we have to take their information and seize their ration booklets."

"How do we know if they're pleasure driving?"

Thomas looked up.

"They'll have a smile on their face—"

They were interrupted by a knock, and Captain Vitti walked in wearing a coat. With the station low on oil, he had ordered all the thermostats turned down. They weren't supposed to go below fifty-five to avoid the pipes freezing. But in such an old drafty building it was impossible to control the temperature, and some floors were worse than others. The lobby was so cold the captain had let the secretary go home early.

"Gentlemen," he said, steam puffing from his mouth. "The weather bureau is now saying it's gonna go below zero tonight."

"Good time for the Germans to attack," someone joked.

They all chuckled, but mostly as a courtesy. With the Germans retreating on almost all fronts, no one was worried about an invasion anymore. The only thing people still feared were U-boats. Only a week before, a fishing boat had been torpedoed off the Maine coast. The men had been saved after a trawler had spotted smoke and had come to their rescue.

"We've got shelters all over East Boston. The high school has two hundred cots set up. Women and children are a priority. We don't want a tough situation to turn into a disaster. We need to protect our people..."

Everyone smiled, and Thomas was filled with a warm elation. For men who felt left out of the war, it made their work sound like a mission.

"If you see any bums, get them off the street. The YMCA has got beds and a soup kitchen. I don't wanna be scraping up bodies with ice picks in the morning..."

They all laughed out loud, a moment of dark humor.

"Lastly, I know everyone's been working a lot of hours. But when the shift ends, I need you to ask your men if they can work tonight. If they say no, and only if they say no, tell them they have no choice."

With that, the captain slapped his hands on the desk.

"Understand?" he asked, then he waited for everyone to nod. "Good."

......

THOMAS HAD BEEN out for almost twelve hours straight. Even with a sweater, overcoat, hat, and gloves on, he shivered so much it hurt. The heat in the cruiser was better than the Ford, but he couldn't run the engine all day. Even if they'd had coupons for unlimited gas, a lot of service stations were out, and many had closed due to the cold. At the request of Mayor Tobin, the Army had donated a few thousand gallons to the department, delivering them to precincts around the city in five-gallon jerry cans.

Thomas sat parked on the corner in Day Square. Whether it was the cold or the ban on recreational driving, hardly any cars were out. All he saw were fuel trucks, racing through the streets, bringing that life-saving liquid to desperate families. Over in South Boston, barges arrived around the clock with kerosene, and it still wasn't enough.

Some barrooms were open, and the lights over at Jeveli's were on.

But Thomas hadn't seen a single person in over an hour. Looking at his watch, he saw it was almost eleven. Some men would have to stay on overnight, but he got to go home. The one rule that had kept them all from being worked to death was that no officer could work three shifts in a row.

As he went to start the car, he heard a tap on the glass. He rolled down the window, and it was an old woman. She was short and stout and wore a hooded wool coat and big mittens.

"Ma'am?"

"Help, please," she said with an accent.

She glanced over her shoulder, and he saw a five-gallon drum on the sidewalk. Then she looked toward the top of a house, a towering triple-decker that was dark and rundown.

"You want me to bring that up for you?"

She nodded.

He took the keys out of the ignition and got out. Walking over, he grabbed the handle of the jug, and it was heavier than he had expected.

They went up the front steps and stepped into a small foyer with shabby wallpaper and cracks in the ceiling. When she turned into a stairwell, he followed her up three flights and into a cramped apartment. The air was chilly, and there were candles scattered on tables, chairs, and windowsills, giving the eerie impression of a séance. Above the mantle was a painting of the Madonna and Child. On a cabinet, Thomas saw a picture of a young man in uniform.

"Grandson," the woman said before he could ask.

Suddenly, there was loud hacking.

"Who's that?"

"Sick," she said, sounding more like "seek."

"Your husband?"

The man coughed again, sending a shudder up Thomas's spine.

"Mario."

"Has Mario seen a doctor?"

She shook her head.

"No doctor."

"Can I see him?"

She hesitated, looking down.

"I can get him help," he added.

"Okay, help."

She led him down a hallway, and they turned into a bedroom that reeked of vomit. The only light was from a candle, which Thomas was horrified to see lying on the floor. He picked it up and put it on the dresser, knowing how quickly fire spread in old houses.

When he walked over to the bed, an old man peered out from a pile of dirty blankets and quilts. His beady eyes were glassy; his forehead was damp despite the cold. He tried to say something, but it came out as a grunt.

Thomas turned around.

"He needs to get to a hospital immediately," he said.

The woman fidgeted with her hands, looking down in shame. In any emergency, one of the hardest jobs for cops was giving help to people who wouldn't take it.

Finally, she nodded.

"Okay, hospital."

"Do you have any heat?" he asked, although he knew the answer.

"No heat."

"I'll be right back."

He flew out the door, down the stairs, and out to the street. Searching for a callbox, he spotted one at the corner and ran toward it. He opened it with his key and grabbed the receiver, cringing as the cold metal touched his ear.

"Central," a woman's voice said.

"Central, Precinct Nine. There's an old couple here. They're outta oil. The husband is sick. Real bad."

"Location please?"

"Four-hundred and sixty-eight Saratoga Street."

"Precinct Nine, we'll dispatch the first ambulance to become available."

"Any ETA?

The woman paused.

"We'll dispatch the first ambulance to become available," she repeated.

Thomas slammed the receiver down. He didn't like her tone, but he knew all the city services were strained.

"Nolan?"

When he turned around, Sergeant Silva pulled up in a cruiser.

"Everything okay?"

"There's an old man on the third floor," Thomas said, pointing up. "I think he's got pneumonia. He looks like death."

"Well, we got a real death."

Thomas frowned.

"Someone reported a body. A young girl."

"A girl?"

"Like...a woman, but young. You know?"

"Where?"

"Under the Neptune Road bridge."

"Is it suspicious?"

Their eyes locked.

"Unfortunately, no."

To anyone else, it would have sounded like a contradiction. But Thomas knew what he meant. With the cold crisis, everyone feared an epidemic of fatalities from exposure.

"I'll follow you."

Thomas ran over and jumped in the car. He sped across the intersection after Silva, and they got to the scene in seconds. As they approached the bridge, he was disappointed to see no witnesses or bystanders. People were quick to report trouble, but most didn't want to get involved.

He slowed down, careful not to slide on the ice, and stopped behind Silva. Reaching into the glove compartment, he grabbed the flashlight and got out.

"Who reported this?" he asked as Silva and his partner walked over.

"Don't know."

The old passenger line had been shut down two years before, the tracks now a jungle of weeds and litter. Thomas leaned over the railing and pointed the flashlight. Sweeping it through the darkness, he saw a figure lying beside the abutment.

"C'mon!" he said.

They scrambled down the snowy embankment and went under the bridge. Thomas' heart pounded, and he got a nervous exhilaration. In his short time on the force, he had seen a few dozen bodies. About half had been murders and the other half had been either accidents or suicides. But it never seemed to get any easier, something a veteran cop had warned him about when he had started.

Crouching, Thomas walked over, broken glass crunching under his feet. As he got closer, he realized she had a blanket over her and assumed she was homeless. Then the moment he flashed the light on her face, he froze.

"What's wrong?" Silva asked.

"I know her."

"You know her?"

Thomas nodded.

The patrolman walked over, knelt down, and felt for a pulse. Glancing back, he shook his head and confirmed what they already knew. With temperatures close to zero, no one could have survived outside for long.

"Who is she?"

"Angela Labadini," Thomas said.

"What the hell is she doing under here?"

They both looked down at her. Her head was tilted, and her eyes were closed like she was sleeping. She even looked peaceful, a phrase Thomas used to scoff at when people said it at wakes and funerals. He thought back to when she had dated George two summers before. As a couple, they had been as wild and reckless as Bonnie and Clyde. He always knew she had problems, and with a brother like Vin, it was no surprise. But he had never expected her to end up frozen to death under a bridge. Gazing at her face, he felt a gut-wrenching sadness that, in many ways, was as much for who she was as for what she represented.

Someone tapped his shoulder, and he flinched.

"C'mon," Silva said. "The ambulance is here. We're done."

As they walked away, two men came out of the shadows with a stretcher.

"Where's the coroner?" Thomas asked.

The men looked at each other.

"We're pretty busy tonight, sir," one of them said, which was probably an understatement. "The body will be at the Southern Mortuary until someone is available."

Thomas and Silva climbed back up the embankment and stepped over the guardrail.

"Should we inform next of kin?" Silva asked.

The death was tragic enough, and now they had to tell the family.

"Naw. I can do it in the morning," Thomas said, kicking the snow off his boots.

As Silva lit a cigarette, Thomas looked out toward the airport and harbor. The entire coastline was dark, with only a few tiny flickers from patrol boats. His hands were stiff, and he coughed more in the cold. But there was something hypnotic about the darkness that kept him there. Or maybe it was the silence.

35

In all her life, Abby could never remember a colder night. The only good news was that the snow had stopped, and there was no wind. Wearing a uniform, sweater, and two scarves, she was so bundled up it was hard to move. Her hat was pulled down, but she couldn't feel her ears. And each time she breathed, she got a tickle in her throat that made her gag. Over her shoulder, she carried a duffel bag filled with blankets. The warmth they added made up for the extra weight. Otherwise, she felt like she would have frozen to death.

"It's sort of romantic if you think about it."

Abby glanced back at Frances and the two new girls. Maureen lived just over the bridge in Chelsea, and Betty had moved up from South Carolina to be with her husband, who was stationed at the Coast Guard base in the North End.

"What's romantic?" Abby asked.

"Wandering around in the bitter cold. Saving lives."

"That's one way to look at it," Betty said.

"Personally, I'd rather be home with my feet on the radiator," Maureen added.

While Abby laughed at the sarcasm, she realized that for the first time in weeks, Frances wasn't complaining. It may have been a sign she was recovering from her grief, although Abby was sure the alcohol helped. Her friend had brought a bottle of Puerto Rican rum that looked expensive. More than mischievous, it felt vulgar to be drinking on the street even if it was just to stay warm. Abby had taken a few sips, but she had never liked straight liquor.

For the past five hours, they had been out on patrol, and for once, it wasn't to enforce the blackout regulations. They were going door to door, handing out blankets and taking the names and addresses of families who had no heat. There were only four of them, but it was a citywide effort that included the MWDC, the Red Cross, the Committee on Public Safety, and even the Army.

Abby put her bag down and went up the steps of a triple-decker. Walking into the vestibule, she pressed the buzzer for the first floor. Seconds later, the door creaked open, and a woman looked out. She was in her late thirties with small lips and sunken eyes. She wore a heavy coat and what looked like a man's hat.

"Yeah?"

"Evening. Abby Nolan with the Women's Defense Corps—"

"What do you want?"

"We're walking around to make sure everyone is safe."

"I'm safe. Why wouldn't I be?"

Abby hesitated.

"We have blankets. We can get oil if you need it."

"I've got coupons."

"Coupons won't do much with the shortage."

"I don't need charity, honey," the woman said, and she slammed the door.

Abby blinked, stunned but not insulted. Everyone was cold and miserable, and she was used to people being unfriendly.

She tried the other two apartments, but no one answered, so she turned around and walked back out.

"How'd it go?"

"Would you believe I was invited in for tea?" Abby said.

Mauren and Betty both grinned, and Frances said, "I'd love some hot tea."

They continued up the road. They were supposed to take turns, but Abby did most of the knocking. By the time they reached Bennington Street, her duffel bag was almost empty. Even some of the people who wouldn't accept help would take a free blanket.

They stopped at the corner, and a guy approached carrying a jug. As he walked by, he reeked of kerosene and alcohol.

"Privates," he said with a salute.

Maureen blew him a kiss, and they all laughed. There was a strange camaraderie in the air. Abby never would have walked around certain parts of East Boston at night, and now she felt completely safe. It was so cold even thugs and thieves stayed home, although Betty had a heavy military flashlight just in case.

"So, tell me about this pilot," Maureen said.

Caught off guard, Abby looked at Frances, who shrugged her shoulders. The question was forward, but unlike Betty, Maureen was single. Men were as much in short supply as anything.

"His name is Arthur."

"Arthur? Sounds distinguished. And where is he?"

"The South Pacific."

"The South Pacific is a big place, honey," Betty said in a southern twang.

"I...I don't know exactly."

A black Chevy Special Deluxe pulled up. It had a shining chrome grille and white wall tires. While the "Massachusetts Women's Defense Corps" sign on the door seemed amateurish, Abby had to respect the generosity of members, especially the senior staff. They donated their cars, homes, and money.

Lieutenant Hastings rolled down the window, and they crowded around it to get some heat. She was one of a dozen MWDC officers who had been driving around delivering supplies and evacuating families.

"Ladies," the Lieutenant said.

Betty handed her the list of people who needed help. It was mostly for oil, but two families had no baby formula, and one old man's pipes had burst.

"When can we go home, Miss?" Maureen asked.

Hastings looked at her watch.

"Did you check the scrap yards along Chelsea Street?"

"Yes," they said in unison.

"How about the cemetery?"

Again, they nodded.

For a woman from Beacon Hill, the Lieutenant was starting to know East Boston like a local.

"We need to be thorough," she added. "If any homeless, strays, or drunkards are out there, they won't last the night."

Abby stood shivering, only half-listening and eager to get out of the cold. She wasn't unsympathetic, but anyone who was still out was either foolish or looking to die.

An oil truck sped by, and its headlights flashed across the car. Abby noticed a woman in the backseat with her arm around a boy. They both looked weary, with flat expressions and downcast eyes. She gasped when she realized it was the student who had been teasing Chickie at school.

"Very well, girls," the lieutenant said, and Abby knew she was getting cold. "Good work. You're all dismissed."

With a quick salute, she rolled up the window. They all watched as she turned around and sped off into the night.

......

ABBY TRUDGED up the front steps, Frances straggling behind. They were so cold they hadn't spoken the entire walk back. Abby had no sensation in her feet or her cheeks. And her throat was so dry that she struggled to breathe. The feeling was an eerie reminder of the night of the fire.

She walked in the front door and moaned in relief. It wasn't as warm as she wanted, but it was better than being outside. Glancing over to the living room, she saw her mother sitting with a book. Other than the lamp, all the lights were off.

"You're up?" Abby said.

"I couldn't sleep."

"Do you mind if Frances stays the night?"

"Not at all."

"Hi ya, Mrs. Nolan," Frances said, stepping in.

They both knelt to take off their boots.

"Did Thomas shovel the stairs?" Abby asked.

"No. Henry came by. Can you believe it? What a peach."

"Henry?"

"Mr. Schultz."

"So, you're on a first-name basis now?"

Her mother frowned and closed her book.

"May I use your toilet, Mrs. Nolan," Frances asked.

"You know where it is, dear."

With a curtsy, Frances dashed upstairs.

"How'd it go?" her mother asked, walking over.

"A few hard cases. Thankfully, a lot of people still use coal."

"Your father is continuing to prove us all wrong, even in death."

Abby smiled. Her mother was the only person who could joke about him.

"I suppose I should go fill the bath."

"You don't have to do that."

"It's for me, love," her mother said, and she went up the stairs.

As Abby hung their coats up, she heard someone on the porch. She opened the door, and Thomas rushed in with his hands in his pockets, his collar upturned.

"God dammit," he said, shivering.

"Watch your language."

"Why? Where's Ma?"

"Upstairs."

"Thomas? Is that you?" their mother called.

"I'm just gonna check the furnace."

Abby followed him into the kitchen, and he went down into the basement. She laid the wet hats and gloves on the radiator and then opened the icebox for something to eat. But at this point, she couldn't look at anything cold. So she went into the cabinet and got a tin of Saltines, taking out a few to have before bringing the rest up to share with Frances.

Moments later, Thomas returned smelling of coal and soot. There were lots of things Abby envied about men, but having to do the dirty jobs wasn't one of them.

"Is there enough?" she asked.

He nodded.

"Hey," he started.

In his voice, she could sense some dread or regret. As twins, they always knew what the other was thinking or feeling.

She stopped chewing and put down the biscuits.

"What's wrong?" she asked.

"I've got something to tell you."

"What?"

When he wouldn't look her in the eye, she knew it was bad news.

"Angela Labadini," he said, finally.

Abby's face dropped. He didn't have to say more because she knew.

"How?"

"Probably exposure. We won't know until we get the coroner's report."

"Where?"

"She was found under the Neptune Road bridge."

Abby leaned back against the counter, her arms limp and mouth wide open. What she felt was neither shock nor sadness, but more the empty satisfaction of hearing about something she had always feared would happen. She had known Angela was troubled since they had first met on Point Shirley the summer before the war. Sarah had introduced them. Now they were both gone.

"I just saw her on Monday. She got kicked out of her house."

"I can't say I'm surprised."

"She asked about George."

Thomas hesitated, his expression torn.

Angela's relationship with their brother had been destructive, and they had all been relieved when it ended. No one knew if what they had was love, lust, or just the mutual attraction of two lost souls. But her death now added a cold finality to anything it might have become. For the first time, Abby was glad George was away because she didn't know how he would take it.

"How's Ma?" Thomas asked, washing his hands in the sink.

"She seems alright."

"Alright?"

"Better, I'd say."

"Did you get the medicine?"

"Yeah."

"Good."

Without another word, he walked out, plodding toward the foyer. It was after midnight, and Abby knew he probably had to work the next morning. Moments later, she felt a chilly draft and heard the front door close. He was gone. Standing alone in the kitchen, she dropped her head and fell into a fit of quiet sobbing.

36

The cold spell continued like a scourge upon the city. While the mayor had declared a weather emergency, the real crisis was the oil shortage. Anyone could handle severe temperatures if they had heat. Cars wouldn't start and pipes froze up. With the schools closed, kids in the poorer neighborhoods wandered the streets. A few people, mostly elderly, had been found dead in their apartments from hypothermia.

The beauty of winter was long gone. Icicles hung from roofs and gutters; smoke from chimneys hung in the air like a bitter fog. In past years, leftover decorations from Christmas brought some festive color to the grayness of January. Now everything just looked bleak.

Thomas drove along the harbor toward Jeffries Point. At seven in the morning, the dockyards were already bustling. Cranes hoisted pallets of cargo; sparks flew from welders. But for the first time in months, he saw more civilian vessels in port than military ones. He didn't know if it was a good sign, or if it meant the Navy was running out of ships to send overseas.

He passed Bethlehem Steel and turned up a side street of plain wooden rowhouses. The curbs were covered in snow, so he cut the wheel and made a spot. Getting out, he stepped carefully and watched for ice. He was anxious and didn't want to fall. While he dreaded what he had to do, he also knew there was no one at the station more equipped to do it.

The door had no doorbell, so he knocked. Moments later, it opened, and Vin Labadini looked out. His chin was scruffy, and he had on gray coveralls, boots, and a flat cap. Thomas knew he was headed to work.

"Nolan?"

"Vin. Can we talk?"

Labadini looked up and down the street.

"Sure," he said, and he waved Thomas in.

Inside was a small parlor with a couch, rocking chair, and Philco console radio. The only thing new Thomas saw was a table with some family photos and a model ship. He had been there once before to identify Labadini for a meat robbery. For some reason, he had lied and told the detective it was the wrong guy. There were days he wished he hadn't. That favor had led to an association with Labadini that he had come to regret.

"Is your father home?" Thomas asked.

"No. He went out hunting U-boats last night."

"How's he like the picket patrol?"

Labadini's expression sharpened. Like any thug, his instincts were good enough to know Thomas hadn't come to chat.

"What do you want, Nolan?"

"I've got some unfortunate news."

"Then let's hear it."

"Your sister was found last night under the Neptune Street Bridge. Dead."

The room filled with a tense silence. For the first few seconds, Labadini was strangely calm, but it didn't last.

"Bastard!"

He smacked a ceramic statue off the table, and it shattered on the floor.

"It wasn't him," Thomas said.

"How the hell do you know?"

"He's gone."

"Whaddya mean gone?"

Labadini punched the coat rack, and it broke in two.

"I told you the black unit was going to Ireland," Thomas said. "I saw the trucks leave last week."

Labadini stood with his fists clenched. His face twitched, and his nostrils were flared. Thomas couldn't tell if he was ready to explode or break down in tears.

"This is your fault!"

Thomas froze.

"What?"

"It's your fault. I told you to tell that bastard to stay away from her!"

"I can't tell a soldier to—"

"You son of a bitch!"

As Labadini came toward him, Thomas backed up. He lowered his hand, pushed aside his coat, and undid his holster.

"Vin, please, don't do anything stupid," he said.

They had fought before, and Thomas had beaten him, but he wasn't sure he could do it again. As a boxer, he knew that skills and determination were no match for rage.

"You lousy mick!"

Just as Thomas went to pull his gun, the front door opened. They both glanced over, and Mr. Labadini stepped in. He was short and thin, with beady eyes and a humble expression.

"What's this about?" he shouted in a thick accent.

Instantly, Labadini collected himself.

"Pa, I got terrible news," he said and then he looked at Thomas. "Go!"

With his heart pounding, Thomas slowly walked across the room, not taking his eyes off Labadini. The moment he got near the door, he darted out and felt a huge relief. It was the first time in weeks that he was glad to be back in the cold.

As he got into the cruiser, he considered coming back with more officers. But it would have been more about pride than procedure. His association with Labadini was already questionable, and there was no purpose in arresting someone who was grieving. He was just glad he didn't have to shoot him.

......

SEATED AT HIS DESK, Thomas looked out to the narrow streets outside Maverick Square. Plumes of smoke rose from the roofs of all the homes, creating a haze of gray. He could tell by the color that most of them were burning coal.

Someone knocked.

"Nolan?"

When he saw it was the captain, he stood up.

"Capt.," he said.

"You busy?"

Thomas didn't know whether to say yes or no.

"What can I do?"

"We've got a bread donation coming in from Charlestown. Can you take it over to the Salvation Army?"

"Why can't they?"

"They don't want anyone to know where it's from or people will expect it."

"Okay."

"Also, some kids just raided Krensky's on Meridian Street."

"I'll send someone over to get a report."

Vitti nodded and walked away.

The holiday lull was over. Most schools were still closed, but everyone was back to work. The new government ration list had just come out and was causing panic. People were buying up goods to stockpile, and criminals were stealing them to sell on the black market. The station had had more calls for canned fruits and vegetables theft that week than for anything else.

Hearing a rumble, Thomas looked out to see a truck with "Bond

Bread Company" on the side. He put on his coat and hat and grabbed some keys off the wall. As he went down the stairwell, he cringed at the temperature change. He burst out the back door, and a heavyset man was unloading crates of bread.

"How much you got?" Thomas asked.

"Four hundred loaves."

"Will they fit in a cruiser?"

"They'll have to."

The driver had a dolly, but the bread seemed light enough to carry. Thomas opened the trunk, and they filled it up, putting the rest in the back seat.

"Thanks."

"Anytime," the man said.

Thomas got in the car and started it, rubbing his hands as he waited for the heat to come on.

The Salvation Army was only four blocks away on Saratoga Street. The brick building looked like a school and probably had been mistaken for one by passersby. In a neighborhood that was almost entirely Catholic, no one knew what the organization did. Abby said they sometimes worked alongside the MWDC; their mother called them "Protestant evangelizers." Either way, they volunteered at hospitals and raised money for the poor. Since the start of the cold snap, they had been sheltering families across the city.

When Thomas arrived, he got out and left the cruiser running. He knocked on the door, and a plump woman with dark hair and glasses opened it.

"Yes, officer?"

"Bread," he muttered.

It seemed abrupt, but it was hard to speak with his lips frozen.

"Can you bring it to the side door?"

He nodded and returned to the car. He backed it down a narrow alleyway where another woman was waiting by the door.

"Afternoon," he said, getting out.

"We're so grateful for your help."

"We do our best."

His sarcasm was subtle enough that she didn't catch it. The last thing he wanted to be doing was delivering bread.

He opened the trunk, and they both took as many as they could carry.

"Lead the way," he said.

He followed her inside, and they went down a dark corridor. At the end, they walked through a set of double doors into a room the size of a gymnasium. Cots were set up in rows from wall to wall, with bags, suitcases, and other belongings around them.

"How many people are staying here?"

"As of today, we have twenty-eight families," the lady said.

Over at a table, a dozen women sat talking and drinking tea. Some held newborns, but any kids that could walk were running around and playing. Thomas didn't see any men, which wasn't unusual. The war economy was booming, and anyone could find a job. Most people were going into shelters because there was no oil for heat, not because they had no money.

They left the bread in a small kitchen, and Thomas went back out for more. He put four loaves on the front seat and carried the rest in. It took six trips, and by the time he was done, he was winded.

"Thank you so much, officer."

"You're welcome," he replied, wiping his forehead.

Watching the kids, he got sentimental, remembering the magic and excitement of his youth. But he also felt a wave of sadness. As a cop, he had seen a lot of suffering, and nothing troubled him more than the plight of children.

"Would you like some coffee or tea?"

Thomas snapped out of his thoughts.

"No, thanks," he said, embarrassed. "I gotta get back to the station."

He turned to go, and a boy plowed into him, hitting him in the groin. While he gasped at the pain, he was more stunned by who it was.

"Hey, pal," he said.

Clarence Morris gazed up, his expression a vague mix of surprise, suspicion, and fear. His clothes were dirty, and he had a scab on his forehead. In the distance, his friends stood taunting him. Thomas gave them a sharp look, and they all stopped.

"Sorry, Officer," the boy blurted.

Then he turned around and scurried away.

37

Abby came out onto Bennington Street and felt a blast of cold air. She winced and kept going, holding her collar together and staying close to the storefronts. As she approached the tailor, she was relieved the lights were still on. Finally, she had a reason to go in. She had lost weight, and her dress for the gala didn't fit.

When she walked in, Mr. Gittell looked up from his sewing machine.

"Abigail," he said.

With his Yiddish accent, her name always sounded funny. Arthur used to imitate him until she had asked him not to.

"Arthur wrote me," she said.

"He wrote to me as well."

She almost asked if it was a V-Mail or a real letter but realized it would sound petty.

"He was ill for some time," Mr. Gittell added.

"I know. Dengue fever. Ten days in the hospital."

"He'll have some stories to tell."

They stood facing each other at the counter. She hadn't seen him since before Christmas, and he looked older. Like anyone who shared a love for the same person, they had a special bond. But it was also hard to see each other.

"How can I help you?"

She opened a paper bag and took out a sleek black dress. She had bought it at Filene's for her graduation, but the school had announced that bare backs weren't allowed.

"Lovely," he said, running his hands along the fabric. "Special occasion?"

"An event. The United War Fund."

"No fit?"

"It's loose here," she said, pointing at the waist and bust.

He peered up.

"I take it in?"

"That'd be swell."

"Pick up tomorrow," he said.

Abby left the shop and went back out into the cold. With the sun almost down, the temperature had dropped even more. The only people out were some guys in front of the pool hall and two old ladies carrying shopping bags. Otherwise, the sidewalks were empty.

She waited for a trolley to pass and then darted across the street. Walking into the corner market, she saw Mr. Schultz standing on a stool. He had moved things around since the last time she was in. The canned goods, coffee, and sugar were all on the highest shelf. Everything else was below. Considering many shops were now keeping their rationed goods in the back, it seemed a polite way of discouraging theft.

"Mr. Schultz," she said gently, not wanting to startle him.

He glanced back.

"Abigail."

He stepped down and turned around, wiping his hands.

"Sorry to bother you," she said.

"No bother. I'm finished."

"Would you have any butter by chance?"

"Hopefully in the morning. All I have now is Nucoa."

Abby grabbed a loaf of crusty bread from the pile on the deli case and a pack of Wrigley's chewing gum from the box next to the register. She was sure she needed more, but she hadn't come in to shop.

Mr. Schultz walked around the counter.

"Anything else?" he asked.

"That'll be it."

"How's Mrs. Nolan?"

"Fine. She was delighted you shoveled our steps on Tuesday."

"I was just passing by."

He rang in the items, and Abby reached into her purse.

"So cold out," he remarked, but that wasn't the reason her hand was shaking.

"Dreadful. I would've stayed home except I had to get a dress tailored."

She handed him a quarter, and he dropped it in the tray.

"A special event?" he asked, and it was the opening she had hoped for.

"Actually...she wanted to invite you to the United War Fund gala this Saturday."

Mr. Schultz stopped and looked up.

"Gala?"

"At Copley Plaza."

When he hesitated, she worried it was too forward. Then a smile broke across his face.

"I'd be delighted."

The relief she felt was like sinking into a warm bath. From the moment she had left her house, she had been anxious about asking. But she knew that anything good or worthwhile required taking a risk. If her mother was ever going to escape her gloom, she had to get out; if she was ever going to love again, she had to at least know who was available to love.

"It starts at seven," she said.

"Seven o'clock."

......

. . .

ABBY WALKED in the door and took off her boots. By now, the mat was covered with slush, a pile of boots, shoes, and socks beside it. Her mother used to put down a towel, but the floors were already warped and cracked from years of water and wear.

"Abby!"

She looked over and saw Chickie reading on the sofa. Considering schools were still closed, she knew it wasn't for homework. Chickie loved books, something Mrs. Nolan had encouraged.

"Where's Gramma?"

Chickie looked up to the ceiling. Abby handed her the gum, putting her finger to her lips. Connie and her mother didn't want her to have anything sweet, worried it would rot her teeth.

"Where's Dada?"

When Chickie pointed, Abby walked into the kitchen, and she could smell something in the oven. Over on the counter, she saw three loaves of bread. With a sour smirk, she put hers next to them.

Thomas burst out from the basement door.

"That goddamn flue needs to be cleaned!"

He had black smudges on his shirt, and he reeked of smoke and coal.

"Nice to see you too."

He walked over, turned on the faucet, and scrubbed his hands.

"Have you seen Connie?" he asked.

"I just got home. Where's Ma?"

"Coming!"

Her mother came down the stairs and into the kitchen. She had bathed that morning and wore a nice dress.

"Ma, that flue really needs to be cleaned."

"I'll call Mr. Donato in the morning. Won't you stay for dinner?"

"Not tonight. Thanks."

"I made Shepherd's pie."

"Thanks, but Connie's still not home," he said, and then he called out, "C'mon, Chickie. Time to go."

Chickie moaned, and Thomas went to get her. Mrs. Nolan got mitts out of the drawer and opened the oven. As she took out the pan, Abby leaned forward to see. The mashed potatoes looked good, but she worried about the meat underneath it. With beef expensive and hard to find, her mother had been sneaking in substitutes. The week before, she had used kidneys and hearts in a stew, which had almost made Abby vomit.

"Would you move those, please?"

Abby took the loaves off the counter and put them in the pantry. Although there was enough space on the shelf, she moved things around like there wasn't. She wanted some time to check the liquor. Seeing that the bottle of gin hadn't been touched was a relief. If the rum was a little lower, it was probably because her mother had put a splash or two in the dish, something she had always done.

When Abby came back out, she heard Chickie and Thomas arguing.

"Where'd you get all the bread?" she asked.

Her mother nodded toward the other room.

"He said someone donated it to the station."

Chickie stamped her foot so hard they felt it in the kitchen. Abby and her mother looked at each other cringing.

"Mr. Schultz said he won't have any butter until tomorrow."

"A wasted trip. I'm sorry," Mrs. Nolan said.

"I didn't just go to buy something."

She said it with enough emphasis that her mother turned around.

"You didn't?"

"I invited him to the gala."

Mrs. Nolan's face dropped.

"You did not."

"I did too—"

"Goddammit! Let's go!"

The roar of Thomas' voice made them both jump. Mrs. Nolan stormed into the next room, and Abby ran after her.

"Here, here," she said.

Chickie stood pouting with her arms crossed. She had matured in many ways, but when she got angry, she went back to acting like a little girl.

"Chickie, darling, it's time to go home," Mrs. Nolan said, and then she turned to her son. "And we don't use that language in this house! You hear me?"

Thomas nodded, staring down with obvious remorse. As Abby watched, she was filled with emotion, feeling inspired. Despite her mother's problems, she still had the pride, confidence, and self-respect to take charge.

"Now get your coats on!" Mrs. Nolan said, and Thomas and Chickie marched over to the foyer. "Hats too. I don't care that it's only next door."

Thomas took his daughter's hand, and they left, gently closing the door behind them. Glancing out the window, Abby watched as their dark figures went up the Ciarlones' front steps and disappeared in the shadow of the porch.

"What's wrong with him?" Abby asked.

"He's just tired. We're all tired."

38

Thomas turned into the garage. He thought it was closed until he saw movement in the office. Six weeks before, the place had been full of cars waiting for repairs, and now it was almost empty. A lot had changed since the tire bust, which had been the day before the Cocoanut Grove fire. At the time, Thomas had just been grateful he and his sister had survived. Now he was starting to see that night as some great dividing line in his life. He didn't know if there was some lesson he had to learn or some atonement he had to make. But after seeing Clarence Morris and his mother in the shelter, he had to do something.

When he walked in, three men looked over. They were crouched around a desk playing either blackjack or poker—Thomas had never cared enough about cards to learn the difference. There was a pile of change in the middle and a few crumpled-up dollar bills, nothing that would have qualified as illegal gambling. A cigar was smoldering in the ashtray, and a bottle of something hard was beside it.

"Sorry to interrupt."

"Ante up, Officer."

Thomas grinned.

"Where's the owner?" he asked.

"The owner lives in Maine."

"Jack Morris?"

The men all looked at each other.

"Jack was just the manager," the heavyset guy answered. "Now it's me till he gets back."

"Back from where?"

"He's been in the Charles Street Jail."

"Still?"

"He didn't make bail. His trial is next Friday, but he's been locked up since Thanksgiving."

The bust had been the day after, but it wasn't important.

"Is that why the lot is empty?"

"Nope. There just ain't much work at the moment."

"Why is that?"

"We can't find parts. Tires are impossible to get."

A skinny guy with a mustache looked up.

"No one's got gas. Who needs repairs when no one can drive?"

"Thanks," Thomas said.

"Anytime."

He walked out, got in the cruiser, and sped away. As he drove through Day Square, he looked over to the restaurant where he had eaten with DiMarco. Everywhere he went now, he was reminded of someone who was gone from his life.

He continued down Neptune Road and crossed over the marsh to Wood Island Park. As he approached the Army checkpoint, he slowed down and rolled down his window. A young soldier walked over, and Thomas remembered him from before.

"Well, well, if it ain't the tree thief."

Thomas rubbed his chin, trying to hide a grin.

"Can you prove it?" he joked.

"What can I do for you, Officer?"

"I wanted to see Major Holdsworth."

Thomas expected him to ask if he had an appointment. Instead, the soldier yelled over to his partner, who got on the field radio and then, moments later, held up his thumb.

"Pull into the base," he said, leaning against the car and pointing. "The Major's in the command barracks on the left."

Thomas drove ahead and pulled into a lot of frozen mud that had a few jeeps and trucks. Getting out, he walked toward the building, and the major greeted him at the door.

"Sergeant," he said, and they shook. "Come in outta the cold."

"I'm used to it."

"Well, I'm not."

Thomas walked into a small office that had a desk with a typewriter, some filing cabinets, and not much else. Everything about the military seemed plain and clinical.

"Not from the Northeast?" Thomas asked.

"Tallahassee, originally. I was stationed in Texas for eight years before the war. What can I do for you?"

"We're looking into the death of a young woman. She was found under the Neptune Road overpass."

Thomas was careful with his words, which was why he didn't call it an investigation. He knew the Army didn't like getting involved in scandals.

"That's unfortunate."

"We believe she was…in a relationship with one of your soldiers."

The major stared at him, his hands on his hips.

"Is this about that negro private?"

Thomas was glad he remembered. It saved him the awkwardness of having to say it.

"Yes, sir."

"That unit shipped out a week ago. They'd be in Northern Ireland by now."

"I know. I just—"

"You suspect foul play?"

"We don't have the autopsy report yet, but no."

"Suicide?"

"I don't think so. She had been kicked out of her house."

Thomas didn't have to explain why. The major got the implication.

"I wish I could help. I can assure you she's never been out here to the base."

"Thanks. That's good to know."

"Speaking of young women," Holdsworth said, his expression changing. "There was a girl out at Deer Island prison last week. One of my corporals gave her a lift home."

"That's not our jurisdiction."

"She lives in East Boston. Civilians really shouldn't be walking out there at night. If the cold doesn't get 'em, one of the trucks might. It's dark out there."

"I can put a call into the chief in Winthrop," Thomas said. "Any idea what she was doing?"

"She said she brings clothes and food to the prisoners."

"Prisoners?"

"The prisoners of war. The Italians."

Thomas felt the hair on the back of his neck stand up.

"And it wasn't the first time," the major added. "The corporal has seen her on the road before."

"Thank you, Major."

......

THOMAS ROLLED up to the bakery and looked inside. Several girls were behind the counter, but he didn't see Connie. He never knew when she was working. With his own crazy schedule, he couldn't blame her, but it still made him uneasy. He punched the gas and sped down Bennington Street.

When he got to Winthrop, he drove across the neck toward Point Shirley. The small summer community was a ghost town in winter, something he still couldn't get used to. Pulsifer's Market was open a few hours a day, but the only person he saw was a mailman, who squinted in the breeze with a bag over his back.

He continued another half mile to Deer Island. As he passed the prison, the yard was empty, the land around it dry and windswept. The road down to the coast narrowed and got bumpier. In the distance, he saw a couple of structures that hadn't been there before. But compared to the base on Wood Island Park, Fort Dawes was more like a camp.

He approached the Army checkpoint where two soldiers stood leaning against sandbags, their faces completely covered. As one of them walked over, Thomas jumped at the crack of gunfire.

"You're gonna have to go back, sir. We're testing the—"

"I just wanted to talk to one of the corporals."

"No one's permitted," he said before adding, "not even the police. I'm sorry."

Thomas appreciated the courtesy. No officer liked being included along with civilians.

"Thanks."

He made a tight U-turn, the car bouncing over the rocks, and headed back. When the road surface got better, he could have gone faster. But he took his time, gazing across the bay at the airport and city. The sun was going down, although it was hard to tell with the clouds. Inside, he felt numb, and it wasn't just from the cold.

After he passed the prison, he saw someone walking ahead. As he got closer, he realized it was a woman. He pulled alongside her and reached across to roll down the window.

"Connie!"

She turned calmly like she expected it to be him.

"Get in," he said, and she did.

He drove on, and they didn't speak. Instead of going straight toward the mainland, he turned down Bay View Avenue. At the end, they came around the bend, and he stopped in front of the cottage. He shut off the engine and gazed across the harbor to East Boston. They sat for a moment in silence until, finally, he cleared his throat.

"Your husband died in Greece, is that right?" he asked.

"Thomas, it's not—"

He whacked the steering wheel.

"Then what is it?"

"Yes, yes, he was killed in Greece. I told you so," she said, her tone defiant.

"Who've you been visiting out there?"

"I bring food and clothing to the soldiers, that's all. A lot of people do it."

"*Soldiers*? Those are our enemies."

"They're still human beings."

"Don't lie to me."

"Thomas, I—"

"Because I'll find out."

"It's my brother!" she shouted.

Thomas looked over, and their eyes met. When she started to cry, he was hit by a wave of guilt. For weeks, he had lived with a suspicion that tore at his heart and soul. In some ways, he had accused her without evidence which, as a police officer, he knew was wrong.

"I didn't know you had a brother," he said.

"Lorenzo is his name."

"Why didn't you ever mention him?"

"It was too difficult," she said, and he could hear the agony in her voice. "He's six years older. When I was in school, he got swept up in the madness of Mussolini. He was in the *Gioventù Italiana del Littorio*, the fascist youth party. When he turned eighteen, he joined the National Fascist Party. My father wouldn't have it. He ordered him to leave the house. My brother never came back. I knew he had joined the Army. By the time the war broke out, I was living with Joseph in Malta..."

Hearing her former husband's name was always uncomfortable.

"How'd you know he was here?"

"My aunt, Maria's sister, wrote to me in November. She was told that his unit had surrendered in North Africa. I had no idea they would be brought to America. There's a woman at the bakery. She had been taking food to the prisoners and mailing letters. One of them asked her if she knew Concetta Ferrara. She said no, but she knew I had been married before. So she asked me my former name. You can imagine how shocked we both were."

"How is he?"

"He was badly wounded in the leg. He can walk, but he's in terrible pain."

Thomas nodded, staring down in quiet shame.

He had the urge to apologize but didn't know how to. So instead, he opened the car door.

"Where're you going?" she asked.

"To see if we left any kerosene here."

He got out and crossed the lawn, the ground cold and hard. When he got to the front porch, he knelt down, pulled on a shingle, and a key fell out. He opened the door and walked in. The rooms were dark, and the air was cold and still.

He went into the pantry and felt along the floor for a canister. All he found was a mop and bucket, some paint cans, and an old pair of ice skates. But he wasn't disappointed. He knew they probably hadn't left any oil behind. At the end of each season, they turned off the water, cleared the icebox, and took everything they could use at home.

In some ways, he had just wanted a reason to come by the cottage. It was the source of his best memories and his happiest times. Standing in the kitchen, he glanced out to the yard, thinking about those long, lazy summers. He remembered when, at ten years old, George had fallen from the tree and broken his collarbone or the time Abby had gotten stung by a hornet and her face had swelled up. In the darkness, Thomas could imagine seeing his father sitting in his chair drinking cream soda. In the silence, he could hear his mother whistling in the garden. Twenty years old seemed too young to miss childhood. But sometimes he thought that, given the chance, he'd go back to it in a minute.

The floor creaked, and he spun around.

"Connie?"

"I didn't want to wait outside."

They drifted together back out into the parlor. The cold was uncomfortable, but the solitude somehow made up for it. It was a cloudless night, the first in weeks. With the moonlight coming through the curtains, he realized he never saw windows without blackout shades anymore. And he was never alone with Connie enough to remember how much he loved her.

"We could start a fire," she said. "Do you have to work in the morning?"

"What about Chickie?"

"She's sleeping at your mother's. She invited Olive to stay over."

Thomas smiled.

"I'll go get matches," he said.

"I'll go upstairs and get blankets."

39

Abby leaned over the sheet pan, her smock covered in white powder. The kitchen was so cold the sugar wasn't sticking to the pastries. The butter had to be warmed by the oven, and the lard which sat in tubs in the basement, was frozen solid. Abby didn't know the exact temperature, but when she got up to check, it was so low the thermometer on the back window had stopped working.

Connie finally showed up, bursting through the back door with a scarf around her face. Although she was late, Eve would never say anything because she was afraid of her.

"How was the sleepover?" Connie asked, unbuttoning her coat.

"Olive said she hadn't been so warm in ages."

"Poor things."

Connie put on an apron and tied her hair up in a ponytail. Her face was flushed, and she had faint splotches on her neck. It could have been from the cold, but Abby also knew she and Thomas hadn't come home.

As Connie walked out to the front, Eve came in. She asked Carlo for more rye bread and then looked at Abby.

"It's pretty slow. You can go home if you'd like."

Abby glanced at the clock, and it was almost eleven. Most Saturdays, she needed the hours, but with the gala that night, she had things to do.

"Sure," she said.

As she took off her hair net, Eve walked over.

"I'll put you in till noon," she whispered.

"Thanks, that'd be swell."

Eve had been nicer since Angela's death, probably out of guilt. Rita had announced it to the staff Thursday morning, and even the girls who hadn't known her had cried.

Abby washed her hands and got her things. Going out the back door, she cringed from the cold, and the dry air made her throat tickle.

She walked around to the street, the sidewalk covered in snow and ice. Her house was only five minutes away, but when she saw a streetcar, she waved it down.

She got home to find Chickie, Olive, and Alfie standing in the yard, their clothes damp. They had built an igloo, a snowman, and some structure that was either another igloo or a tortoise. Mrs. Nolan had taken them to the movies, bowling, and even the YMCA, which was now open around the clock for families. But children were getting bored, and parents were getting frustrated.

"Where're your gloves?" Abby asked.

When Chickie pointed, she saw that one of the snowmen was wearing them.

"He doesn't need them like you do."

"It's a girl," Chickie said.

Abby made a disapproving frown and then walked into the house. It was warmer than usual, and she worried the furnace was up too high. She put down her pocketbook and undid her coat, hanging her scarf and hat on the hook. She had to wear so much clothing now that when she took it off, she felt lighter.

"Ma?" she called out.

"Up here."

She kicked off her boots and left them by the door in a puddle of dirty slush. Walking up the stairs, she clutched the banister. With her socks wet, she didn't want to slip. She turned into the bedroom and stopped.

"You're home early," her mother said.

Seated at the vanity, her mother wore a long purple gown. Her hair was done up in Victory Rolls, and she had pearls around her neck. In the reflection of the mirror, Abby could see she had makeup on too, red lipstick and dark mascara.

"You know the gala doesn't start until seven?"

Her mother stood up and turned around.

"I haven't worn these shoes in years. How do they look?" she asked, sticking out her foot.

As Abby smiled, she got emotional.

"Ma, you look beautiful."

"I wish I felt it."

"You should because it's true."

And it was. With her lean figure, dark hair, and blue eyes, Mrs. Nolan had always been attractive. Abby remembered an uncle telling her how the biggest livery stable owner in East Boston had been determined for his son to marry her. She didn't know if it was just family lore, but it was romantic to think that her father, an Irish orphan, had won her mother in the end.

"I suppose I should take it all off until later," her mother said, reaching to undo her necklace.

"Why's it so warm in here?"

"Your brother brought us some more coal. The Brits are staying over with Chickie again. Connie's going to mind them."

The Brits. She said it out of affection, not ridicule. They all loved Olive and Alfie. The night before, Abby had made cookies with them and Chickie, using honey because they were out of sugar. Then they all listened to *The Cisco Kid*, and Abby had fallen asleep before they had.

"Better not spoil them," Abby said.

As she turned to leave, she noticed her mother's expression change.

"Ma?"

"When I heard they were going to Iowa, I considered fostering them."

By the hesitation in her eyes, Abby knew she wasn't telling the whole truth.

"Considered?"

"I've already contacted the Children's Aid Association."

......

THE BALLROOM at Copley Plaza was as grand and elegant as a palace banquet hall. The endless round tables were covered with lace tablecloths; the mahogany chairs had silk cushions. Crystal chandeliers hung from the ceilings, and the walls were covered in ornate wallpaper. On one side of the room was a hand-carved bar where men in tuxedoes served cocktails and glasses of wine, and on the other, a band was playing. A large banner hung over the stage, "United War Fund Drive." Abby couldn't keep track of all the service organizations, but Frances said the event had raised more than sixty thousand dollars.

Abby sat with her mother and Mr. Schultz, who looked dashing in his three-piece suit. They had just finished a dinner of roast tenderloin, potatoes, and carrots. As the waiters collected the plates and utensils, a few couples got up to dance, but most sat around talking.

The room was filled with important people, including Mayor Tobin and the president of Harvard University. There were men in military uniforms, and women wearing diamond brooches and ruby earrings. Just at Abby's table, there was a banker, a physician, and a stockbroker. She had seen some senior MWDC officers too, but none of them had recognized her.

In their small corner of East Boston, her family was considered respectable, maybe even upper class. But at Copley Plaza, they were commoners. Since they had arrived, her mother had been anxious, her leg shaking. But she hadn't had any alcohol. To make her less self-conscious, Mr. Schultz had gotten her a Roy Rogers in a highball glass. Since picking them up, he had treated them both like ladies, something Abby was sure her father would have approved of.

When she glanced back, Frances waved, her hand in a white glove. She was sitting a few tables away and not with her mother, which Abby found strange. Instead of a tailored dress, she wore a loose gown, and for good reason.

The band stopped playing, and the musicians left to take a break. Mrs. Farrington walked out onto the stage, and Abby wasn't surprised. Frances' mother seemed to be at the center of everything.

"Ladies and gentlemen," she said, and the room went quiet. "Thank you all for coming out on this dreadfully cold night to support the efforts of the United War Fund…"

When Abby crossed her arms, her mother tapped her shoulder with a scolding look.

"First, I'd like to announce that, in light of the current oil crisis, our organization, in partnership with the Boston Committee on Public Safety, will be providing funds to keep shelters open across the city for families without heat."

The audience clapped.

"This has been a difficult year for all Americans. At times, we suffer in ways that are not always obvious. For me, one example that comes to mind is a friend who is here with us tonight. The summer before last, her husband lost his life in a crane accident that was very much a consequence of our country's preparations for war…"

Abby froze.

"Now her son is serving bravely with the U.S. Army. Even after all she has sacrificed, she still finds the time to sell War Bonds, plant Victory Gardens, and knit clothing for Bundles for Britain, an organization very much committed to alleviating the suffering of our civilian allies across the Atlantic."

The room broke into a wild applause. But Abby didn't blush or panic. Mrs. Farrington hadn't said her mother's name, so no one knew who they were.

"Some notable mentions for tonight's gala," Mrs. Farrington went on. "Lester Amory, Adjutant General of the Massachusetts National Guard is here with us, as well as Major Victor Holdsworth of the 241st Coast Artillery Regiment. We'd also like to recognize the generous donation from..."

Abby listened, but nothing could match the touching tribute to her family. When she looked over, her mother had a smile that went beyond mere pleasure or satisfaction. She looked happy for the first time in months.

Once the speech was done, the band returned and went into a light waltz. Frances scurried over holding a glass of wine, and Abby could see she was tipsy.

"Hello, Mrs. Nolan," she said before turning to Abby. "Come say hello to Richard Alden. He's back on leave."

"Richard Alden?"

"You met him last year at my house."

Abby hesitated, not wanting to leave her mother. Then Mr. Schultz stood up, gave a slight bow, and extended his hand.

"Care for a dance, Mrs. Nolan?"

In those few seconds, it felt like the world stopped.

"Why, I'd be delighted."

40

THE TEMPERATURE HAD RISEN TO THIRTY DEGREES FOR THE FIRST TIME in weeks. The weather service was calling it a "warm spell," ironic considering it had snowed four inches the night before. With the tires on most of the cruisers now bald, Thomas took the Ford to work. But it didn't help much. The streets were awful. On the way, he had seen three accidents, including a collision between a trolley and a truck loaded with scrap metal. He would have stopped, but cops had already been on the scene.

When he walked into the station, the secretary was on the phone. She said something to the caller, covered the receiver, and looked up.

"The captain would like to see you," she said.

"Thanks."

He continued through the doors and went down the hallway. He hoped it was about Angela Labadini, the autopsy report confirming she had died of exposure. But he knew it was probably about the new driving restrictions. With the governor's policy of Gasless Sundays, OPA agents were pulling people over, and departments were expected to help.

When he got to the captain's office, he stopped in the doorway. A

State Police officer was seated across from the captain. He was tall, with wide shoulders and a buzz cut.

"Capt.?" Thomas said.

"Sergeant. Please, sit."

Thomas walked in and took the only other chair. He knew something was wrong because Vitti looked anxious, rubbing the scar on his face.

"This is Lieutenant Calderwood," he said.

The man nodded but didn't offer to shake hands. He opened up his briefcase and took out a folder, flipping through some papers.

"Sergeant Nolan," he said, "we've come into possession of a number of gas ration coupons that were used by you."

Thomas frowned.

"Who doesn't use gas coupons?"

"The ones in question have been forged."

"What makes you think they're mine?"

"We have the serial numbers and records from the service stations where they were redeemed. You do own a black Ford Coupe, registration number 159-441?"

"Yes, but look," Thomas said, getting defensive, "we come across contraband all the time. Last week, I caught some kids with enough sugar rations to feed an army…"

As he tried to explain, justify, and make excuses, the lieutenant just stared.

"You can dispute the allegations, but it will open up a full investigation into the matter."

Thomas' heart sank, and he looked over at Vitti.

"Thank you, Lieutenant," the captain said. "I can take it from here."

Calderwood put everything away and got up. Without another word, he walked out, and the room went silent.

"I'm sorry," Vitti said.

"What's next?"

"A suspension."

Thomas sank into the chair.

"But—"

"Thomas, I have no choice. The feds are cracking down on the OPA, the OPA is cracking down on the State Police, and the State Police are cracking down on us. Shit rolls downhill."

"For how long?"

"One week. It won't affect your job. You're already a sergeant for chrissakes. Once the war's over, no one will even remember."

Thomas had to chuckle. Everywhere he went, people talked about life after the war like some future salvation, a time when all sins would be forgiven or forgotten, and the world would live in peace.

"When?"

"What's on your docket?"

"A lot."

"Then you tell me."

As Thomas sat thinking, he remembered something.

"I'm supposed to be in court Friday for the tire case," he said.

"Then how about next week?"

"But I'd rather not show up."

"If you don't, it will likely get quashed. The DA can't prosecute without the lead officer."

"That's my hope."

Their eyes locked.

"You don't think that case is solid?"

"I think I made a mistake," Thomas said, keeping it vague.

Vitti looked confused, but he didn't ask any more questions.

"Okay, okay," he said. "The courts are overloaded anyway. We've got other things to worry about. So you'll take the suspension?"

"Sure. I could use a week off."

Vitti opened up a folder, turned it around, and pointed to a line. Leaning forward, Thomas scanned the small print, but he didn't bother reading it. He had suspended men before and knew the routine. After he had scribbled his name, he felt something that, while not quite relief, seemed to lessen the shame.

THOMAS DROVE through the streets in a stupor. Despite the suspension, it was hard to think he wasn't working. He was still in uniform, and the captain hadn't taken his pistol. In many ways, the job was his life now, and the idea of a week off terrified him.

Any humiliation he felt was more personal than technical. Vitti was right when he said no one would remember. The department had been a mess since the start of the war. With all the new policies, rules, and responsibilities, it had to be strict sometimes. Thomas had seen men get suspended for everything from tardiness to having their ties too loose.

He accepted the punishment, and he didn't blame the captain. He knew he shouldn't have been using confiscated ration tickets anyway. The station had plenty for officers to take. He had gotten cocky, something Coach Fidler had warned was always the downfall of any good boxer.

Still, he couldn't escape the feeling that he had been betrayed. So when he passed by Sonny's and saw Labadini out front, he didn't have the sense or self-control to keep driving. Slowing down, he turned at the corner and slid into a spot. He shoved his gun under the seat and put his badge in the glove compartment. Whatever happened, he didn't want to be accused of police brutality.

He got out and stormed down the sidewalk, so overcome by rage that a lady walking by looked scared. As he approached the bar, he knew Labadini's friends could tell because one of them pointed, and they all turned.

Then something happened.

"Hey, Thomas!"

Hearing the voice, he stopped. In the fury of the moment, he thought he had hallucinated. But when he looked over to Maverick Station, he saw a figure that he knew was no dream or delusion. All at once, his body went limp.

"G...George?" he muttered.

His brother ran toward him across the street, a duffel bag over his shoulder. One of his arms was in a sling and his other hand was wrapped in a bandage. They hugged awkwardly in the shadow of the lamplight. For two brothers who had never gotten along, it was the most heartfelt embrace they had ever shared.

"What happened?" Thomas asked, gasping.

"Broken arm and frostbite."

"You're back."

"For now. When the captain heard I'd be out of commission for a few months, he gave me leave to recover. I hopped a troopship from Anchorage to Seattle, caught a C-47 to Camp Dix in New Jersey, and a train up from New York."

Thomas shook his head, too shocked to speak.

"Hey, look at this," George said.

He reached into his coat pocket and took out a medal. It had the Coat of Arms of the United States and a red, white, and blue ribbon.

"Distinguished Service Medal," he said before Thomas could ask.

"How—"

"I'll tell you. But get me outta this cold. You driving?"

"Right there."

Thomas nodded toward the Ford, which was sticking out from the corner.

"Damn. She's still kicking?"

"New tires too."

As they walked toward it, Thomas glanced back to Sonny's. He was relieved to see that the men had left. Going after Labadini could have ended his career or worse. He had no proof that anyone had snitched on him; he had only been looking for a scapegoat. In an instant, all that rage had been replaced by a warm gratitude for having his brother back safe.

"You wanna drive?" Thomas joked.

"You know I would try."

Thomas smiled, and they got in.

"You...you didn't write," he said, pulling out.

"I couldn't. I was lost."

"Lost?"

"Well, not lost. We were stranded. Four weeks..."

George took out a cigarette, and Thomas held the lighter for him.

"In November, me and eight guys from my unit volunteered to install a radio tower on a small island. Not an island, really. More like a volcano. Not more like. It was a volcano. You wouldn't believe how fuckin' desolate this place was."

"Why there?"

"The Army wants to put a landing strip on Amchitka, the next island over. They needed comms. We left in the middle of the night on a PT. The ride over was nuts—seventy miles in open ocean. We got knocked around somethin' fierce. It set us back almost two hours. When we finally got there, the sun was coming up. We were about a half mile from shore when we hear something. We look up and see two Jap Zeros. I don't know if they got lucky or what. We were sittin' ducks. The captain guns it and heads straight for the island. We're doing thirty knots in ten-foot seas..."

Thomas didn't know any of the lingo, but the image gave him chills.

"Suddenly, I feel my stomach in my throat. We hit rocks. Sergeant Colbert fell overboard. We never saw him again. I got knocked into the radar mast—"

"Is that how you broke your arm?"

Geroge turned with a giddy smile.

"No. That was from chasing a bird," he said.

"A bird?"

"To eat. Thomas, there's nothing on this island. Just birds. Some foxes. But I only saw one."

"I was wondering why you look so thin."

"The boat starts taking on water," George continued. "We grab anything we can and jump out. The water is freezing and rough. But it's shallow. We're wading toward the shore when the Zeros come in and start spraying us. Helmstetter was killed instantly. Ballentine took one in the shoulder. Forbes got hit in the chest bad. I put him over my shoulder and got him to the beach."

He stopped.

"He didn't make it," he said.

The emotion in his voice got Thomas choked up.

"What about the planes?"

"We were lucky. There was enough fog for cover. We thought the Zeros might circle around and come back, but they never did. We fixed up the wounded, and set up a camp in a gorge, out of the wind. We survived by eating birds. Me and Nicholson swam back to the PT and got some water jugs. But it wasn't a good idea."

"Why not?"

"He got hypothermia and died."

"Sorry," Thomas mumbled. "How'd you get rescued?"

"On New Year's Day, one of the guys spotted a recon plane. We sent up a flare. It shook its wings, so we knew they saw us. The next morning, a Navy Catalina came and got us. Now I'm home."

As he said it, they pulled up to the house.

"How're things here?" George asked. "I heard about the Cocoanut Grove fire."

"We...we were there."

"Who's 'we?'"

"Me and Abby, and some other people."

Thomas parked and shut off the engine.

"George," he said, looking over. "Sal died."

Somehow it didn't sound so terrible or tragic, or maybe he was just used to it. Either way, he was sure that after all his brother had been through it would be hard for him to be stunned by anything.

"Sal was a good guy," George said.

"That he was."

Thomas got out and grabbed the duffel bag from the backseat. As they walked up the steps, he felt like he was in a dream. He opened the door and stuck his head in. Connie was setting the table in the dining room, and Abby was lying beside the radio with Chickie and the two British kids.

"Thomas," Abby yelled, jumping up and running over. "We just got a call from the Children's Aid Association. They said Olive and Alfie can stay—"

She stopped midsentence, and her face dropped.

"What's wrong?"

"Who's that?" their mother called from the kitchen.

Thomas opened the door wider and extended his arm. The moment George stepped in, Abby fainted. Connie lunged and caught her before she fell. Their mother walked in and shrieked, throwing her arms around her son. Chickie started to cry, and Alfie and Olive just stood in the middle of the room confused.

Thomas helped Connie carry Abby over to the couch. He smacked her on both cheeks, and she came to.

"George?" she said.

"Didn't you hear? The war's over."

"Well, it is for me," their mother said.

"What happened?" Abby asked, and Connie helped her sit up.

George looked down at his cast.

"I was chasing a petrel—"

"What's a petrel?"

"A bird," Thomas said.

"I fell over a cliff and broke my arm in two places. The ulna was sticking right out of the—"

"Okay, okay," Mrs. Nolan said who always got squeamish. "Thomas, please go put some more coal on."

"Is there enough?"

"There's enough for now. We're all gonna sleep warm tonight. My boy is home."

41

Abby woke to the smell of bacon. Outside it was still dark, a light wind shaking the windows. But the house was warm, and the radiators had been creaking all night. She put on a dress and sweater and splashed cold water on her face.

When she went downstairs, George was lying on the floor beside the radio. He looked thin, almost fragile. Just seeing him without socks on made her shiver. But after what he had gone through in the Aleutians, none of them could complain about the cold.

"Our boys shot down a hundred and thirty-eight Jap planes in New Guinea."

"Is that good?" Abby asked, half-joking.

All the numbers and statistics meant nothing to her.

"Of course, it's good."

She went into the kitchen where her mother was cooking. In the back hallway, the washing tub was filled with dirty clothes. Abby couldn't help but notice that her mother always seemed happier when she was busy or had someone to take care of.

"Can I help?" she asked.

"Ask George if he wants onions in his omelet."

"I can hear you, Ma," he called. "And the answer is the more the better."

They looked at each other and smiled.

Thomas burst through the front door carrying kerosene. He kicked the snow off his boots and walked in. His face was red, and he was out of breath.

"Here's five gallons," he said, dropping the can beside the stove. "That should tide you over."

"Thank you, dear."

"Are you working today?" Abby asked.

He gave her a sharp, almost suspicious look.

"Why?"

"I just need a lift to Maverick Station, that's all."

"I'm leaving in ten minutes."

"I'll only be nine," she said.

She ran up to the bathroom and saw a green canvas bag open on the sink. It was an Army grooming kit with shaving cream, tooth powder, a comb, a razor, and even a pack of matches. After months of living alone with her mother, she had to share the house again. George had always been a menace, and she used to hate him for it. But somehow his survival had made up for all those years of antagonism. Even if she never liked him, she loved him. She never wanted him to leave again.

When she got back downstairs, George was at the dining room table. Around him was more food than Abby had seen since Thanksgiving. It would probably take him weeks to put on the weight he had lost; he had always been skinny anyway. But she had no doubt her mother would help him do it.

Glancing out the window, she saw exhaust from the car and knew Thomas was waiting. She quickly put on her coat and scarf.

"By, Ma!"

"By, deary-o," George said, mimicking their mother's voice.

Abby frowned, but she had missed his sarcasm.

She walked out and scurried down the steps. When she got into the car, Thomas pulled out before she closed the door. For the first few minutes, they drove in silence.

"Ma is gonna take in Alfie and Olive," Abby said.

"Take in where?"

"They're gonna stay with us until the war's over."

Abby watched his expression to see if he was excited.

"Then what?" he asked.

Considering he and Connie had adopted Chickie, she had expected more sympathy.

"Then they'll go back to their parents in England."

They stopped at a light, and he turned to her.

"Abby, what makes you think they're even still alive?"

......

ABBY WALKED through the archways and into the grand lobby of North Station. Even with all the shelters across the city, families were sleeping on benches. A group of soldiers stood by the ticket booths, their uniforms pressed. Since the war, train and bus stations had become more than just travel junctions. They were places where people parted with their loved ones, often for the last time. Abby would never forget the day George had left or when just two weeks before, she had said goodbye to Harold and Mr. Glynn.

"Abigail?"

Looking over, she saw Frances and was surprised that her mother was with her. She put on a bright smile and walked over. Knowing it was going to be awkward, she wanted to change the mood.

"George is back," she blurted.

"Home?"

Abby and Frances hugged.

"That's your brother, I presume?" Mrs. Farrington asked.

"One of them."

"I can't believe it," Frances said.

"He was in the Aleutians. He got injured...he's okay. But they sent him home."

"My dear, that's wonderful news," Mrs. Farrington said.

Frances had on a fitted Chesterfield coat and a suitcase in the same color blue. With her hair in curls, she looked like she was headed off for a tour of Europe.

An announcement came over the loudspeaker, and Frances reached down for her bag.

"Concord, New Hampshire? Abby asked.

"I'll be just outside. It's a lovely area. You'll have to come visit this summer."

"Ha," her mother said with a haughty laugh. "If this girl doesn't give birth by June, it's straight to City Hospital."

Abby froze and looked at Frances.

"It's fine, Abby. My mother's not the person I'm trying to appease."

"No," Mrs. Farrington said. "That would be your father. And anyone else who might be inclined toward gossip or malignance. I'm not happy about the situation, but Salvatore was a fine young man. I would've been proud to call him a son-in-law."

"Thank you, Mother," Frances said, getting teary.

"That's quite broad-minded of you, Mrs. Farrington."

"Hardly. My daughter is twenty-one. Her father and I've been married twenty years...or were, should I say. The math is fairly plain."

Frances swiped at her mother, wiping her eyes with a tissue.

"Mother, please."

Abby chuckled, and they walked out to the platform.

"Goodbye, love," Abby said, and they hugged again.

"It's goodbye for now."

"Right."

"And let me know if you hear from Harold."

"I will."

Frances then kissed her mother.

"Toodle-loo," she said, and she stepped onto the train.

As Abby watched her go, she felt a mix of emotions. She hated that her friend had to go hide like a criminal, but she also admired her courage. She thought about the baby too, the great wildcard in the whole affair. Children always suffered the most from the mistakes and misfortunes of adults.

Abby walked with Mrs. Farrington back into the station, relieved to be out of the cold.

"Can I get you a taxi?"

"No, thank you," Abby said. "I can get the subway to BU."

They stopped at the doors by a line of newsboys. With the freezing temperature, it was better to say everything before going out.

"Abigail, there's a rally for the United War Fund at the Boston Garden next Friday. Seventeen thousand people."

"I heard about it."

"I'd like to invite you. You'll be my personal guest. Some Hollywood stars will be there, Lynn Bari, Elyse Knox, Maria Montez…"

When Abby hesitated, it was more out of fear than reluctance. She had never been to an event that size or that important.

"I'd like that," she said.

"Good. I'll have my driver pick you up at seven."

42

As Thomas pulled off the highway, he looked over at the directions he had scribbled on a napkin that morning. He wasn't familiar with Quincy, a city of eighty thousand people just south of Boston. While parts of it felt suburban, it had a naval base, several factories, and one of the biggest shipyards in the northeast. It was the birthplace of two presidents, and a decade earlier, Amelia Earhart had flown with a flight club at a local airport.

He turned onto a tidy street of single and two-family houses. It was nicer than he had expected, not quite professional but not working class either. Coming from East Boston, any place with backyards and trees felt upscale. The neighborhood was far enough from the coast that the homes didn't have blackout shades. In some of the windows, he saw blue star flags and even a yellow one, which always gave him chills. At this point, there wasn't a person alive who had not been affected by the war.

The address wasn't hard to find, a small brick Tudor on the corner. He parked out front and walked up to the door where he saw a plaque that read "The Lerners."

Thomas hadn't known Sarah was half Jewish until DiMarco had told him. The magic of summers on Point Shirley was that people came from all over, leaving behind their prejudices and presumptions. No one cared where you were from or what your background was. When he was a boy, Sarah had just been one of the endless kids with scuffed knees and sunburnt faces. His father had called them "ragamuffins," a term of endearment, and his mother had known them all by name. Over the years, Thomas had watched Sarah grow into a beautiful young woman.

He knocked, and a middle-aged man with balding hair and thick eyebrows opened the door.

"Yes?" he asked.

"Mr. Lerner?"

"That's me."

"Thomas Nolan. I'm a friend of Nick's."

The man's expression changed, not quite a smile but something less guarded.

"Please, come in," he said. "Have you heard from Nicholas?"

"It's only been a month. I don't think he's out of basic training yet."

Thomas took off his hat, and they walked into a living room with a couch and leather club chairs. There was a walnut coffee table with an ashtray and some magazines: *Life*, *Harper's*, and *The Atlantic*. On the mantel over the fireplace, Thomas saw a framed picture of a young man in uniform.

"My son Francis," Mr. Lerner said. "Last we heard, he's in North Africa."

Thomas started to say his brother was home but stopped. He had come to console Sarah's family, not to gloat about his own.

"Roosevelt thinks it'll all be over by the end of the year."

Mr. Lerner gave a friendly but skeptical look. It was obvious he didn't want to talk about the war.

"Alan?"

Thomas looked over and saw a woman on the stairs. She wore a long white robe, and her hair was in rollers.

"Madge, this is Thomas Nolan. A friend of Nicholas'."

When she smiled, Thomas saw the resemblance to her daughter. She tiptoed over with an embarrassed grin.

"You'll have to pardon my—"

"Not at all," Thomas said. "I would've called, but I didn't have your phone number. I wanted to come by to say how sorry I am."

"Well, thank you."

"I was at the Cocoanut Grove that night."

Mrs. Lerner put her hand to her mouth.

"Did you see Sarah?" she asked.

"Earlier in the night. We were all there together, but it was a big group."

Thomas had struggled over whether to tell them, worried it would make things worse. He was relieved when she said, "Well, at least she wasn't alone."

A poignant silence filled the room. Thomas got uncomfortable enough that he started fidgeting with the hat in his hands.

"Can I get you anything? Coffee or tea?" Mrs. Lerner asked.

"No, thanks. I have to get back to work."

The guilt he felt lying about the suspension was almost as bad as the humiliation.

"Maybe another time then."

"I'd like that."

"I should go finish getting ready," she said, backing away with a smile.

"Nice to meet you."

"Likewise."

When she walked upstairs, Mr. Lerner led Thomas to the door.

"Thank you for coming by," he said.

"I told Nick I'd drop by to see if you needed anything."

"What we need, you can't give us, unfortunately," he said, and at first, Thomas got offended. "But I can tell you that your visit means more to us than you know."

"Thank you."

"Are you on the police force? Is that how you know Nicholas?"

"Yes. But we also went to high school together."

"Thanks for all the work you do. Our boys overseas have had a hell of a time, but the war hasn't been easy on you guys either."

Thomas looked up, and their eyes met.

"I appreciate it."

......

THOMAS PARKED in front of the school and got out. Everything had been shoveled and salted, but it was too cold for students to go outside at dismissal. With his busy work schedule, Connie had been getting Chickie, and he hadn't been there in weeks. The scrap pile had gotten bigger, and the flag was at half-mast for a local soldier who had died over the English Channel.

He walked in just as the last bell rang. A dozen parents were waiting, but most kids walked home by themselves. Standing by the door, Thomas cringed when he saw Mrs. Giaconni leave the office. The last time he was there he had been rude, and he wanted to avoid her.

Turning away, his eyes caught someone. Across the lobby, Jack Morris was leaning against the wall with his daughter. For a second, they stared at each other, but Thomas wasn't sure he even recognized him. Cops looked different out of uniform. Either way, he got some private satisfaction in knowing the man was free. Despite the government regulations, selling tires over the price ceiling was no high crime. Thomas could admit he had raided the garage for his own gain.

He was distracted when the students started coming out. They walked in perfect lines and were quiet, which was a lot different than Thomas remembered. He and Abby had gone to school there during the Depression, a time that had all the irreverence of the Twenties but with none of the prosperity. With the country at war, discipline and order were back in fashion.

Chickie walked over, and he hugged her.

"How was your day?"

"Tired," she said, putting her head against his shoulder.

As they went to leave, she stopped.

"Wait for Olive and Alfie."

The British children scurried over. Their clothes were ragged, but they always looked clean.

They left the building and got into the car, and Chickie sat in the back with her friends. As they drove away, Thomas saw Clarence Morris walking home with his father and sister. He didn't know if the tire case had gotten dismissed, but at least they were together again.

"Olive and Alfie are coming to live with us," Chickie said.

Thomas looked in the rearview mirror and smiled. He was always amused at how she blurted things out.

"Is that right?" he asked.

"We're pleased about the invitation," Olive said.

"We don't want to go to Iowa," her brother added.

"Really? What's wrong with Iowa?"

The boy just gazed out the window and didn't respond.

They were home in two minutes. As they got out of the car, Connie was leaving the house. Thomas knew she wasn't just going next door because she was bundled up.

"Going to see Gramma!" Chickie said.

She waved to her friends, and they all ran up the steps.

"*Togliti gli stivali alla porta!*" Connie yelled over.

Once the door shut, everything seemed to go quiet. The only sound was the faint breeze and the distant hum of traffic on Bennington Street. It was almost peaceful.

Connie walked over with a paper bag in her arms.

"You didn't work today?" she asked.

Throughout his life, any time he had lied it had been for convenience, never to cause harm. If he had taken favors, it was only because every officer did. He realized now that all dishonesty was wrong. Hard times were no more an excuse for graft than good times were for excess. His father had once said that people were nothing more than the sum total of their principles and their actions, and Thomas finally believed it.

"I got suspended," he said.

Her eyes narrowed.

"What means this? *Suspended*?"

"It means I can't go to work for a week."

"Is that bad?"

"No, not really."

And it wasn't. Vitti said no one would remember, and Thomas agreed. The war was a nightmare society would someday wake up from. There was enough blame to go around, and one slight on his record wouldn't ruin his career. He wasn't even sure he wanted to be a cop forever. But that was a consideration for another time.

He leaned forward and looked in the bag to see loaves of bread and cans of vegetables.

"Where're you going?" he asked, although he already knew.

"To see my brother."

Reaching into his pocket, he took out his keys. He would never let her take the bus out to Deer Island again.

"Let's go."

"Are you sure?"

"My mother wanted me to stop by the cottage anyway," he said, taking the bag from her.

"Why?"

"To get pillows and sheets for the Brits."

He opened the passenger door. As she got in, he went to shut it, and she stopped him.

"Does it bother you that the children will live here?" she asked.

Thomas looked over at their houses, almost identical and separated by only a few feet. As a child, he could never have imagined the great saga that would unfold between them. Now they felt more like a single fortress than two homes, some defense against the threats and uncertainties of a chaotic world.

The battle people fought every day on the home front wasn't bloody, but the losses were painful. With George back, Thomas' family was together again, and if they could help anyone else displaced by the war, it was their duty.

"It doesn't bother me," he said, finally. "It'll be nice having the little ragamuffins around."

"What's a ragamuffin?"

"I'll tell you on the drive out to Point Shirley."

"Can we start a fire?" she asked.

Thomas smiled.

"Yes."

I'd love to hear your feedback! Consider leaving a review by following the link below and scrolling down to the review section.
www.amazon.com/B0BWBZ9PWV

ALSO BY JONATHAN CULLEN

The Days of War Series
The Last Happy Summer

Nighttime Passes, Morning Comes

Onward to Eden

Shadows of Our Time Collection
The Storm Beyond the Tides

Sunsets Never Wait

Bermuda Blue

The Jody Brae Mystery Series
Whiskey Point

City of Small Kingdoms

The Polish Triangle

Love Ain't For Keeping

Sign up for Jonathan's newsletter for updates on deals and new releases!

https://liquidmind.media/j-cullen-newsletter-sign-up-1/

ABOUT THE AUTHOR

Jonathan Cullen grew up in Boston and attended public schools. After a brief career as a bicycle messenger, he attended Boston College and graduated with a B.A. in English Literature (1995). During his twenties, he wrote two unpublished novels, taught high school in Ireland, lived in Mexico, worked as a prison librarian, and spent a month in Kenya, Africa before finally settling down three blocks from where he grew up.

He currently lives in Boston (West Roxbury) with his wife Heidi and daughter Maeve.

Made in the USA
Las Vegas, NV
05 April 2024